PUMPKIN RIDGE

PAMELA GRANDSTAFF

PUMPKIN RIDGE

2017

Books by Pamela Grandstaff:

Rose Hill

Morning Glory Circle

Iris Avenue

Peony Street

Daisy Lane

Lilac Avenue

Hollyhock Ridge

Sunflower Street

Viola Avenue

Pumpkin Ridge

Ella's New Hat and Her Terrible Cat

June Bug Days and Firefly Nights

Terry Lee's Home for Bluebirds

Printed by Createspace

ISBN-10: 1979113033
ISBN-13: 978-1979113038

ACKNOWLEDGMENTS

In the middle of this tumultuous year, little Josie was born, and she's made a dark time seem hopeful and bright. I am so thankful for her parents Ella and Adam, her big brother Jackson, and her grandparents Linda, Bruce, Kate, Richard, and their families.

Also brightening up the dark was an October wedding where my nephew, Michael, added Brittany to our family, joining Terry, Greg, Colin, and Emily. I'm also grateful for my own little family, my mother Betsy and dogs George and Gracie.

Thank you to everyone who reads my books, takes the time to write reviews on Amazon, and sends me sweet emails.

Thank you to Tamarack: The Best of West Virginia, for selling my paper books in your beautiful building.

For June Bug

CHAPTER ONE - MONDAY

Ava substituted her husband's sleep medication with the stronger sedative that would ensure he stayed unconscious for the next few hours and then delivered it to him in bed, where he reclined in his pajamas, going over some business documents.

"I wish I didn't have to take anything," he said. "I don't know why I can't sleep like a normal person."

She watched him swallow the capsule with a sip of white wine.

"You probably shouldn't drink wine with that," she said.

"It's only one glass," he said. "It helps me to relax."

"Don't blame me if you never wake up," she said.

"I wouldn't be in a position to blame anyone, then, would I?" he said. "Why don't you lay down with me for a while?"

He patted the bed.

"I need to check on the kids," Ava said. "I also have several emails to return and some household accounting to go over."

He reached out and grasped her hand.

"Confess," he said. "You're bored with me."

"On the contrary," she said, "I'm mad about you. I just can't let you know that or I'd lose what little power I have."

"You're my queen," he said, and then kissed her hand. "I'd slay dragons for you; you know that."

She leaned over, kissed him lightly on the lips, and adeptly evaded his attempt at a deeper embrace.

"Ava, I miss you," he said.

"This weekend when you get back from Concord," she said. "You won't need any sleep meds when I'm through with you. I promise."

"I'm going to hold you to that," he said, and then yawned.

"Sleep tight," she said and closed the door behind her as she left the bedroom.

Ava went downstairs and crossed the vast central hub of the house to the southern wing, which housed the children's rooms. Two-year-old Olivia was sleeping soundly in her crib, her left thumb in her mouth, the other chubby hand clinging to her blankie: a pastel-pink, hand-crocheted rabbit head with a crocheted blanket for a body, its ears lined in white polyester satin, which Delia Fitzpatrick had made for her. Unfortunately, Olivia had bonded with the wretched thing before Ava could hide it in the trash.

The Irish nanny, Siobhan, was in the next room reading to seven-year-old Ernest, who was tucked up in his bottom bunk amidst various stuffed animals and toy trucks. Siobhan glanced up at Ava with wary eyes and a polite smile, but Ernest didn't take his eyes off the book.

"It's awfully late for him to still be up," Ava said.

"Yes, Miss," Siobhan said. "He's had a bad dream."

"I see," Ava said. "My husband's sleeping, so I know you'll help me make sure nothing disturbs him.

"Yes, Miss," Siobhan said.

Even though Ava detected a hint of willful resentment in her nanny's tone, she trusted it was nothing to worry about. They paid the young woman well, well enough to guarantee she wouldn't dare leave her charges to wander about the huge house at night, let alone poke her nose into Ava's private business. They had imported her directly from Ireland, she had no friends here save the housekeeper, nor was there a boyfriend to distract her from her duties.

Gail, their housekeeper, had gone home after preparing their dinner. Their security manager, Karl, was in the apartment over the garage, where Ava assumed he would drink himself into a stupor. She had deliberately turned a blind eye to Karl's continual thievery of alcohol, having instructed Gail to lock up the good stuff where he couldn't get to it. As a wealthy man, it made Will feel better to have someone nominally in charge of security. As someone with a vested interest in autonomy and privacy, it made Ava feel better not to have someone wandering around at night with a flashlight and a gun.

Ava crossed back through the central section of the house, which contained a spacious formal living room, family room, formal dining room, casual dining room, media room, kids' playroom, Will's home office, and a huge kitchen, all connected by a soaring two-story foyer. She took her time as she climbed the stairs to the north bedroom wing, and then tiptoed to the doorway of their bedroom.

Will was still wearing his glasses, but he'd dropped the papers he'd been reading. His head was resting on the pillows behind him, his steady, shallow breathing signaling he was deeply unconscious. She slid his glasses off and placed them on the bedside table. She took the papers away and put them in his open briefcase on the dresser.

Her hand on the light switch, she regarded her husband. His thick auburn hair and full red beard disguised the baby face of a man almost ten years younger than she. He was confident, intelligent, and loyal, and she never had a moment's worry that he would stray or betray her trust. A successful businessman, a loving husband, and a devoted father; Ava could not have chosen more wisely.

He was also ridiculously wealthy.

In her elegantly appointed dressing room, Ava undressed and took off all her jewelry, including her diamond-encrusted wedding band and the hefty emerald-cut diamond engagement ring, all of which she dropped in a china saucer on top of the dresser.

She placed her cell phone, sound muted, next to the saucer of jewelry. Will was a bit of a techno wizard, and although he said he had complete trust in her, he also had the means with which to track her phone, and thus her movements, should he choose to. Ava often "forgot" to take her phone with her, a mistake for which she was often lovingly reproved and immediately forgiven by her husband.

She entered the adjacent, luxurious spa-like bathroom, tiled floor to ceiling in various permutations of Carrera marble. She took a leisurely bath in the deep soaker tub, blissfully free from any opportunistic connubial interference. She performed her feminine ablutions with pleasure, anticipating the appreciation of the intended audience.

After her bath, she blew-dry her long dark hair but did not apply any makeup or scent. She donned black panties and a bra, both only slightly more substantial than a cobweb, and slid on close-fitting black leggings and a long, black cashmere tunic.

She watched the clock, which always seemed to move more slowly in the evenings after Will fell asleep. Her blood seemed to hum through her veins, so anxious was she to get to where she was going. Instead, Ava curled up in a chair in her parlor and took up a book where she had left off reading the night before. She went through the motions of reading, but her mind was already across the river.

A 1:30 a.m. Ava slid her arms into a black winter parka and tied the laces of her sturdy, waterproof boots. She punched in the code that turned off the house alarm, flipped the hood up over her head, slid outside, and locked behind her the northern side door, which led to a slate-paved veranda. From there it was a near-vertical slog down the steep hillside on a muddy gravel path, guided only by a pin-light flashlight Ava kept fastened to the zipper pull of her parka. She slid several times and was thankful for the handrail she had insisted Will have installed for the children.

At the bottom of the hill, she walked out onto their dock and took the cover off a small boat with an outboard motor. She got in and untied it from the pier, but didn't turn on the spotlight that was fastened to the bow. The lights from Rose Hill were bright enough to guide her, even through the fog that hovered over the river. Across the river, there was a red light attached to the reciprocal dock behind the bicycle factory her husband owned. She started the motor and aimed for it.

After she killed the engine and tied up the boat behind the bicycle factory, she made her way around to the front of the dark, mammoth, red brick structure, walking on the former railroad tracks that had been converted into a rail trail. Security cameras mounted on the factory walls monitored the area, but Ava knew that there were no security personnel employed there, and no one would review the footage unless there was an attempted break-in. During the four years the factory had been in business, there had never been a break-in.

She walked up Pine Mountain Road until she reached the alley behind Rose Hill Avenue. She kept her hood over the top part of her face and her head down, only seeing the next steps she needed to take. There were security cameras affixed to various businesses in town, and she wanted to remain indistinguishable from the many students from Eldridge College who frequented the area late at night.

She made her way up the alley to the dumpster behind the Rose and Thorn. She hid behind it until she heard the waitress from the pub throw the trash in, and then unlock and drive away the car she kept parked outside the side entrance.

The light above the side door to the bar went out.

Ava made her way to the door and pressed the button that rang the bell. It was always at that moment when she wasn't entirely sure he would open the door, that Ava felt panicked. Although, from a lifetime of experience she was pretty confident about her effect on men, and this man, in particular, she still had that small flash of doubt, and it was deliciously terrifying.

Ava could get through the other part of her life, she believed, only if she had this small part to look forward to, and then to remember until she could have it again.

She heard the lock turn, and the door opened, which always gave her a satisfying thrill. It was dark inside. She could smell Patrick, even though he had backed away from the door.

She slid inside and closed the door behind her. In the back room behind the bar, lit only by the light from the front room, Ava shed her parka, her boots, her sweater, and her leggings. She climbed the steep ladder to the cold attic space, where a nest of blankets and pillows on a futon had been placed under the eaves. Ava lit a candle he kept there and put it on top of a crate. She lay down and pulled the blankets up around her. The bed smelled of them, enough so that she almost swooned with the scent of it.

This part, where she anticipated him joining her, was incredibly erotic in its intensity. She could hear him lock up and close the door between the back room and the bar. She heard his boots hit the floor as he took them off, one after another. Then there was the creak of the ladder under his weight and the appearance of his dark-haired head as he reached the attic.

His blue eyes, pupils dilated, glinted in the candlelight.

"Patrick," she said. "I've missed you."

"I don't want to hear it," he said.

She turned back the covers, and there was his quick intake of breath, the groan that always accompanied his first look at her. It quickened her pulse like nothing else.

It had been almost ten years since the first time they made love, but for Ava, nothing had changed.

Ava was asleep when the crash happened. Patrick was up, dressed, and descending the attic stairs by the time she was fully conscious. Ava blew out the candle, hurried down after him, and pulled on her clothing, her boots, and her coat. She went out the side door, which Patrick had left ajar.

She ran up to the junction of Rose Hill Avenue and Peony Street, where she could see a coal truck had wrecked into an electrical pole in front of PJ's Pizza, directly across the street from the Rose and Thorn. The pole had broken in half, and the street light attached to it had shattered. There were electrical lines down, and any lights left on at night in the various businesses and houses east of Rose Hill Avenue were out. The next sound she heard was dozens of automatic backup generators starting, and then some of those lights came back on.

Patrick had climbed up the side of the cab, had the driver's side door open, and was talking to the driver. He looked back as Ava approached and pointed to the other side of the truck, gestured for her to go around to that side.

She walked up to the front of the truck, where she could see a man lying flat on his back in the PJ's Pizza restaurant parking lot. He was situated just outside the glare of the truck's headlights. There was a dark puddle spreading out from the back of his head onto the frosted pavement.

She took her tiny flashlight and shone it on him.

He was dressed in dark pants, an insulated jacket, and hiking boots. A black balaclava covered his face, except for his mouth and eyes, which were wide open but unfocused. When Ava shone the light in them, his pupils did not contract as they should have. She lifted the edge of the balaclava and felt for a pulse in his throat. It was barely discernable, but it was there.

She searched his coat and found his wallet in the inside breast pocket. In it were his drivers' license and a laminated State of Pennsylvania private investigator's license.

Ava's pulse quickened, but she did not allow herself to panic. Momentarily paralyzed as adrenaline flooded her nervous system, she was conscious of the ticking of the truck engine, her exhalations making steam in the frigid air, and the wet feeling of the man's blood, which had soaked through one knee of her leggings.

She needed to work fast.

Ava stuck his wallet down in the pocket of her own coat. In an outside pocket of his coat, she found a keychain with several keys attached. She pushed the lock button, and although she could hear a faint beep, she didn't see any car lights flashing in the immediate vicinity.

Using her tiny flashlight, she searched the area until she found his phone, the screen cracked, lying a few feet away, and put that in her coat pocket as well. A few yards beyond that she found his camera. Although the body was cracked along one edge, she was still able to scroll back through his photographs. The most recent snaps were of her entering the side door of the bar this evening. Scrolling back further, she found more of her entering or leaving the side door on previous nights. She hung the strap around her neck and tucked the body of the camera down inside the front of her coat.

She heard voices from up the street at the fire station, and the sound of the station garage door rolling up. Any second there would be witnesses all over the place.

She looked at him.

She went back to his side and knelt down next to him. She put her hand on his chest and could feel it barely rising with each slow, shallow breath. With her fingers, she felt up to the base of his neck until she reached the soft indentation over his windpipe. She could feel his pulse more clearly there as she pressed lightly.

"I'm sorry," she whispered. "I don't have any other choice."

Using both hands, she pressed her thumbs down hard and didn't let up until he had stopped breathing. Then she counted to ten, still holding down. When she finally lifted her thumbs and checked for a pulse, there was none.

Voices came closer. Ava stood, leaped over the puddle of blood, ran toward the restaurant, went around the rear corner of the building, and waited there, in the shadows, to watch what happened next.

She saw the flashing lights of the EMT truck as it left the fire station, rolled down the street, and turn into the parking lot where the man lay. Other emergency personnel ran up the street and converged on the scene. Patrick climbed down from the truck to talk to one of them.

A paramedic knelt down next to the man, and Ava heard the woman say to her partner, "Get the bag."

With so much noise and activity focused on the scene of the accident, Ava wasn't worried about attracting notice. She needed to get as far away from the scene as possible and establish herself as having been there all night.

She turned and almost walked right into the back of a parked car with Pennsylvania plates. She took out the man's keys and found the fob that unlocked the door. She slid into the driver's seat and looked around. His leather gloves were on the passenger seat. She put them on.

She started the car, put it in gear, and drove down the alley to where a lane intersected with it behind the Dairy Chef. She turned left, drove up the lane, and then turned right into a parking area behind what used to be her home and bed and breakfast business.

She got out of the car and went around to the side of the garage, which had an apartment over top of it. By the base of the stairs was a flower pot sitting on a ceramic tray. She lifted the pot and took the two keys on a key ring out from under it. She used one to open the garage door. She backed her old van out of the garage, parked it behind the B&B, and then drove his car inside.

She turned off the engine, got out, put his keys in the pocket with his phone and wallet, and put the garage door down with her inside. She took a rag from the rim of the utility sink, wet it, and used it to wipe down every part of the car she had touched with her bare hands.

Once she was convinced she had erased any evidence of her fingerprints, she took the rag and his gloves with her as she departed the garage, closed and locked the door behind her. She shoved the rag, gloves, and garage keys in the coat pocket that was empty.

Ava walked quickly down the alley behind Fitzpatrick's Service Station. She turned right at Pine Mountain Road and crossed Rose Hill Avenue, her head down, the hood of her coat up, trying not to run. Ava's heart rate sped up as she crossed the street, every second expecting someone to call out for her to stop. When she passed the diner, outside their line of vision, she ran. At the entrance to the alley, she stopped and threw the rag and gloves in the trash dumpster behind the antique store.

She ran the rest of the way down to the river and made her way along the rail trail to the dock. When she reached the boat, she stepped in, untied it, and started the motor. She aimed at the red light of their dock on the other shore.

She was halfway across when there was a jolt of impact, and the boat went up and over what she quickly realized was a mostly submerged tree floating down the river, hidden by the dense fog hovering over the water's surface. The blades of the outboard motor foundered in wet wood, and the engine whined to a crescendo before it sputtered and died in a noxious cloud of oily smoke.

Ava was now floating down the river with the tree, headed for the dam below town. She pushed with all her strength but could not separate the boat from where it was lodged in the top limbs. Ava watched helplessly as she floated past the red light of her home dock. She didn't know if the boat and tree would get hung up on the dam or go right over it.

She only had moments to decide what to do.

She unzipped her coat and shrugged out of it. She took the man's car keys, wallet, and phone out of her coat pocket, and tucked them into her bra under her sweater. She slung the camera by the strap across her body. She eased over the side of the boat just as the top of the tree met the edge of the dam.

The plunge into icy water took her breath away. She clung to the upstream side of the tree as the trunk with its widespread roots swung toward the western river bank. As soon as the tree stopped moving, and was lodged solidly against the dam, she made her way, using the branches, knot holes, and then the roots as handholds, and pulled herself through the water until she was close enough to the shore to let go.

She pushed off the tree roots and lunged toward some Rhododendron branches that hung out over the water. The brittle stems snapped, but she was able to grab onto a sturdier branch behind them. The smaller, prickly stems tore at the soft skin of her hands and arms as she pulled herself up through the bush toward the muddy shore.

The current pulled at her sodden sweater, dragging her backward. She couldn't free even one hand to take off the sweater, for fear she would lose her grip, but it was keeping her from pulling herself to safety. She felt her strength flag, but the fear of drowning made her adrenalin surge. She kicked her feet and immediately felt mud beneath them. She almost laughed, realizing how close she had come to drowning in a few feet of water.

She stood up, and by using the branches of the bush to assist her, she crawled up onto the bank. She looked back and saw the tree was still foundered against the dam, the boat along with it, water pouring over and around it. She wrung the water out of her sweater as best she could, and then made her way through the dense brush toward the red light of the boat dock. She had just reached it when, with a mighty crash, both the tree and the boat went over the dam.

She turned away and started the climb back up the muddy path to her house. Without her small flashlight, she could only feel her way. She fell a few times, tearing her leggings. There was a stabbing pain in her knee¬, but she ignored it.

Soaked to the skin, racked with chills, covered in mud, and gasping, she reached the side veranda, where she was startled to see headlights shining from the front driveway and courtyard. She ducked down low and followed the stacked stone wall to the drive, where she could see Will's white Range Rover. The engine was on, the driver's side door was open, and the light was on in the cab, where the seatbelt warning was dinging insistently.

Ava stood up and approached the SUV. The driver's side headlight was broken, the front grill was bent, and from the front panel to the back end, there was a long, deep dent blackened by whatever it had sideswiped. Will was still inside, passed out across the front seats. He was barefoot, in his pajamas.

"Will," she said.

He moaned.

"Will, you're sleepwalking," she said. "Wake up."

He moved, and then pushed himself into an upright position. He turned to look at her but seemed to have difficulty focusing his eyes.

"Ava?" he said.

"Come on, sweetie," Ava said. "Let's get you back to bed."

He turned so that his legs were dangling out of the car.

"What's going on?" he asked. "Why are you so wet?"

"Out for a walk in the rain," she said. "You're still asleep. Let's go back in the house."

He slid out of the car, attempted to stand, and immediately lost his balance. Ava struggled to support his body. She considered waking Karl to help her, but decided against it; the fewer complications, the better.

With her help, Will slid down and sat against the back tire while she turned off the headlights and removed the keys from the ignition. She shut the door and locked it.

"What's happening?" Will asked. "Are we outside?"

"You're dreaming," Ava said.

"Well, it's a weird one," he said.

"Help me," Ava said. "You have to get up and walk. I'll steady you."

Once she got him to stand, he leaned on her, and they walked, or rather, lurched toward the house. Ava took him around to the northern veranda entrance, hoping they wouldn't wake anyone in the opposite wing.

It took a long time and much coaxing, but Ava eventually got Will inside the house. She decided there was no way she could get him up to their bedroom, so she took him to his office, pulled off his now wet and muddy pajamas, and got him to lay down on the leather chesterfield.

"Don't go," he said. "Please don't leave me."

She wrapped him up in a woolen throw and murmured soft words to soothe him until he relaxed. He had been gripping her hand so hard it hurt, but he finally let go.

Ava stood up and crept to the door.

"Ava," Will said.

Ava jumped, startled, and turned around.

His eyes were still closed.

"You're asleep," Ava said softly. "You're dreaming."

"Is the driver okay?" he asked.

"What driver?"

"The truck driver," he said. "Is he okay?"

Ava's heart raced. Had he actually driven to Rose Hill and back?

"You're dreaming," she said. "Go back to sleep."

She waited until his breathing became shallow and steady before she turned off the light and closed the door.

Ava unslung the camera strap from around her, kicked off her muddy boots, and then peeled off the wet sweater and leggings, leaving them in a heap on the tile kitchen floor. It was then that she realized that she did not have on panties. In her haste to dress, she must have left them in the attic of the Rose and Thorn.

She removed the man's possessions from her bra, retrieved the camera, and ran upstairs to the master bedroom wing. In her dressing room, she assessed her injuries. Her knee was cut and bleeding, and her hands and arms were scraped and scratched, but nothing required stitches.

She concealed the camera, wallet, keys, and phone in a handbag in the back of her closet, covering the contents with a silk scarf. It was then that she realized she had left the garage and apartment keys in the other pocket of her coat, which went with the boat over the dam.

She took a hot shower, scrubbed herself raw, dried off, treated her knee, and bandaged it. Her hands and arms, with their multiple superficial cuts, scrapes and developing bruises, she could cover with long sleeves and gloves.

She dressed and went back downstairs. She put her leggings, muddy boots, wet sweater, and Will's pajamas in a garbage bag and placed it underneath the other garbage bags in one of the cans outside the garage. She put Will's Land Rover in the garage next to her matching one.

Back inside, she retraced her steps, cleaning up the water, mud, and debris she'd left in a trail from the side door to Will's office to the kitchen and then up the stairs to her bathroom.

She reset the house alarm.

She checked on Will and found him sound asleep, but noticed his skin was muddy everywhere she had earlier touched him. She took some baby wipes from the hallway powder room and cleaned his hands, face, and feet. He didn't wake up.

No one would be surprised in the morning to find Will naked in a different room than the one in which he went to sleep. Everyone associated with the household knew his sleep medication sometimes had disturbing side effects, such as sleepwalking.

He had once called his mother and had an entire conversation with her that he didn't remember the next day. Another time he ate a whole pie and then left the refrigerator door open, thereby spoiling the entire contents.

Everyone counted on the house alarm system to alert someone if he ever tried to leave the premises, but Ava had turned that off when she left.

The alarm company would be able to produce a report showing what time the alarm was turned off, what exterior doors were opened and closed, and what time the alarm was turned back on. Ava wasn't worried about being questioned; whatever had happened, she could blame it on her sleepwalking husband. If he could make a phone call in his sleep, he could turn off an alarm. She'd have to think up a plausible reason why she didn't hear any of this going on, but she would worry about that later.

Ava was relieved Will had acceded to her request that there be no video surveillance equipment installed in or around the house. She had told him it would make her feel like she was being asked to live in a prison, the subtext being that she might not live there if he insisted upon it. The compromise had been the motion sensor system that could be turned on and off, connected to a 24-hour alarm company, and a video-monitored electronic gate at the entrance to their driveway. And Karl.

Thinking about the gate reminded Ava that she could check to see when Will had left the grounds. She went to Karl's office, a small room off the garage, turned on the laptop kept on a desk there, and using it, backed up the digital recording to the time she had left the house.

Sure enough, about forty-five minutes after she left, there was Will's car, driving past the camera. Although she couldn't see his face, who else could it be? A sensor in his Rover opened the gate automatically when his vehicle approached it, and a timer closed it again a few seconds afterward. She forwarded the video. Almost two hours later he was back. Ava brought the recording back to its end and left it the way she'd found it.

Where did Will go, what did he see, and if he saw anything, how much would he remember? He'd asked about the truck driver, but he hadn't been outside when Ava left the Rose and Thorn.

Ava wanted, needed to talk to Patrick, but she didn't dare.

Instead, she went to the housekeeper's small parlor behind the kitchen, where Gail kept her things and sometimes napped on a daybed. Gail also liked to listen to the police scanner, like all the old people in Rose Hill seemed to. Ava turned it on and scrolled around, looking for the correct frequency.

Finally, she found the channel on which the paramedics and police were communicating and eventually discovered the two things she needed to know: the coal truck driver was alive, but the man he hit was dead.

She could destroy his belongings, but there was still the matter of his car. She could ditch it out in the woods somewhere, but then she would need some way to get back. It might be a better idea to take the car to Pennsylvania to find and destroy any other evidence related to her.

She could leave his car in the B&B garage for a day or two, but any longer would be dangerous. She would need to take it out under cover of darkness, would need an excuse for being gone several hours, and she couldn't take her phone, would have to "forget" once again to take it with her.

Years ago, Will had tracked Ava's daughter, Charlotte, through her phone when she had run off with her boyfriend to New York. Ava knew he wouldn't hesitate to do that to his wife, especially if he couldn't find her and was worried. It was all cloaked in husbandly concern, of course, but Ava knew that what Will wanted to do was to control her. No matter how much she reassured him, he was never sure of her or of their marriage. His insecurity made him clingy and overprotective, and it sometimes felt to Ava as if he were slowly smothering her to death.

Ava returned to Will's office to check on him, but he was still asleep. Looking out the window through the fog and trees she could see the lights of Rose Hill gleaming dully in the darkness. Ava thought about her coat with the garage keys in the pocket, still in the boat that had gone over the dam. She couldn't face going back out tonight, hadn't the strength to, and by tomorrow morning the tree and boat would have been discovered. She would have to deal with that some other way.

She wasn't thinking about the man she killed, or the man she loved, except in an abstract way: the first as an obstacle to be removed from her path, and the second as the prize to which that path led.

Tomorrow she could start to deal with the consequences of this night, but meanwhile, she needed to rest. She needed to look her best, could not afford to have puffy or dark-circled eyes if questioned. She must think of the children. She must keep up her strength. Ava made her way to their bedroom, got in bed, and within minutes, fell sound asleep.

CHAPTER TWO - TUESDAY

Melissa changed her clothes for the fourth time. Later that morning, a reporter from the Pendleton paper was coming to the law office where she worked to interview her, and she couldn't seem to get exactly the right look. She wanted her appearance to say, "I am a professional person with a career," but not "I am a man in a business suit."

She finally settled on a form-fitting black sweater, a short black and gray tweed skirt, black tights, and black knee-high boots that appeared to lengthen her legs. She dithered over accessories for a few minutes before coming back to the mother-of-pearl and onyx-studded silver necklace and chunky silver hoop earrings her friend, Claire, had recommended for this particular outfit.

Following Claire's tutorial, she loosely braided and then wound her long blonde hair into an intricate knot at the back of her head, where she secured it with bobby pins. She applied her makeup as Claire had taught her. She reviewed the results in the bathroom mirror and was pleased with the result. Not as good as Claire's work, but passable.

She thought she looked like one of those girls in the photos on Pinterest that Claire had pinned for her to be inspired by. On the inside, Melissa still felt like the dirt-poor Tennessee ragamuffin she had been at twelve-years-old, but if she watched what she said and how she said it, she might fool anyone.

In addition to helping her choose potential outfits and teaching her how to apply work-appropriate makeup, Claire had also manicured her nails the evening before; they were now a rosy taupe color that Melissa never in a million years would have chosen for herself. Melissa liked bright colors; they were more cheerful.

She went down the hallway to the front room of her mobile home, where Patrick was snoring on the couch, wrapped in a fleece blanket, his beagle Banjo curled up in the V behind his knees. He had come home around 4:00 in the morning, even though he closed the Rose and Thorn at 1:30 am, after which he usually cleaned and walked the half a block home to arrive by 2:00 am.

This wasn't the first time he'd slept on the couch, which he claimed to do in order not to interrupt her beauty sleep. Lately, however, it was happening more often than not. She tried to remember the last time he had slept in the bed with her. Two weeks ago, a month?

Earlier this morning, when she heard him come in, she had not been able to go back to sleep for a long time. She knew she should say something, but she was afraid to. There had been an uneasy tension between them for a while now, and more and more she found him short-tempered, or not listening when she talked. Her mind raced through the possibilities, from mundane to dramatic, but she always ended up wondering if Ava had anything to do with it.

Beautiful, perfect Ava, married to her multi-millionaire Prince Charming, who had built her a hilltop palace on the other side of the Little Bear River, from which she could look down upon the peasants of Rose Hill.

Ava was also Patrick's widowed sister-in-law, with whom he had been involved while his older brother, Brian, Ava's first husband, had been missing for several years. While Brian was away, Patrick had acted like a father to her two children, Charlotte and Timmy.

Years later, after Brian had returned to Rose Hill and then died suddenly, Patrick had broken it off with Ava due to his mother's wishes. Bonnie Fitzpatrick adored her sons, and her apron strings were like barbed wire around Patrick's neck. He had confided all this to Melissa, his good buddy and waitress at the Rose and Thorn, where he bartended. Although it hurt to hear how much he loved another woman, Melissa had tried her best to hide her own feelings.

Melissa and Patrick had met when she went to work at the Rose and Thorn over 16 years ago. As far as Patrick was concerned, they had only been co-workers and friends, but Melissa had nursed a crush on him for years. She had witnessed his devotion to Ava, watched him pine for her after they split, had been a shoulder for him to cry on, and finally, happily, a soft place for him to fall. In return, when her life had fallen apart, Patrick, along with his family, had been a lifeline for Melissa to cling to.

Melissa put on her bright red wool coat and wound a long woolen scarf around her neck. She made Banjo go outside to do his business, cleaned it up, fed him, and then watched as he jumped back up on the couch to snuggle in with his beloved Patrick. She took one last look at the sleeping giant who held her heart in the palm of his hand, and then left the trailer as quietly as she could.

It was October, but winter was making its intentions known with light snow and freezing temperatures. She started her vintage Mustang to warm it up. She scraped the heavy coating of frost off the back windshield of the 1965 Caspian Blue Ford, which Patrick had restored for her as a gift to celebrate her graduation from Pineville Community College the previous May.

She heard Maxine, a neighbor, calling to her. The older lady, wearing a floral housecoat and curlers in her white hair, was leaning out the door of her trailer, waving to get Melissa's attention. Melissa walked over to the edge of the rickety porch Maxine's husband had built (not well) onto their mobile home many years before.

"I guess you heard about the wreck," Maxine said.

"No," Melissa said. "What happened?"

"Coal truck run into a light pole up on Rose Hill Avenue," she said. "You know my Bruce is a night owl; he heard the crash and went up to see what happened. I turned on the scanner and got the details. The driver said he swerved to avoid a white SUV, but there weren't no SUV anywhere when Bruce got up there. Either that man was hallucinating, high on drugs, or the other driver must've run off."

Melissa was relieved to have a reason for Patrick's late arrival home.

"That's a shame," Melissa said. "Was the driver hurt?"

"Not too bad, but the fella he run over died at the scene."

"Who did he run over?"

26

"Some fella standing on the sidewalk there," Maxine said. "Although why anybody would be standing on Rose Hill Avenue after 3:00 in the morning, I don't know. Them college kids got more money than sense, and no matter what they do the law in this town just looks the other way."

"Was that when it happened? At three?"

Maxine nodded.

"I heard on the scanner the fella had no ID on him; they don't know who in the heck he was or where he comes from."

"That's odd," Melissa said, although she thought that if Maxine was right about the time, Patrick had just lost his alibi.

"I'm surprised your man didn't tell you all about it," Maxine said.

The older woman's expression had turned sly.

"I was asleep when he came in, and I didn't wake him up this morning," Melissa said.

"Well, I don't like to gossip," Maxine said, "but Bruce said there was somebody with Patrick—a woman—but he only caught a glimpse of her. He didn't know who she was."

Melissa's chest hurt, and she felt like she might throw up.

"That's odd," she said and looked away so Maxine couldn't see how she felt.

"I didn't know whether to say anything or not," Maxine said. "I hope I done right."

"No worries," Melissa said, and waved as she turned away. "Have a good day."

Melissa made herself calmly walk back to her car and finish scraping the melting ice off of her windshield while she held back her tears and willed herself to be strong, to be made of stone.

She got in the car and gripped the steering wheel. She could go back inside and confront Patrick, but she would be late for work if she did. She couldn't very well meet a reporter with the swollen cry-face she anticipated she would be wearing as a result.

She had a choice to make.

She had been ignoring the signs for weeks, possibly months. Could it have been going on for years?

For the past three years, Melissa had been working full-time in the law office while also going to school to become a paralegal. Patrick worked at the family-owned service station all morning and the pub from noon until two in the morning. Consequently, she and Patrick hadn't spent a lot of time together, and their love life had suffered, but she had thought it was just a bump in the road, like all grown up relationships were supposed to have, and if they were strong, to survive.

If Patrick had been having an affair with Ava all this time, it meant he had never stopped being in love with her, and that Melissa hadn't ended up with him as she assumed she had. He apparently (allegedly, her interior paralegal reminded herself), didn't have the loyalty to Melissa that she had toward him. Patrick was (allegedly) happy to cheat and lie, and not even hide it very well. He loved Melissa, she knew he did, but evidently, she (allegedly) could not hold a candle to the love of his life, Princess Ava.

It now seemed possible to Melissa that (allegedly) he had only been using her to cover up his relationship with Ava.

She wondered how many people knew.

Patrick's sister Maggie hated Ava, and would not have covered for her brother. Maggie's cousins, Hannah and Claire, were friends of Melissa's, and she hoped one of them would have told her rather than let her find out this way. Her boss Sean was Patrick's brother, but the brothers were not close. His mother Bonnie couldn't know, or she would have taken after him with a rolling pin. If Patrick's best friend Sam knew, he wouldn't tell anyone, including his wife Hannah. Sam was a dark horse.

Three years previously, Ava and Will had eloped and immediately left for a month-long honeymoon in Europe. At the time, Melissa had wondered if that was so no one in the Fitzpatrick family could attend a wedding ceremony. She had wondered if Patrick would have stood up in the church and declared himself. He had certainly been a moody son-of-a-bitch that month, but Melissa had been patient, which she knew how to do better than most. Sometimes, she knew, a heart has to wait for a long time, standing outside in the cold and dark, looking in at the warm fire of its beloved burning for someone else.

Hadn't she waited all this time to be his one and only? Hadn't Ava finally marrying someone else broken the spell? She had thought so. She had believed him when he said he loved her, that she was the most important person in his life.

All lies, apparently (allegedly).

She reminded herself, as Sean so often cautioned his clients, not to let her emotions take the place of facts and evidence. So far, all she had to go on was gossip from a nosy neighbor married to a senior insomniac who did not have perfect eyesight. There were lots of people in the small town of Rose Hill who knew the old gossip about Patrick and Ava, and Lord knows, they did so love to stir something up whenever they could, if only for their own amusement. Maxine and Bruce were no different.

To confront or not confront?

"To hell with him," she finally said to herself.

This morning, she would do what was best for her and no one else.

"Are you excited?" Sean asked Melissa.

"I'm nervous," Melissa said. "When I'm upset or worried I sometimes forget my grammar."

"You'll do fine," Sean said. "Telling your story may inspire others to believe in themselves despite their circumstances. You'll probably never know how many people you'll help."

"That's the only reason I agreed to do it," Melissa said. "I sure don't need to stir up old gossip."

The reporter from the Pendleton Press arrived, and Sean and Melissa greeted her and shook her hand. Although from her wrinkled hands Melissa could tell she was in late middle age, she was dressed like a much younger person, her hair long and blonde, her shoes the highest of heels. Her face looked a little meddled-with. Her eyebrows were hiked up in a permanent expression of surprise, her upper lip was much larger than the bottom one, her forehead was unnaturally smooth and shiny, and her cheekbones stuck out too far to be believed. Melissa wondered what was worse, being pitied for trying to look younger or being pitied for looking your age. It seemed like either way a woman couldn't win.

"I'm Sabrina Dowd," she said. "You may have heard of my husband, Melvin Dowd."

"He owns most of the car dealerships in this county," Sean said. "I've seen the commercials and the billboards."

"Five dealerships over the whole northern part of the state, actually," Sabrina said, as she flipped back her hair. "This column is my hobby; I don't have to work. I certainly don't need the money."

"This is Melissa," Sean said. "Your subject."

Sabrina looked her up and down.

"Well, aren't you pretty as a picture?" the woman said, but her smile did not reach her eyes.

"Thank you," Melissa said. "May I get you some coffee?"

"Nothing for me," Sabrina said. "I'm all about protein smoothies these days."

"I'm going to leave you ladies to it," Sean said. "Melissa, why don't you use the conference room? I'll stay up front to catch the phones and anyone who comes in."

Melissa waited for the older woman to seat herself at the conference table before she sat down. Sabrina took a little notebook and a gilded pen out of her large logo-covered handbag, which was accented by chunky, shiny gold hardware and a gold metal logo dangling from one strap. That logo was one Melissa certainly couldn't afford to have dangling from anything she owned.

"The photographer will be along in a little while," Sabrina said. "We're stretched pretty thin right now, what with budget cuts, so he's at a crime scene down the street. Did you bring a few outfits to change into?"

"I'm sorry," Melissa said. "I just have what I've got on."

Sabrina raised a critical eyebrow.

"I guess that will do, although black is not ideal for newsprint," she said. "How tall are you?"

"Five-two," Melissa said.

"So petite," Sabrina said. "What's your dress size?"

"Four, I guess," Melissa said. "Sometimes two."

"What designers do you prefer?"

"I can't afford designers," Melissa said. "My friend picked all this out."

"So we'll say you have a stylist," Sabrina said. "Where does she shop for you?"

"Online," Melissa said. "I don't have an eye for stuff like she does."

"What handbag are you currently carrying?"

"A canvas tote for my files," Melissa said. "I also have a laptop bag that used to be Sean's."

"You're not making this easy," Sabrina said.

"I'm sorry," Melissa said. "I thought this story was about my paralegal degree."

"Sure, I'll mention it," Sabrina said. "But my column is about fashion. It's called The Fashionista Report. Haven't you read my column?"

"I've been going to school and working full-time for three years," Melissa said. "The only things I've been reading are textbooks and legal case studies."

Sabrina's face reddened, and her lips tightened.

"Do you even care about fashion?"

"Not really," Melissa said. "I'm sorry if I've wasted your time."

Sabrina put her pen away and closed her notebook. She smirked at Melissa.

"That's all right, my dear, I've only wasted my whole morning driving to this godforsaken place when there are plenty of other women who'd be thrilled to be in my column," Sabrina said. "It just goes to show, I guess, that you can't make a silk purse out of a sow's ear."

She stood up, slung her handbag over her shoulder, and looked Melissa up and down.

"It's a shame you don't make more of what you have," Sabrina said. "A woman who looks like you shouldn't have to work. You could catch a wealthy husband."

"I want to work," Melissa said. "I want to support myself."

"That's sweet, honey," Sabrina said. "When you're older you may wish you'd been more sensible about it, but who am I to tell you anything about how the world works? You have a degree!"

"I'm terribly sorry," Melissa said. "I didn't mean to offend you."

Sabrina rolled her eyes.

"Right, well, I'll be off then," she said. "Good luck with your career."

Melissa felt her eyes fill with tears, although she wished with all her might that she wouldn't cry at work. Her female classmates had all agreed that was the worst thing you could do. No one would ever let you forget it. You had to be tough. You had to demonstrate the fierce determination to surmount all obstacles, outwit the competition, and soundly defeat all who opposed you.

Anger was all right. Crying was for losers. Everyone knew that.

Melissa couldn't help it, though. Her son Tommy had gone away to college in August, and it was now the end of October; she missed him like someone had pulled off her arm. That combined with her worries about Patrick, plus a looming financial decision she needed to make had drained the fight out of her.

"What happened?" Sean asked from the doorway.

Melissa wiped her eyes, trying not to smear her mascara.

"It was supposed to be a story about my clothes and pocketbooks," Melissa said. "Not about my degree or my history. Plus I think she called me a dirt-poor pig."

"You're kidding me."

"It's probably my fault," Melissa said. "I guess I misunderstood."

"That's ridiculous," Sean said. "I'll call the editor."

"No, Sean, please don't," Melissa said. "I'm embarrassed enough. You'll only make it worse."

"Are you sure?"

"Yes," Melissa said. "I just want to forget it ever happened."

They heard the front door open, and Sean left to see who it was. When he came back, he said it had been the paper's photographer.

"I told him the story was canceled," he said.

"Good," Melissa said. "Now we can get back to work."

Just after lunch, Ava's husband Will came in. He had dark shadows under his eyes, his cheeks were sunken, and his clothes hung on his tall frame.

"Hi Melissa," he said. "Is the contract ready?"

"Sean has it on his schedule to review this afternoon," Melissa said. "I'll call you as soon as he approves it."

"I'll be glad to have that property sold," he said. "It's been nothing but trouble."

"Could I get you some coffee or something?" Melissa asked. "Sean should be back any minute, and you could wait for him."

Will sank into a chair and rubbed his face.

"Thanks, yes," he said. "I'll take you up on that."

Melissa made a fresh pot of coffee while Will checked messages on his phone. He thanked her when she handed him a large mug.

"You remembered how I like it," he said. "You're good. Sean's lucky to have you."

"Are you feeling okay?" Melissa asked him. "I hope you don't mind me asking. You look sorta peaked."

"I have terrible insomnia," he said. "The medicine I take lets me get a little sleep, but then I have the worst hangover the next day. It's a vicious cycle."

"Worrying about this sale probably hasn't helped."

"We've been through this so many times in the past three years," he said. "It was on the market for almost eighteen months without any offers. The first offer fell through, the second buyer lost her financing at the last minute, and then I had to drop the price way below market value to get any further interest."

"It's a beautiful house," Miranda said. "You'd think someone would want to run a B&B business here. There are always people looking for a place to stay in Rose Hill; students, their parents, skiers, tourists. I guess nobody wants to take the financial risk."

"These people both just retired from federal jobs in DC," he said. "I don't care if they're making a big mistake or not; I just want it off my hands."

"It should all be fine," Melissa said. "How are Ava and the kids?"

"Charlotte's at Oxford now, studying Art History," he said. "Timmy's settling in at Exeter; the first few months are always difficult, but I have no doubt he'll do fine. Ernest is in the grade school here in town, and he seems to be doing well. Olivia's in the preschool at Sacred Heart; she'll have put herself in charge there by Christmas, no doubt; she certainly rules our household."

"And Ava?"

Will appeared forlorn for a moment, but then took a deep breath and gave Melissa a rueful smile.

"She's a little bored, I think," he said. "I wonder if I shouldn't give her a job of some sort. She says she's fine, but I think she could do with a project."

"We don't see her very often these days."

"If the city had let me put the bridge to our property at the bottom of Pine Mountain Road like I wanted, you'd see her all the time," he said. "Unfortunately, I lost that battle, and because I didn't want to lose the P.R. war, I let it go. It still galls me that it takes a half hour to get to Rose Hill by car, even though I can see it from my back deck."

"Unless you use your boat."

"I don't mind the dinghy, but Ava's not keen; she worries about the little ones going overboard."

"Your house is so beautiful," Melissa said. "I saw the Christmas tour photos in the Pendleton paper last year."

"We like it," he said. "I tell Ava all the time that we should have the Fitzpatricks over for a house-warming. We've meant to do that ever since we moved in; my schedule is just so hectic now that I'm running my father's business as well as my own."

"What was it he did?"

"Lots of things, actually," Will said. "He and my uncle would buy factories, make them profitable, and then sell them. My uncle eventually left to start his own business, as a defense contractor to the government. By the time my father died he'd sold all of the businesses he'd purchased except the one they had started with, the one my grandfather had owned. It's a boiler manufacturer, commercial and residential. I could sell it, but it employs a lot of local people in our hometown in New Hampshire, and I didn't want a new owner to sell it for parts or move production out of the country."

"Everybody I've talked to that works at your bicycle factory only has nice things to say," Melissa said. "I guess that's just small potatoes compared to your other companies."

"It's the smallest, but it's my favorite," Will said. "The happiest I ever was in my life was when I went to Eldridge College and mountain-biked the trails here with my friends."

He got lost in a reverie for a moment but then snapped out of it.

"Up until I married Ava and we had Olivia, of course."

"Of course," Melissa said. "How's your mother?"

"She's settled in Palm Beach," he said. "She has lots of friends there."

Sean came in and greeted Will before they went back to his office.

Melissa had tried not to seem like she was grilling the man, but it was hard to ask innocuous questions when what she really wanted to know was if his wife was sleeping with her boyfriend and if she was home all night the previous evening.

At the end of her workday, Melissa was shutting down her computer when Ed walked in.

"What are you doing here?" Melissa asked.

"Claire told me about your interview with the Pendleton paper."

"I should have expected it," Melissa said. "Nobody takes a woman seriously when they talk like me and look like me."

"There's not a thing wrong with you," Ed said. "She was probably just jealous."

"It doesn't matter what I do or how I dress," Melissa said. "It's like I've still got dirty feet, wearing a hand-me-down dress, and all those rich ladies can see it."

"That's all in your head, I'm sure," Ed said.

"I guess you'd have to have ovaries to know what I'm talking about," Melissa said. "You ask Claire; she'll tell you."

Ed laughed.

"If you have time, I'd like to interview you for the Sentinel."

"You don't have to do that, Ed," she said. "It's sweet of you, but I'm over it."

"I think your story is one that people would be interested in," he said. "I'd feel privileged to have it in my paper."

"Your students would laugh."

"No, they wouldn't," he said. "They'll be disappointed they didn't get the opportunity to interview you."

She thought for a moment. She had wanted to share her story, to vindicate herself, maybe, but also to inspire someone like her who needed to hear what she had to say. Tommy had wanted her to do it; his college application essay had been their story.

To hell with what anyone else thought. She'd do it for him.

"What do we need to do?"

Ed took out his phone, pressed the screen a few times and sat it on her desk.

"We talk," he said.

He took a seat in front of her desk.

"You know my story," she said.

"Pretend I don't."

"How do we start?"

"Where were you born?"

"Chattanooga, Tennessee," she said. "My mama's family was poor, her mama had run off, and she was too young to have a baby, so her aunt raised me."

"Did you see your mother very often?"

"Not really. Mama moved away to Oklahoma when I was in second grade," Melissa said. "I saw her a couple times after that, but then she died in a car accident when I was nine. I can barely remember her."

"What was your aunt like?"

"Religious and strict," she said. "She always said I'd end up just like my mother."

"Did she have children of her own?"

"No, she never married, and she didn't like kids," Melissa said. "She cleaned houses for a living. I don't want to talk bad about her. It was pretty grim, but she did the best she could. She didn't have to take me in, but she did. There's some that wouldn't have, and I could have ended up with a lot worse."

"Did you like school?"

"I hated it," she said. "The big boys would never leave me alone. The girls hated me and teased me, called me trailer trash."

"Did you tell your aunt?"

"She said I was lucky to have a home at all and she didn't want to hear any bawlin' or squallin'. She said it was my fault, anyway, that just because I was pretty didn't mean I should

40

flaunt myself. I didn't flaunt myself, though. I was like a lamb with no shepherd; I just attracted the wolves. When I was twelve, she caught some boys trying to peek in my bedroom window. Pretty soon after that, we moved to Pennsylvania."

"Was that any better?"

"It was worse," she said. "There I was the new kid who didn't wear the right clothes or shoes, and I talked funny."

"How did you do in school? Did you like any of the subjects taught?"

"I had one teacher I liked," she said. "Mrs. Abraham. She taught music. She was kind to me, said I had a lovely voice, and didn't let anyone pick on me in her class. She told me not to pay attention to it; if I didn't react, they would stop."

"Easier said than done."

Melissa nodded.

"She was the only one I said goodbye to before I ran off," she said. "She was sad about it and wanted to know if she could help in any way; said I could come live with her if I wanted to. She cried, and it made me cry. She gave me some money."

"What happened to make you want to run away?"

"I was lonely, going to school was daily torture, and there was this boy in the neighborhood who was nice to me. He had quit school and was working for his father's construction business. My aunt said if he showed up on our porch she'd have him arrested, so we had to sneak to see each other. His family was even worse than mine. His daddy liked to drink too much and beat everybody up. He seemed like a grown up at sixteen, and he said he'd take care of me."

"How old were you?"

"Fourteen," she said. "I can hardly believe it now, looking back. We were both just kids."

"So you left."

"We packed up his car one night and drove south. He'd had a falling out with his father and been fired, kicked out of their house. He had an uncle in Clearwater who said he'd take us in if we got married. We got married in Tennessee, where there wasn't an age requirement; I forged my aunt's name on the paper you have to have, to allow it. I didn't reckon on them calling her, but she still gave her permission, told them to say I was not welcome back to her house when it didn't work out."

Ed was quiet, waiting for her to continue.

"So, we went to Clearwater, where he worked for his cousin's family, washing boats at their marina. Later, he worked at their boat tour company, taking people on water tours of the Gulf Coast."

"Did you work, too?"

"I waitressed at a diner in Largo, off the books on account of my age."

"Were you happy?"

"For a while I was," she said. "I loved being free, and I liked the people I worked with. My husband's aunt took me under her wing, was motherly to me. Until he fell out with them I had it pretty good, I'd say for about two years. I was sixteen when we got kicked out of their house."

"Why did that happen?"

"My husband was using their boats to run drugs, and they found out."

42

"What happened then?"

"We moved into a ratty apartment near the beach. I waitressed in a hotel there, and my husband sold drugs."

Ed was silent but looked at her with compassion and affection.

"He took up with some pretty bad characters," she said. "There was one couple who cooked meth in their rental house at the beach. They had a baby."

Melissa looked at Ed, who smiled sadly but said nothing.

"I'm not sure I want to include this part," she said.

"Only if you want to share it."

Melissa paused and took a deep, shuddering breath.

"I offered to take care of their little boy during the day, before my night shift. They didn't care about him; all they cared about was the crack and meth or anything they could smoke out of a pipe, snort up their noses, or poke in their veins. I kept him at our apartment during the day, and our neighbor kept him until I got off work in the night. I fell in love with the little fella. He was starved for affection, and they had neglected him something awful. I got him fattened up and cleaned up, and over time, I started feeling like he was mine."

Ed nodded, and Melissa continued.

"His mother got arrested for possession with intent. Her folks were rich, and they talked the judge into rehab instead of jail. When she got out of rehab, she wanted her baby back, and I had no choice. The police came, and I had to let her have him."

Melissa paused, tears in her eyes.

"It was easy to keep track of them, on account of my husband lived over there. He ratted out some bad people to keep from going to jail, so he was scared all the time someone was gonna kill him. They went back to smoking crack, and when they weren't too high, they were cooking meth and selling it. Before too long, Tommy's mama was even worse than before.

"One morning I woke up, went over there, and took the baby. It was the weirdest thing. I just woke up knowing what I was going to do and I went and did it. He was so glad to see me. He was sitting in his crib, soaked with pee and covered in poop. His little voice was hoarse from crying. His mother was so out of it she didn't even notice what was happening. My husband and her boyfriend were passed out. I took the baby back to the apartment, cleaned him up, and my neighbor agreed to hide him if the cops came."

"Did they?"

"No one came because no one cared."

"What happened then?"

"Not too long after, they blew the house up, with them and my husband in it."

"How did you find out?"

"I heard it happen; we didn't live too far away. I knew what it was. I was with my neighbor, sitting outside, watching Tommy play with her little daughter in their baby pool. We both heard it. She said, 'what was that?' and I said, 'Lord, Connie, they've blowed their selves up.' I left Tommy with her and went over there.

"The flames were shooting high up in the air. There was an awful smell. Miranda's fancy car was just sitting there, parked at the curb. I got in it, and there was her purse, full of money, crack rocks, pipes, and her IDs. I only intended to take what cash there was, for the baby."

Melissa paused.

"On her driver's license she looked so much younger, so much prettier," Melissa said. "She looked a lot like me."

"I heard the sirens, and I had the idea. I didn't think about it for more than a few seconds. People were gathering around, watching the fire, so I had to hurry. I put the money and her IDs in my pocket. I got out of the car and waited with the crowd for the police."

Ed was silent. Melissa heard the furnace kick on, felt the warm air from the vent. Outside, some college students were talking loudly as they walked past.

"After the police came, I went up to the friendliest looking one and told him I used to live in that house, and I knew who was in there. He asked for my ID, and I showed him her driver's license. He looked at it, looked at me, and handed it back. And just like that, I was Miranda.

"I told him Melissa had been in the house with her husband. He wanted me to come down to the station to give my statement. I said I had a baby that I had to pick up from the sitter. He wanted to know how to get in touch with me. I gave him a fake number and address. There was another explosion, and while everybody was freaking out, I took off.

"I could feel the heat from the fire on my back as I walked away. There was another loud bang, and I heard the police shout for everyone to get back. I kept waiting for someone to call out, to stop me, but no one did. I went home, packed up my things, put Tommy in my car, and left Florida."

She took another deep breath and blew it out.

"First I drove to Chattanooga. I wanted to see the house I grew up in, but it had been knocked down, there was a drugstore there instead. I was having trouble with my car, so I stopped at a gas station, and the man there replaced something but told me it wasn't going to last long. We slept all night in the car in his parking lot but left before he came to work the next morning.

"I drove north to Pennsylvania. I decided to show up at my aunt's house. I thought if she saw Tommy she wouldn't turn us away. When I got there, her neighbor told me she had died.

"I didn't know what to do so I just drove. We were just about broke, and I was worn out from nerves. I was on the highway just north of here when the car broke down. A cop stopped and called for a wrecker. It was Curtis Fitzpatrick who showed up to tow us."

"That was some good luck."

"The best," she said. "Curtis took us to the service station here in Rose Hill and then his brother, Ian, the chief of police, came to look us over. I was in tears by that point. I told him my fake story, said I was Miranda, showed him her ID. I expected he would arrest me, then and there. Instead, he offered us a place to stay overnight."

"He was a good man."

"He was like a father to me," Melissa said, "and a grandad to Tommy. He and Delia saved us."

"Did he ever question your story?"

"He never believed a word of it; I heard him talking to his wife about it that night when they thought we were asleep. My car registration was in my husband's name, him who died in the explosion. I fully expected to be arrested that next morning. Instead, he told me Curtis said my car repairs were going to be expensive and offered I could stay with them until it was ready, and work at the Rose and Thorn to pay for it."

"Did you consider running away?"

"I didn't know what else to do, and where could we go? You know Ian and Delia's son died when he was young, and Claire was in California with her husband, Pip. Delia and Tommy got on like a house on fire, and she offered to watch him while I worked at the bar.

"Come to find out, the car was a lost cause, only good enough to sell for parts. Curtis knew that right off, but he and Ian knew we were in some kind of trouble, so they put off telling me. Everyone was so friendly to Tommy and me. Ian and Delia said we could stay as long as we wanted. Somehow, we fit into their family, and because of them, we belonged in Rose Hill."

"Did Ian ever talk to you about what had happened in Florida?"

"Not until the truth came out, and then he just wanted to help," Melissa said. "Later, when he got the dementia he started calling me Mandy, again, and we all just let him do it."

"Did you ever regret what you'd done?"

"Not once."

"So, fast forward a few years. Tommy's a young man, and you're virtually a member of the Fitzpatrick family. What changed?"

"You know what changed."

"Pretend I don't."

"I don't want stuff about me and you in the paper."

"It won't be," he said. "You can trust me, you know that. We'll call that information 'off the record.'"

"Well then, off the record, I took up with the editor of the newspaper," she said with a rueful smile. "It didn't work out, but I don't think it was meant to."

"I agree," he said. "But with no regrets."

"If you're too nice to me today I'll cry," Melissa said.

"I'll try to reign it in," he said.

"There were some letters stolen from the post office; you remember that business with Margie, the postmaster. The new chief who took Ian's place, Scott Gordon, found her stash of stolen mail, and in it was a letter from Miranda's mother, who was looking for her. Scott looked into it, figured out who I was and what I did. He confronted me with the evidence, and I confessed. It felt good to tell someone, actually, and you know Scott, he was kind about it."

"What happened then?"

"I called Miranda's mother and confessed to her. She had been hoping her daughter was still alive somewhere, so she was pretty ticked off by what I'd done. She called the cops. Scott took me to Florida to turn myself in. Tommy stayed with Delia and Ian. You know all this."

"Keep going."

"Miranda's mother was dying of cancer. She met me, heard my confession, and went to Rose Hill to meet Tommy. She wanted to withdraw the charges but the law is the law, and I broke it. Kidnapping and identity theft are felonies. She ended up pleading with the judge on my behalf, and I got a lesser sentence because of it."

"What was your sentence?"

"Three to five, but I got out after three for good behavior, with a year of parole."

"What was that like, going to prison?"

"Scaredest I ever been in my life," Melissa said. "Sorry. Don't put that in. Say I was frightened."

"Done."

"I lucked out again, though. My cellmate was an embezzler from Orlando, named Glenda. She was big enough no one messed with her, but she wasn't mean on the inside. She was my friend, and she set me on the right path."

"Prison has a right path?"

"It sure does," she said. "She told me you can get harder and meaner or you can use your time to prepare for getting out. I got my GED and took secretarial courses."

"Did anyone come to see you?"

"Miranda's mother did until she got too sick. Some Rose Hill folks came; all the Fitzpatricks, and you."

"What happened to Tommy?"

Melissa rolled her eyes.

"Pretend I don't know," he said.

"Miranda's mother took him to Florida, but she knew she was going to die soon. She asked him who he wanted to live with other than Delia and Ian, who she thought were too old to raise him. He chose Ed Harrison, the editor of the Sentinel, who lived next door to Delia and Ian. It was the right choice."

"He never blamed you or hated you for what you did. He understood."

"I know," she said. "But three years is a long time for a boy to go without his mama. Four visits per year were no substitute."

"Did you resent me?"

"Sometimes," she said, "but I know he loves me. He will always be mine."

They were both silent for a few moments.

"What happened after you got out?"

"I came home," she said. "Rose Hill was home, and I was still welcome here. Turned out most folks felt like I did the right thing rescuing a little boy from dying in an explosion, even if what I did afterward wasn't legal."

"Was it hard to transition to being on the outside?"

"Of course it was," she said. "I had to learn how to think for myself again. I was used to somebody telling me what to do and when to do it all day every day. I had got used to being part of a noisy crowd of angry people, watching my back all the time, while guards with guns watched us every minute."

"What was it like for you here, after you got out? What were your challenges?"

"One of the hardest things at first was how quiet it was at night. It made me jumpy. I wasn't used to a soft bed; I had to sleep on the floor for the first few nights. Food tasted so good I gained ten pounds working at the bakery. Bonnie didn't say anything, either; she just let me eat everything in sight. Wearing clothes washed in fabric softener, long, hot showers, and privacy. Oh, Lord, to have privacy. I never knew how important that was. Then there was grocery shopping, all the choices. Cold beer, Dairy Chef ice cream, PJ's pizza. Just everything.

"The first time I drove somewhere by myself in a car I was so nervous; I felt like any minute I was going to be pulled over and put back in prison. I felt like everyone was watching me, waiting for me to make a mistake; I still have that feeling sometimes."

"How was your relationship with Tommy?"

"Harder for him, probably," she said. "I wanted things right back the way they were, but he had got used to living with you. I cried about it, but whatever he wanted I wanted."

"He didn't love you any less."

"I don't want to talk about Tommy anymore," she said. "I miss him so much I can hardly breathe when I think about it."

"You couldn't work at the bar because of your parole."

"Bonnie hired me back to work at the bakery."

"But you weren't satisfied with that."

"I love that family," she said. "I owe them more than I could ever repay. Claire got me this job working for Sean, or I would never have left the bakery, just out of loyalty. Here I can use my brains and my education, and I'm still helping the Fitzpatricks."

"Sean's a good boss, I take it."

"The best. He encouraged me to go to Pine County Community College, and then to get my paralegal license. He helped me pay the tuition. He believed in me even when I didn't think I could do it. He was all the time asking me test questions. By the time I took the big test, it was not exactly easy, but I knew enough to pass it."

"So now you're helping him with his cases."

"I still answer the phones and do the secretarial stuff; we can't afford another person just yet. I do the research related to his cases; I keep it all organized; I get the paperwork filled out and filed on time. Eventually, he's going to make me a partner, so I got something to work toward. I mean, I have something."

"You've accomplished so much," Ed said. "Is there anything else you'd like to do?"

"There is, but I don't want it in the paper."

"Off the record, then," he said and ended the recording.

"Miranda's mom left me and Tommy some money; Tommy's was for his college education, and mine is invested. I can't touch the principal, but I've been saving my dividends. I've got me a big nest egg."

"That's great," Ed said. "What are you going to do with it?"

"That's just it," Melissa said. "Patrick wants to buy the building next door to the Rose and Thorn, and expand the business. He hasn't asked me to help, but I think he'd accept if I offered."

"What do you want to do with it?"

"I want to buy the trailer park."

"The Foxglove?"

"Yep," she said. "The owner died last year, and the estate is just about to settle. I've talked to his son, and he's agreed to give me first refusal. They got it appraised, and I have enough to buy it outright. The son wants me to buy it, rather than some real estate developer. Somebody else would just put expensive condos on it, and it's one of the few places left in Rose Hill where poor folks can afford to live. He grew up here, and he wants other low-income families to have that same opportunity."

"What will you do with it?"

"Fix it up, take care of the old folks and the decent people who rent there. I'll keep out the drug dealers and the no-accounts who trash up the place."

"I think that's a great plan," Ed said. "When you do that, I want to write about it in the Sentinel."

"Keep it just between us right now; don't even tell Claire. If I for sure decide to do it, I gotta pick my moment to talk to everyone else about it. They're not going to be happy about it."

"Surely they'll support you in pursuing your dreams, not just theirs."

"That's wishful thinking, but I appreciate you saying it."

"Well, I wish you the best of luck," Ed said. "I won't say a word about it."

"Thanks," Melissa said. "And if I haven't already, I want to thank you for all you've done for Tommy and me. I haven't forgotten. I owe you big time."

"You don't owe me anything," Ed said. "Getting to be a father to Tommy was a gift no one else could have given me."

"And now you've got four little girls to run after."

"It was kind of an instant family and for sad reasons," Ed said. "I'm grateful, though, and Claire is so good with them, it's just overwhelming sometimes. There's a lot of princess paraphernalia. I wouldn't tell just anyone, but my toenails regularly get painted, and right now they are bright pink."

"Don't worry, your secret's safe with me," Melissa said. "As soon as the maternal grandparents sign off on the consent to adopt, it won't be long before it's official."

"I figured Pip's mother wouldn't want them," Ed said. "She was just disappointed there was no life insurance for her to collect. Jessie's parents are certainly taking their time deciding."

"They don't want those kids," Melissa said. "They'd just hire nannies to raise them if they did take them. They like to travel all over the world on their private jet."

"All we can do is hope they want what's best for the girls and not what they think makes them look the best."

"As soon as we hear anything I'll call you," Melissa said. "Sean was going to wait another few days before calling their attorney again."

"Keep your fingers crossed."

"I'm not much of a prayer, but I'm doing that, too."

Ed prepared to leave, and Melissa, who had been debating internally, gave in to her need to know.

"Hey," she said. "You know anything about that accident in front of the Thorn last night?"

"The driver says he swerved to miss an SUV driving on the wrong side of the road," Ed said. "Nobody saw it happen, there was no SUV anyone could find, and I guess the driver blew a point-one-five on the breathalyzer."

"I heard he killed somebody."

"Yeah, that's a mystery," Ed said. "The victim had no ID, no car that anyone can find; nobody seems to know what he was doing on the street at that time of night. They're going to run his prints, circulate a photograph, and check missing person reports."

"I know Patrick was there," Melissa said.

"I read that in the police report," Ed said. "After we're through here I'm going to the Thorn to interview him."

Melissa hesitated, agonized, but finally spoke.

"My neighbor Maxine said her husband saw a woman there," Melissa said, and couldn't look at Ed.

"A woman?" he said. "I talked to Malcolm and Skip, and neither mentioned a woman being there. It wasn't in the police report, either."

Malcolm Behr was the fire chief and Skip was a deputy policeman.

"Bruce is old and maybe doesn't see too well," Melissa said.

"Are they the type to make up gossip?"

"Yeah," Melissa said. "I reckon they are."

"I wouldn't put too much stock in that, then," he said.

"Do you think Malcolm or Skip would lie for Patrick?"

"Have you talked to Patrick about it?"

"Not yet."

"Melissa," Ed said. "I can't imagine Patrick doing that to you. Maybe you're just feeling insecure about things right now?"

"Maybe," she said. "Anyway, don't ask Patrick about it."

Ed hesitated.

"Please," Melissa said. "As my co-parent. As my friend."

"I won't," he said. "But you should."

After work, instead of walking home, Melissa crossed Rose Hill Avenue and then took a left down Pine Mountain Road. At the intersection where the road crossed Marigold Avenue, she looked across the Little Bear River. It was almost dark now, and the trees had lost their leaves, leaving a forest of white, gray, and brown trunks sprouting out of a blanket of dark, damp fall color.

Through the woods, she could see lights on in Ava's grand house on the hill, and Melissa wondered if she was in there and if she was thinking about Patrick.

CHAPTER THREE - WEDNESDAY

Melissa yawned and rubbed her eyes. It had been a long time since she'd stayed up until Patrick got home from work. She had tried watching television, but every show irritated her. They all seemed to be about selfish rich people's problems, and she didn't have the patience for that. Banjo, the beagle, was trying to sleep, but Melissa's fidgeting was interfering; she could tell by his deep sighs.

She had taken up the book Patrick's sister had given her, titled "Wuthering Heights." After a slow start, it had gotten interesting, even though it seemed as if on every page she had to use her phone to look up the meaning of a word she didn't understand. Now her eyes were watering as she repeatedly yawned, blurring the words on the page.

She must have dozed off because the sound of his key in the door startled her awake. He came in and looked at her, and Melissa could tell by his expression that he was both surprised and a little scared.

"What are you doing up?" he asked.

He shrugged off his coat and sat down at the kitchen table to untie his boots. His face was lined, and there were shadows under his eyes. Melissa was tempted to put off the confrontation she had intended to have, but the thought of going through one more day not knowing was unacceptable.

"I haven't seen you in weeks, it seems like," Melissa said. "I wanted to talk to you."

"That can't be good," he said. "What'd I do now?"

The expression on his face was wary but also closed down, as if Melissa were the enemy, not an ally. Up until that moment, Melissa hadn't realized how far apart they had drifted.

"I wanted to ask you about the wreck," she said.

"Oh, that," he said. "The driver was high as a kite, ran into the utility pole outside of PJ's. Killed some dude, they don't know who; he didn't have an ID on him. He said he swerved to avoid a white SUV driving down the middle of the road, but if there was one, he was long gone by the time I got out there. I think he probably passed out and lost control of the truck. The electric was out for everybody east of Rose Hill Avenue and north of Sunflower Street. They just got it back on around noon today."

Patrick got up and looked in the refrigerator.

"How come there's never any food in this place?" he asked. "Where's that pizza?"

"It was a week old, so I threw it out," Melissa said. "If you want there to be food in this place you could always buy some."

He huffed at that.

"That'll be the day," he said. "I work fourteen hours a day, and you work eight."

"I heard Ava was there last night," Melissa said.

Patrick froze, but then turned to the pantry and rifled through its contents.

"Where'd you hear that?" he said, but he wasn't looking at her.

"People saw her, Patrick," she said. "I know she was there."

"People also lie, Melissa," Patrick said, and then looked right at her. "She wasn't there."

"Have you been seeing her?"

"I see her," Patrick said. "She's a citizen of this town, and sometimes our paths cross. She's the mother of my brother's children, so she sometimes brings the kids to visit members of my family."

"Are you still in love with her?"

"No," he said. "Is that all you wanted to know? Can I go to sleep now? God, I'm starving."

"I'm countin' on you to tell me the truth," Melissa said. "We've known each other a long time. We're friends, Patrick. I knew she was the love of your life. I just thought it ended when I came back."

"Melissa, I'm tired. I was up all night last night. I've got a lot on my mind," he said.

"What's on your mind? Tell me. You used to tell me things."

"It's just the tea room next door. I want to buy it, but it's complicated. The owner has stipulations I can't agree with."

"You've been talking about buying that thing for years," Melissa said. "You've got the down payment, you've been pre-approved by the bank, why don't you go ahead and buy it?"

He sat down on a bar stool by the kitchen counter.

"Mom wants me to buy the bakery," he said.

"She does? Since when?"

59

"She has to have knee replacement surgery on both knees," he said. "She's almost seventy; she wants to retire."

"But you don't want to run the bakery."

"This isn't about me," he said. "This is about my mother wanting to keep a family business in the family."

"You already run a family business."

"The Thorn is Aunt Delia's," he said. "If I buy the tea room and expand the place, we'll be partners, but it will never be all mine unless I can come up with the dough to buy it from her."

"Then that's what you should do."

"Except I need you to run the restaurant side," he said. "That was the plan, I thought, until you decided to play office with Sean."

"You supported me going back to school," Melissa said. "You supported my decision to get a degree."

"But I thought you would eventually want to work with me, not my brother," he said.

"If you had bought the tea room three years ago, when you could have, we'd already be in there together," she said. "What was I supposed to do, sit around and twiddle my thumbs while you couldn't make up your mind for three years?"

"I waited for you," he said.

"I know," she said. "And I'm grateful. I love you, Patrick. Isn't that what's important, not whose business I work in?"

"I can't believe you like doing that job. Isn't it all paperwork and suing people?"

"The paperwork is a big part of it, but I like it. I'm using my brain, my education, and we don't just handle lawsuits, we help people do all kinds of things. We're helping Claire and Ed get custody of Pip's kids."

"You're the one who's changed," he said. "You used to want to help me."

"My life is bigger than just you," she said. "Why can't I have what I want, too?"

"We had a plan."

"You couldn't commit."

"I've proposed to you a thousand times," he said. "Don't say I can't commit."

"To the restaurant plan, I meant."

"You're never going to marry me, are you? How can you say you love me when you won't marry me and you won't help me achieve my dream? It's you that can't commit."

"If I believed you were really done with Ava, I'd marry you. You're not, though, are you?"

"Why are you so obsessed with Ava? She's married to a gazillionaire, living in a mansion. What would she want with me, anyway?"

"She was there, wasn't she? Swear she wasn't on your mother's life."

"You're crazy," he said.

"Swear Ava wasn't with you last night," Melissa said. "Swear it on your mother's life."

"I'm going to Mom's," he said. "I need to get some sleep."

He stuck his feet down in his boots, grabbed his jacket, called the worried-looking Banjo off the couch, and left the trailer, slamming the door behind them.

Melissa was momentarily paralyzed by what had just happened. The atmosphere in the room was still buzzing from the tension. Her heart began to pound, and tears welled up in her eyes.

She didn't know what she had expected, but what she had always feared would happen, just had.

That morning, Melissa did her best to cover up her swollen eyes and red nose with makeup, but she didn't fool Sean.

"What's wrong?" he asked.

"Just a fight with your stupid brother," Melissa said. "I'll be fine."

"All right," Sean said, but he didn't sound convinced. "Let me know if there's anything I can do."

Melissa knew Sean well enough to know he was relieved not to find out more about what was going on. Sean didn't like drama, didn't like emotional scenes, and sure didn't want to get involved in Melissa's personal life if he could help it. Sean went back to his office, and Melissa looked at her to-do list for the day. There was plenty to keep her busy, and she was glad. She didn't want to think about anything else.

At nine o'clock realtor Trick Rodefeffer came in.

"Hey, jailbird," he said. "What's up?"

"The sale documents for the B&B are ready and Will can do the closing at 2:30 tomorrow," she said. "I called your buyers, and they will meet you for a final walk-through at 1:30. Be sure to bring the keys to the house, garage, and apartment with you when you're through."

"I was just over there, and the keys to the garage and apartment are gone. I guess you don't have them."

"No, Trick, I don't have them," she said. "You want me to call a locksmith?"

"No, they're probably in my office somewhere," he said. "I'll keep looking."

"Please be on time tomorrow. Will can only stay for a half hour; he has to go out of town for work."

"Well, far be it from me to hold up Mr. Moneybags," Trick said. "I can hardly believe we finally unloaded that money pit. I'll be glad to accept my commission and be done with it."

"When's Sandy coming back?" Melissa asked. "I don't mind pitching in while she's gone, but I have a lot on my plate this week."

Trick was uncharacteristically silent, his hands stuck down in his pockets. Melissa noticed his thinning blonde hair needed a trim, he'd missed a few places shaving, and his tie was stained.

"Trick," Melissa said. "Is Sandy coming back?"

He shrugged.

"She's leased a house on Anna Maria Island," he said. "I don't think that's a good sign, do you? I mean, when a married woman takes all her clothes and her little dogs and rents a house in Florida, it doesn't bode well, does it?"

"What does Stacy say about it?"

"My daughter is not exactly talking to me right now."

"What'd you do to her?"

"She wants me to pay for a Hawaiian wedding. I told her, 'Baby Doll, I don't have that kind of dough; we're Rose Hill rich, not Hawaii rich.' All the family assets are tied up in a trust, my house is mortgaged way beyond what it's worth, nobody's buying lots to build homes in Eldridge Point anymore on account of the sewage issues, and now I've got Anna Maria Island to pay for. I can't bankroll some swanky shindig. I could pay for a fried chicken picnic in a park shelter, maybe."

He sighed, and his shoulders slumped.

"I'd feel sorrier for you, Trick, if I didn't know what a low-life cheater you are."

"Go on," he said. "Kick me when I'm down."

"If you could keep it in your pants for five minutes you might be able to get your wife back."

"Men aren't made to be monogamous, jailbird," he said. "We have to spread the seed far and wide just to keep the species going. It's in our DNA; we can't help it."

"I tell you what, Trick, when the fool killer comes you better be hiding in the tall grass," Melissa said. "Listen to me; you need to hire somebody to do Sandy's job because I'm not going to keep doing it forever."

"I can't afford to hire anyone; business is too slow," Trick said. "Those national outfits are stealing all my business."

"Only because you're so do-less and no-account," Melissa said. "You just need to work harder, Trick, that's all."

"I need somebody to kick my ass every day," he said. "I need my wife back."

Melissa could not believe her eyes, but Trick had tears in his.

"Then straighten up and be a good husband," Melissa said. "Show her you want her back bad enough to change."

"She wouldn't believe it even if I could do it," he said. "The truth is I'm never going to change. She knows it, and I finally ran out of do-overs. She's never coming back. She's just hanging on for half the dividends. She'll collect them all when I die. Which might be soon. I don't see any point in living like this."

"I'm not going to feel sorry for you," Melissa said. "You're the only mule in your own barnyard."

"I know it," he said. "You need me for anything today?"

"Nope," Melissa said. "Just make sure you show up at the B&B at 1:30 tomorrow."

"Alrighty then," he said. "I'm going to forward my calls to voicemail, crawl into a bottle, and not come out till I have to."

Melissa shook her head but didn't comment as he left.

Just before noon, Claire Fitzpatrick came in holding the littlest of her ex-husband's children by the hand. The previous summer, Pip and his second ex-wife Jessica had disappeared while on a mountain climbing expedition in Tibet, and were assumed to have perished from falling into a mountain crevasse during an avalanche, although their bodies had not been recovered. Pip and Jessie's four girls, aged five to eleven, had been living with Ed and Claire ever since.

Pip's mother was only interested in the girls if there was money to be had. Jessie's parents weren't willing to pay her to care for the girls, and there was no life insurance to be collected. Jessie's parents, who were wealthy California film industry executives, were not interested in taking them on, either, although they were dragging their feet about signing the papers to make it legal. Claire and Ed were not asking for any money, which was unheard of in L.A. circles, so the grandparents' attorneys were using many valuable billable hours to explore every nuance of the suspiciously amicable agreement.

Five-year-old Pixie was wearing a pink tutu, a pink fleece jacket, flowered leggings, and purple fleece-lined boots. Her long curly hair was pulled up on top of her head in a loose knot. She was adorable.

"Hi, Pixie!" Melissa said as she came around the desk for a hug. "How you been, girl?"

All four of the girls were blonde like their mother and had beautiful hazel eyes flecked with gold, just like their father. Pixie flew into Melissa's arms and hugged her. Then she looked up and smiled, showing her missing tooth.

"You lost it!" Melissa said.

"And you'll never guess what!" Pixie said. "The tooth fairy gave me a whole dollar, and I'm gonna buy a new book. Claire says I can have any book I want."

"That's awesome," Melissa said and exchanged winks with Claire.

"We thought you might join us for lunch," Claire said.

Sean came out of the back and said, "I thought I heard a fairy princess out here. Where is she?"

Pixie ran to hide behind Claire and peek out at Sean, who stooped down low to the floor.

"Are you still afraid of me?" Sean asked. "What am I going to have to do, Pixie-Lou-Who?"

Pixie hid her face against Claire's leg.

"Sean's silly, isn't he?" Claire said to Pixie and then hoisted her up into her arms. "Pixie's just feeling a little shy right now, and she doesn't have to talk to anybody if she doesn't want to; isn't that right?"

Pixie nodded and threw her arms around Claire's neck, burying her face in her hair. Claire rolled her eyes at Sean and Melissa.

"We're having a day together, just Pixie and me," Claire said. "The other girls are in school, and we're playing hooky."

Sean stood back up.

"Well, you tell Pixie that someday I'd like to take her to the park and push her on the swings," he said. "But we'll wait until Ed can go, too."

"Would you like that?" Claire asked the little girl.

Pixie just gripped Claire harder and shook her head.

"Sorry," mouthed Claire.

"Don't worry about it," Sean said. "I'm sure eventually we'll be friends."

"Do you mind if I run out with these two for lunch?" Melissa asked.

"No, go on," Sean said. "But bring me back something, I don't care what."

Claire and Melissa took Pixie to Little Bear Books, where she finally let Claire put her down. Pixie ran back to the kid's section while Claire stretched out her shoulders and back.

"She's getting heavy," Claire said as they got in line on the café side.

"Is she okay?" Melissa asked.

Claire shrugged.

"She's clingy, and panics when she's not with me, Ed, or my mother. She cries so hard when I leave her at preschool that I can hardly

67

bear to do it. I'm sure it's normal considering what she's gone through; we're just being patient and working through it."

"Poor little orphans," Melissa said. "They're lucky to have you."

"It's been an adjustment for everyone," Claire said. "Lily's having bad dreams at night, Daisy's counting everything, and Pixie's our little Klingon. Bluebell's doing the best, so far, so of course we're worried that's not healthy."

"They're just darlin'," Melissa said. "And you're a natural at this motherin' thing."

"Ed adores them, of course," Claire said. "I don't know what we'll do if Jessie's parents decide to take us to court."

"Sean will roast them alive in court," Melissa said. "The family was officially living here so the hearing would have to be held here. There's not a judge in this county who would find in their favor."

"I hope it doesn't come to that. The girls have had too much upheaval already."

"Sean doesn't think the grandparents want them. He thinks they're afraid of how it looks not to want them, and their attorneys are billing them a thousand an hour while they take their time decidin'."

"I hope that's all it is."

"Sean's going to follow up with them this week. We'll keep you posted."

They placed their orders and sat down at a table near the back, where they could keep an eye on Pixie. The only child in the store, she was seated in a child's rocker, looking through a picture book.

"She would be happy to do that for hours," Claire said. "She's my little bookworm."

Their lunch was served, along with Sean's bag lunch to go.

"You look great, by the way," Claire said. "It's a shame that idiot from the Pendleton paper got it so wrong."

"It was sweet of you to send Ed over," Melissa said.

Her eyes filled with tears and she blinked several times to try to control them.

"Are you okay?" Claire asked.

Melissa's eyes spilled over, but she rolled them at Claire before dabbing at them with a paper napkin.

"If you can't talk about it I understand," Claire said. "But let me know if I can do anything."

Melissa blew her nose and then laughed at herself.

"Actually, I'm dying to tell somebody," Melissa said. "But you've got your own stuff going on."

"Please tell me," Claire said. "It will take my mind off my own problems. Is it Patrick?"

Melissa nodded and cleared her throat.

She told Claire everything, and Claire nodded and prodded in all the appropriate places. When she was done, Claire narrowed her eyes at Melissa.

"What does your gut say?"

"That he's cheating with Ava, maybe has been for a while, and I've just been too busy to pay attention to what's going on right under my nose."

"Sounds about right," Claire said.

"You think so, too?"

"I trust your instincts," Claire said. "What are you going to do about it?"

"I thought about spying on him."

"That's natural," Claire said.

"But I think he basically admitted it last night."

"If it's true," Claire said. "If you caught them in the act, what would you do then?"

"I'd kick him out, but he already left," Melissa said. "If he wants to be with her he shoulda broke up with me first and then did what he wanted."

"What about Ava, though?" Claire said. "Is she likely to leave Will for him?"

"I don't know," Melissa said. "Maybe they were just happy sneakin' around on us."

"She was not in the police report," Claire said. "That's something."

"Why do people cheat?" Melissa asked.

"Lots of reasons," Claire said. "I cheated on Pip because I was young, stupid, starved for affection, and desperate for attention. I should have just left him, but we were so tangled up together working for Sloan that I felt stuck. It's different in the entertainment business. Everyone was either good-looking and ambitious or ugly and powerful. Although it's reprehensible, sex was the coin of the realm."

"Would you ever cheat on Ed?"

"I hope not," Claire said. "I don't think so now, but people change, relationships change. Right now we're in parental mode, and all our energy is invested in the kids. Later on, who knows? I love Ed, and I'd like to think I could be faithful till death do us part, but the truth is, I'm not a for-better-or-worse kind of person. When things get worse, I tend to bail."

"You didn't bail on your mom; you'd never bail on your girls."

"That's different," Claire said. "They depend on me. My relationships with men always seem a little more tenuous. I invest all my emotion and energy, but if nothing is returned, eventually I'm done."

"Ed would never cheat on you."

"I know," Claire said. "He's a much better person than I am."

"Let's face it," Melissa said, "Ed's better than everybody, but we love him in spite of it. When are y'all gettin' hitched?"

"He's finally divorced from Eve," Claire said. "Nothing is stopping us, and I know it would make him happy. I'm just afraid I'll screw it up. I love him, but I don't trust myself."

"If you get custody of those girls you might change your mind," Melissa said.

"Maybe," Claire said. "You know, Maggie told me when she and Scott were estranged that she kind of knew Scott was the one for her, but she just didn't feel compelled to do anything about it. At the time I thought that was horrible, but now I kind of get it. Things are fine the way they are. Right now Ed and I are committed to each other and the girls, but the thought of putting a wedding together is exhausting."

"You did a great job on Maggie's wedding," Melissa said. "It was fun, too."

"Maybe I got it out of my system that way," Claire said. "Anyway, unless I find some way to get excited about it, it probably won't happen."

They finished their drinks and Claire went to get refills. Melissa noted that even though Claire didn't dress up as fancy as she used to, and looked as tired as she felt most days, she also seemed happier than Melissa had ever known her to be. Settled, somehow, and content. She had kids now, which she had always wanted, and Ed was, for all his nerdy faults, a steady, supportive person who was deeply in love with Claire. If Claire was a little more pragmatic about their relationship, it was only because she'd been out in the bigger world, and knew life was messy and strange; Ed had only ever lived in Rose Hill and was terminally idealistic.

Melissa wondered if she'd made a mistake not sticking with Ed, but quickly reminded herself that his non-stop talking had bored her silly, and she only half understood the stuff he went on and on about. At the time, he was lonely and sex-deprived, she wanted a husband for herself and a father for Tommy, and their sexual chemistry had been off the charts. When the heat wore off, however, they would have both realized they made a big mistake. Their brief infatuation had thankfully turned into a real friendship and a cooperative co-parenting operation, and she was sincerely glad that he and Claire had got together.

What would happen to her if she actually broke up with Patrick for good? Would there ever be anyone else? What would she even look for? It was hard to imagine someone could be as steady as Ed and as exciting as Patrick.

Who would be interested in her, anyway, with her background and prison record? Patrick already knew all that and still had loved her. How could anyone else be expected to understand and accept her past? Just the thought of telling someone about it made her incredibly tired.

When Claire sat back down, she resumed their conversation.

"We need to find out who the guy was that was killed," Claire said.

"And what was he doing hanging around town at that hour?" Melissa asked.

"Ed says they have no idea."

"That's weird as hell," Melissa said. "What man do you know goes anywhere without his wallet or keys?"

"You should get Hannah involved," Claire said. "You two could investigate both things."

"I don't know," Melissa said. "She and Maggie are awful close, and Patrick being Maggie's brother ..."

"I'm just saying, if you want to find out if anybody else saw Ava the other night, Hannah is the person who can help. She knows everyone, she's snoopy as hell, and she hears all the gossip. If I were you, I would trust her."

"Thanks, Claire."

"Meanwhile, I'll see what I can find out from Ava's housekeeper."

Late in the afternoon, while Melissa was prepping that day's correspondence to go out, she received a call from Bonnie Fitzpatrick, asking Melissa to come to see her after work. Melissa was nervous as she walked down Pine Mountain Road to Marigold Avenue.

The Fitzpatricks' ramshackle two-story four-square house sat at the end of the street near the alley known as Daisy Lane that, along with a high brick wall, separated Eldridge College from Rose Hill. On the Fitzpatrick's house, the shingles were curling, the paint was peeling, the porch rail was leaning, and parts of the porch floor had already rotted and caved in. As Melissa walked up the creaking steps, she wondered how safe they were.

Bonnie answered the door and gathered Melissa in a fierce hug, which was, to say the least, uncharacteristic. Bonnie was a stout, formidable woman with thick, white curly hair and intense blue eyes. She was wearing a pinny over her clothes, which were worn and faded from many years of washing in the hottest water and cheapest laundry detergent you could buy. The family may have been poor, but they were always clean.

"Get in here," Bonnie said. "It's freezing out there. We're supposed to have snow this weekend, maybe three inches."

She led the way toward the kitchen, which smelled like cinnamon, vanilla, and melted sugar. They tiptoed past Patrick's father, whom everyone called Fitz, who was snoring in a recliner, swaddled in sweatshirts and old threadbare quilts. He looked a lot thinner than the last time Melissa had seen him, just a few weeks before. The TV was on, blaring a sports talk show, but it didn't seem to disturb him.

Their big, shaggy Irish Setter, known as Lazy Ass Laddie, was sprawled out on the floor by the gas heater, sound asleep. The fur on his face was white with age. Patrick's beagle Banjo hopped off the couch and wagged all over at the sight of Melissa. Bonnie shooed him out of the kitchen.

"We'll just shut this door," Bonnie said, "so we can talk."

Melissa felt a shiver of dread cascade through her body, but she dutifully went in and sat down at the kitchen table. The Formica was peeling, and the vinyl seats of the chrome chairs were patched with duct tape. Bonnie had spread wax paper over the table's surface, and it was sticky with pieces of dough and dusty with flour.

"Why are you baking on your day off?" Melissa asked her.

"I can't sit still," Bonnie said. "Unlike some people, I can't just sit and vegetate in front of the television for hours; I have to be doing something. My knees have got so bad I can't go upstairs to clean, and I can't go downstairs to do laundry, so I'm baking."

"I'd be glad to do some laundry for you," Melissa said.

"You're a good girl," Bonnie said, "but Delia's coming over later to do it. Since Ian died and she quit working she's at loose ends, poor thing, and if she's not minding Pip's children, she's over here minding us."

"I can still hardly believe Ian's gone."

"Well, the Ian Fitzpatrick I knew had been gone a couple of years before he died," Bonnie said. "It's a crime what dementia does to people. It's a mercy he died when he did, and I don't mind anyone hearing me say so. Before his family went broke and lost their health in the caring of him. He wouldn't have wanted that, do you agree?"

"I do," Melissa said.

"We all go when it's our time and not a minute earlier. I hope when it's my time the Lord will spare me a few moments to explain why wicked rich people have such an easy time of it and us poor but good folks have to suffer."

"Please sit down," Melissa said. "Let me wait on you while you rest your legs."

"You're as good as gold," Bonnie said. "I don't mind if I do."

Bonnie proceeded to boss her around for an hour while Melissa made coffee, cleaned the kitchen, put a load of dish towels in the washer, and then put the cinnamon rolls that had been proofing near the gas box heater into a hot oven to bake. If it felt right, and it felt familiar, it was only because Melissa had worked for Bonnie in the bakery for so many years.

When Melissa finally sat down with a freshly baked cinnamon roll and a hot cup of coffee of her own, Bonnie dove right in.

"My son came home early this morning," she said. "I didn't expect him."

Melissa knew Bonnie well enough to know she wasn't supposed to speak until she was asked a direct question, so she started unwinding her cinnamon roll instead. She liked to eat them that way.

"I couldn't get a word out of him, as usual," Bonnie said, "but I know what the problem is, and I'm finally going to have my say. I've kept my tongue in my mouth for a long time where you two are concerned, but look where that's gotten us. I didn't say a word when he moved in with you, on account of it's a new century and I had hopes that there would be a wedding and some grandchildren soon after. But that hasn't happened.

"I know he's got some pie-in-the-sky dream about adding on to that bar and having a restaurant and a dance place, but you and I both know that's never gonna happen. You may think you know why, but I do know why, and I'm going to tell you.

"I'm also going to tell you why he can't get Ava's hooks out of him. He won't talk to me about it, but something's got to change. I'm being done out of a wonderful grandchild, and an innocent child is being done out of a perfectly good grandmother, while Will's mother can't be bothered.

"I'm also going to put you on the spot about the bakery. If you and Patrick don't take it over, I'm going to have to sell it, on account of Fitz's kidneys are failing, and I need new knees, and there's no way we can afford any of that without selling. We have no savings. Social Security and Medicare may be yanked away from us at any minute, depending on how big of a tax cut those millionaires in Washington give the billionaires that own their souls, so I have no choice. Maggie knows a catering lady who wants to buy it and will pay us enough money, but I would like it to stay in the family.

"There's this house to consider. It's falling down around our ears as we speak. I don't think we could get but what the land underneath it is worth if we sold it and that's next to nothing. I talked to Ruthie down at the Mountain View Retirement home in Pendleton, and we can give them this house and move into a small apartment there, but I still need the money from selling the bakery. I would have liked to leave our business and home to one of our children, but Maggie's got her hands full at the bookstore, Sean can barely make toast, and Patrick thinks he's going to make a million dollars hiring bluegrass bands to entertain college students.

"You're a sensible girl. I feel like you're a niece to me, just like Hannah and Claire. I had hoped to call you daughter-in-law, but it looks like Patrick's going to fool around and mess that up, too.

Bonnie took a deep breath, but never took her fierce blue-eyed gaze off Melissa.

"So," Bonnie said. "What do you want to tackle first?"

"Tell me about Ava," Melissa said.

Bonnie took another deep breath.

"You want to know anything about Ava, you ask Delia," she said. "Delia worked at the B&B for her while Brian was missing and she saw everything. Ava's a beautiful woman, and a wily one, and she's used to manipulating men to get what she wants. She's also a good mother, I can't fault her there. But she's greedy, and she wants to have her cake and eat it, too."

"Will and Patrick."

"Don't ask me how I know, just trust me that I was tipped off by a dear friend," Bonnie said.

Now it was Melissa's turn to take a deep breath. She knew better than to cry in front of Bonnie; it would just make her mad.

"How long has this been going on?" she asked instead.

"Who knows?" Bonnie said. "I don't know what it is about that woman; she must have a trick coochie."

"I figured they were together while I was gone," Melissa said. "But I thought it stopped when we moved in together and I for sure thought it ended when she married Will."

"I don't think he ever stopped," Bonnie said. "I'm sorry, I know that's not easy to hear. But somebody needs to tell you the truth, and I guess that's me."

"You don't think she'd leave Will for him?"

"Why should she? She's got it made, swanning around in her expensive clothes, driving a fancy car, going on exotic vacations, and living in that big house. Not that anyone in this family has been invited to see it."

"I guess there's nothing I can do about it," Melissa said. "I'm going to have to let him go."

"Don't be so hasty," Bonnie said. "There's more to tell."

Melissa got them both some fresh coffee and changed out the laundry. They folded dish towels while they continued their conversation.

"Have you ever seen that little one of Ava's, that Olivia?" Bonnie asked.

"Sure," Melissa said. "She looks just her mother, just like her big sister Charlotte."

"Except for the blue eyes."

"That's not that unusual," Melissa said.

"No, but I'll tell you what is," Bonnie said, and held up her hands.

Her knuckles were gnarled with arthritis knots, the backs were wrinkled and spotted, but the quicks of her nails were a light pearly pink. She held up the first two fingers of each hand.

"Look at this," she said. "Look at your own hands. I'll bet anything the index finger is shorter than the bird finger, just like mine. Go on, look."

Melissa held out her hands.

"See?" Bonnie said. "Now, if we were to go in there and wake up his majesty, and ask to see his fingers, on each hand you'd see an index finger longer than the bird."

"Like Patrick's."

"Like Brian's, like Patrick's, like Maggie's, like Sean's," she said. "All my children have the long index finger, and it's rare. Neither of Fitz's brothers has it, and none of their children do. It's from some pirate way back, one of those Spaniards who showed up in Ireland and seduced his great-great-grandmother."

"So you're saying Olivia has it, too."

Bonnie slapped the table and pointed at Melissa.

"You bet your sweet bippie, she does. That child has my eyes and my husband's finger. Now, how do you think that came about?"

"She's Patrick's daughter."

"And my granddaughter by blood. But do I get to see her and cuddle her and feed her good baked things? I do not. Meanwhile, that useless mother of Will's can't be bothered to even visit that child. If it weren't for Ernie being my blood grandchild, I'd never see him, either. Charlotte, she shipped off to Europe three years ago, and just this past August she sent my precious Timmy to a boarding school in New England, of all places, where those Yankees are mean to him."

"How do you know that?"

"He calls me and cries," she said. "It breaks my heart."

"But you say she's a good mother."

"When they're young. When the babies are young and don't give Ava any lip, or ask too many questions, or get in the way of what she wants to do, she's a marvelous mother. But the minute one of them gets difficult or sees what's really going on with their mother and the men she's involved with, then it's off to rich children boot camp, and we never see them again. She did that with Charlotte, and she did that with Timothy, but I'll be damned if she does that to Ernie or Olivia, not on my watch. I've had enough of Ava's shenanigans, and I aim to put a stop to it."

"But how?"

"I don't know yet," Bonnie said. "I need your help."

"What can I do?" Melissa said. "I'm nobody."

"Patrick loves you, I know he does," Bonnie said. "If he could get free of Ava I think you two would be just fine."

"I don't believe he wants to be free. Why can't he be if he wants to?"

"She's got his child, and something else."

"What's that?"

"She owns the tea room," Bonnie said.

"What?"

"She bought the tea room from Knox's estate after it settled, and owns it through a shell company, so no one but Patrick knows about it."

"Why did she do that?"

"Because she knew Patrick wanted it, and her condition for selling it to him is that he gives you up."

"How did you find that out?"

"Timmy told me," Bonnie said. "He followed her one night to see where it was she went to, and heard her tell Patrick it was time for him to choose. Timmy confronted her, and she shipped him off on a fast boat to Yankeetown."

"And Patrick turned Ava down."

"He loves you," Bonnie said. "He really does."

"I don't know," Melissa said. "This is really twisted."

"If we can find a way to get her hooks out of him, once and for all, the way would be clear for you and Patrick to be together."

"If he loves me so much why does he keep having sex with her?"

"Men are like dogs, my darlin'," Bonnie said. "They like to roll in shit. It's their nature."

"That's malarkey right there," Melissa said. "If Patrick trusted me, he would tell me all this, and we could work it out together. So he quits seeing Ava, so she sells the tea room to somebody else. He could demand a blood test for Olivia and fight her for joint custody."

"Only Ava's husband is a wealthy man, and very much under his wife's thumb. He could sue Patrick into the poorhouse."

"But he'd know the truth."

"Wouldn't matter, he's that far gone. No prenup, and him a millionaire many times over," Bonnie said. "But show your hand to Ava, my darlin', and threaten what she holds dear, and you'll end up just like my firstborn, dead in a ravine."

"You think Ava did that?"

"She had it done," Bonnie said. "You ask Delia about that sometime. She'll tell you."

"You think she's blackmailing Patrick by threatening to hurt me?"

"I don't think she even has to say the words; he knows her better than anyone. You get in between Ava and something she wants, and she will get rid of you. She's rich enough to arrange it, too."

"So, how can we fight that? It sounds like she has us right where she wants us."

"We're going to figure it out," Bonnie said. "We're going to put our heads together and come up with a plan. We have to."

"I'm not smarter than her, and I'm sure not as sneaky," Melissa said.

"But you love my son."

Melissa sighed.

"I do," she said. "Patrick's also my friend; I hate to see this happen to him."

"Then help me figure out how to beat her at her own game."

"We're going to have to have some help," Melissa said.

"We need to be careful," Bonnie said. "We have to keep this close."

"I know who we should get," Melissa said. "Hannah."

"She's leakier than the holiest sieve," Bonnie said.

"Not when it's this important," Melissa said.

"But she'll tell my daughter," Bonnie said. "And do we really want that?"

"I don't know if she'll tell Maggie or not," Melissa said. "But we have to trust somebody, and that person has to be wilier than Ava. Hannah's nosy, she's sneaky, and she's smart."

"And her husband used to work for the CIA or FBI or something," Bonnie said.

"If we need him that would be handy," Melissa said.

"So, I take it you haven't given up on my son."

"I want to help him," Melissa said. "After that, if we're successful, we'll see. That's all I can promise."

"Now, about the bakery," Bonnie said. "I'd really like you to have it."

"I love you," Melissa said, "and I'm grateful for everything you've done for me, but I don't want the bakery. I like what I'm doing, and I'm good at it. I'm helping Sean, and we work together really well. I don't want to give that up."

"He doesn't like girls, you know," Bonnie said. "Don't go falling in love with him; it will only end in tears."

"I'm not in love with Sean," Melissa said. "Don't worry about that. It's just Patrick for me, and if not him, then nobody."

Melissa left Bonnie's house, clutching her coat around her to keep out the fierce wind that was blowing, making her ears sting and her eyes water. When she reached Pine Mountain Road, she could see Patrick's Uncle Curtis driving his tow truck down the road toward her. Curtis stopped and waved her over.

"Hey Lil bit!" he said. "I haven't seen you for a long time. How in the world are you?"

"I'm fine as frog hair," she said. "What's going on?"

"A tree came down the river and pulled Will's boat off the dock," Curtis said. "I don't know how it didn't take the whole dock with it. I'm towing out the tree on the other side of the dam, and Will wants his boat back if there's anything left of it. Seems like he could afford a new one, but he wants this one back; said he bought it for Ava."

"Can I ride with you?" Melissa asked.

"Sure," Curtis said, and Melissa climbed in.

Melissa liked Curtis, who was Hannah's father. He was a quiet, even-tempered man with a keen sense of humor. He had a wife who could place first among hypochondriacs if that were an event in the Olympics, and Melissa felt sorry for him on account of it.

They drove down to Daisy Lane, the alley which ran parallel to the brick wall separating the college from the town. At the end of the alley, where the college wall turned left and fled south, a narrow dirt lane ran between the wall and the rail trail. They bounced over the rutted dirt track to where the top of the dam was, down over the hill, and then right across the tracks, to the base of the dam. The dam spill-over had been adjusted to a minimum, so they could clearly see the rocky bed of the river and the huge tree that had crashed over, carrying the boat.

There were a few men already there, and volunteer firefighter Calvert Fischer, dressed in his scuba gear, was putting his gloves on. They greeted Curtis and consulted with him about how to go about what they were doing. After a few minutes Curtis got back in the truck and drove further downstream, then got out and started unwinding the tow cable. Calvert used a rope held by two fellow firefighters to slip down the steep bank, waded in with the big hook attached to the end of the tow cable, wound it around the top of the trunk of the tree, and then let his fellow volunteers pull him back up the bank.

"The tree is not that waterlogged yet; I think it will hold," he told Curtis.

Someone handed Cal a silver emergency blanket and a hot cup of coffee. He wrapped the blanket around him and then wrapped his hands around the coffee cup.

Curtis started winching the cable, which drug the massive tree closer to the steep bank. Branches snapped off, and the gnarled roots dripped muddy water as the tree left the river bed.

"Not much left of that boat," Curtis said.

Sure enough, Melissa could see the splintered hull of the boat, and something else.

"What's that?" she asked him.

He shrugged, but when the tree was completely winched up onto the bank, Melissa made her way to where the men were waiting with chainsaws to cut it up.

There, in the broken hull of the boat, was something made of cloth.

"Could you hand me that?" Melissa asked one of the men.

He obliged and dragged the sodden lump of black cloth back to where Melissa stood.

"Looks like a coat," he said.

Melissa rolled it up, wrung it out and then shook it out. It was a hooded nylon anorak with a fuzzy lining of gray shearling. Expensive, she thought. There was a small flashlight attached to the zipper pull. Melissa stuck her hand in each pocket of the coat and found a set of two keys on a key ring that looked familiar.

Where had she seen these before?

She tucked the keys into her pocket, took the coat over to the tow truck, and slung it in the back.

"What's that?" Curtis asked.

"A coat," Melissa said.

"I can see that," he said. "Any idea whose?"

"I have an idea," Melissa said. "I'll take care of it."

Curtis shrugged and finished his job.

"They're gonna take the pieces of that boat back to Will; you wanna send the coat, too?"

"Nope," Melissa said. "I'll deliver that personally."

Curtis dropped Melissa off at her trailer, and she took the coat with her inside, where she hung it up on the shower head over the bathtub so it could drip muddy water down the drain. She disconnected the flashlight on the zipper pull and dropped it into the top vanity drawer, and then studied the keys while she wondered where she had seen them before. The tab on the key ring was an unusual shape, a pewter Celtic rose. Holding it in her hand, she closed her eyes and let her mind wander, until she realized these were the keys kept hidden under a flower pot next to the garage apartment behind the Rose Hill B&B that Ava owned. Melissa had once used them to show someone the property as a favor to Sandy Rodefeffer.

These were the missing keys.

She went back outside, got in her car, and drove up to the bed and breakfast, the one that was going to be sold the next day. She parked out back between Ava's old van and the garage with the apartment overhead.

Three years before, a man had died in that apartment, and although it was suspected to be the result of foul play, the case was never solved. That had been right before Ava's daughter had gone to boarding school, Ava had married Will, and her new husband had built the house on the hill.

It was dark now, so Melissa didn't worry about anyone seeing her try one of the keys in the apartment door, which it opened. She stepped inside and turned on the lights. The main room was empty save for some folded drop cloths and paint cans. It smelled like paint and new carpet. The refrigerator hummed, and the kitchen faucet dripped.

She started down the hall but stopped when she thought she heard something in the bedroom at the end of the short corridor. The hair stood up on the back of her neck, and her arms sprouted goose pimples.

She stood still and listened, but could not hear anything. She opened her mouth to say, "Is anyone here?" but a shiver of fear stopped her. If there was someone in the apartment, that person was hiding and did not want to be found. Melissa was alone, with no weapon, and no one knew where she was. Instead of investigating further, she backed down the hallway and let herself out, locking the door behind her. It was then that she noticed the window closest to the door was not quite closed, the aluminum frame bent as if it had been jimmied open.

Out on the small porch at the top of the steps she had the sudden thought that maybe Ava and Patrick met in the apartment. Maybe that was why Ava had the keys in her coat pocket. It would be risky, what with the nosy neighbors that lived on each side. Maybe they were in there now. Then her rational mind reminded her that Patrick was at work at the Thorn right now, so he wasn't meeting Ava in the apartment.

Reminding herself that the obvious explanation was usually the right one, she reasoned that Ava had every right to hold the keys to her property; she might have used them to inspect the work that had been done and left them in her coat.

But why was her coat in the boat?

Melissa went back down the stairs and was walking around the corner of the building to try the other key in the garage door when she was startled to see a person dressed in dark clothing already standing there.

"What are you doing here?" Ava asked Melissa.

Melissa's heart thumped in her chest.

"I was with Curtis just now when they towed your boat up," she said, her words rushed and her voice breathless. "These keys were in it, and I thought I recognized them. I was just trying them to see if they were yours. Trick is doing the final walk-through tomorrow, so we'll need them."

Ava held her hand out, and, after a brief hesitation, Melissa placed the keys in them.

"Thanks," Ava said. "I'll be sure to tell Will how much I appreciate the full service provided by Sean's staff. I'll also make sure Trick gets the keys in time for the walk-through."

Melissa didn't know what else to say, so she half turned and gestured at her car.

"Well, I guess I'll go," she said.

"I heard you and Patrick broke up," Ava said.

Melissa was so taken aback that at first she stuttered, but then found her words.

"I'm sure it's for the best," Melissa said. "These things happen."

"I know," Ava said. "I'm just surprised. I know Patrick was very fond of you."

Melissa had to grind her teeth not to respond in the way she wanted to.

"You've worked so hard to overcome your upbringing and your past," Ava said. "I know everyone's very proud of how far you've come. I'm sure whatever you do in the future, you'll do well. And as far as men go, there are always more fish in the sea."

Melissa could not, would not thank Ava for such a mean compliment.

"I have to go," she said instead and backed away rather than turn her back on Ava.

"Take care," Ava said.

Melissa didn't realize how hard she was trembling until she was safely locked in her car.

It wasn't from the cold.

Back at home, Melissa locked the door behind her, took off her coat, and walked down the hallway to the bathroom. She flipped on the light and immediately saw the coat was gone. The tub had even been rinsed out so no one would believe it had ever hung there. She opened the top drawer of the vanity and saw that the flashlight was gone, as well.

Melissa froze, her scalp tingling in fear. Quickly, she took a spray bottle of toilet bowl cleaner out from under the vanity, and armed with that, she checked every room in the trailer, but no one was hiding anywhere. She finally thought to check the back entrance, which was rarely used, and outside, at the bottom of a substantial drop off, she saw small footprints in the accumulating snow.

Only Patrick and she had keys to that door, which was always kept locked.

Now apparently Ava had one.

Delia seemed happy to see Melissa.

"Come in, sweetie," she said. "This is a pleasant surprise."

Melissa held up a hastily packed overnight bag and said, "I hope you don't mind if I stay for a while."

"Of course I don't mind," Delia said as she hugged her. "You're always welcome in my house for as long as you need to stay. Stay forever; nothing would make me happier."

Melissa dropped her bag and took off her coat. Delia hung it up in the hall closet, saying, "Put your bag in Claire's room. The sheets are clean, and there are extra blankets in the closet."

Melissa went down the hall to Claire's childhood bedroom, which had been Melissa's bedroom when she had lived with Ian and Delia. Tommy had slept in the room across the hall, which had been their son Liam's before he died. She left her bag and then joined Delia in the kitchen.

"I have to confess I was hoping you'd come see me," Delia said. "I was at Bonnie's earlier this evening after you left."

"Bonnie thinks we should do something, but I don't know what to do," Melissa said. "I'm heartbroke, but I don't know whether to abandon Patrick or try to rescue him."

Tears spilled over, and she raised a trembling hand to wipe them away.

"Oh, honey, I'm so sorry."

"I'm plumb wiped out," Melissa said. "I'm down to playin' on one string, and that one's about to pop."

Delia handed her a box of tissues and patted her shoulder.

"Let's talk it out," Delia said. "Ian used to say that it was better to vent in a safe place than to hold it in and explode somewhere dangerous."

Melissa told Delia everything. It still didn't seem real to her. It was more like a nightmare she was still walking around in.

"You poor thing," Delia said when she was done. "I don't doubt for a minute Ava was following that tow truck and then following you. You know I don't throw the word 'evil' around lightly, so when I say you're right to be afraid of Ava, you can believe it."

"Bonnie told me you found that out working for her at the B&B."

"God help me," Delia said. "I think I know how that woman's brain works, although only the Lord knows for sure. Ava was adopted by old parents, and they died when she was still pretty young. She latched onto Brian and finagled her way into our family so she'd feel safe, I think. You can understand that; we Fitzpatricks have our faults, but no one can say we're not loyal. We're established here in Rose Hill. We have our place.

"I remember Ian saying he didn't like the way Patrick looked at his brother's wife, that there'd be trouble on account of it, you wait and see, but I always thought Ian suspected everyone. Turned out he was right.

"I loved Ava, and I felt sorry for her. Brian was terrible to her, blamed her for missing out on his baseball scholarship, and he never let her forget that. She was always a good mother; she adored her children. I was so impressed when she took Ernie in even though he was Brian's child with another woman. I wonder if that isn't part of her camouflage, somehow, her devoted motherhood.

"Ava's beautiful, any fool can see that. She uses that to her advantage. She's smart, and she's a survivor. She has complete control over herself, over her emotions. Ian used to say she was 'self-possessed," and that description is apt on so many levels. Ian said many times she should have gone to Hollywood; she's that skilled of an actress. She fooled me for a long time.

"I saw firsthand how she manipulated an FBI agent to protect her children, and then to get rid of her husband. I saw how, after she got rid of the agent, she latched onto Scott. Ava got her money, left to her by Theo Eldridge, who I'm sure, although I couldn't prove it, she was also involved with; after that, she didn't need Scott, and she wanted Patrick back.

"More than anything, Ava wanted to be respected in the community, and she got that as a Fitzpatrick. All most people really want, when it comes down to it, is to belong, to feel safe and cared for. She had that as a member of our family.

"If she and Patrick went public with their affair, and heaven forbid, got married, it would have been the scandal of the century, and her children would have paid the price. Many people suspected Patrick killed his brother in order to have Ava, and no one would have hesitated to gossip about that. They would have had to leave town. Patrick, for all his good points, is rooted here like knotweed; I don't think he could thrive anywhere else. He's also, please forgive me, more than a little bit of a mama's boy. There's not much he dreads more than his mother's disapproval; if he married Ava, Bonnie would never forgive him.

"I thought after Ava married Will that she'd give up Patrick; I thought to have all that money, a husband who adored her, and another baby would satisfy her. I thought if she belonged to Will's family she could feel safe and cared for in that marriage. I was wrong."

"So why doesn't she leave Will and marry Patrick? She'd get half his money in the divorce."

"I don't think she loves Patrick, sweetie, so much as she thinks Patrick belongs to her. She wants him to always be available, and she sure as hell doesn't want anyone else to have him. That's not love, that's control."

"So why didn't she bump me off years ago?"

"Let me ask you something," Delia said. "How did Miranda's mother find out that someone with her daughter's name was living in Rose Hill?"

"She hired someone to look for me," Melissa said. "He got a tip and followed it up."

"Who do you think provided that tip?"

"You think Ava did that?"

Delia shrugged.

"We'll probably never know. It's certainly possible."

"So why didn't she pay for me to have an accident?" Melissa said.

"Patrick's not completely blind," Delia said. "He'd have known it was her doing, and she would have lost him."

"He must still love her," Melissa said. "I saw what he was like all those years when they were sneakin' around, and even three years ago when she married Will. She's the love of his life. I'm just the one he's been biding his time with."

"I can't speak for what's in Patrick's heart," Delia said. "Of course Bonnie thinks Ava's using some sort of witchcraft on him; her precious son would never willfully be involved with anyone she didn't approve of. He might love her and love you, too. It's not necessarily one or the other. He can love Ava even if he sees what she really is. It speaks volumes, however, that he wouldn't sacrifice you for her."

"Why do men have to fool around?" Melissa asked. "Can they just not help it?"

"It's a choice they make, men or women," Delia said. "If satisfying their sexual needs outside the marriage is more important to them than the consequences to the people they love, then that's what they'll choose to do. When it comes down to it, they're selfish, and they think their desires are more important than anything or anybody else."

"Patrick and I never talked about it," Melissa said. "Maybe we should have."

"The desire is there inside of everyone; only the weak give into it. Ava is Patrick's weakness."

"That doesn't make me feel any better."

"I know, and I'm sorry," Delia said. "I'll always be honest with you, even if it hurts."

"I don't know what to do," Melissa said. "Claire says I should get Hannah involved, to try

95

to find out if Ava was really there that night of the accident."

"Hannah may already know," Delia said. "It wouldn't hurt to get proof. It might help you figure out what to do."

"I'm so tired my eyes are crossing," Melissa said. "Is it okay with you if I go on to bed?"

"You go on, and I'll set the alarm," Delia said. "You're safe here."

Melissa changed into her nightgown and then layered extra blankets on the bed. As she snuggled down in, she looked around the room where, from the moonlight through the window, the shadows from the tree outside were dancing on the wall. Melissa breathed in the familiar smell of Delia's laundry detergent. It felt like home to her. She belonged, she was safe, and she was cared for. Her last thought before she fell asleep was that she wished Tommy were in the room across the hall.

Then it would be perfect.

CHAPTER FOUR - THURSDAY

Melissa was nervous about the B&B sale closing because she didn't know whether or not Ava would be there. On Ava's behalf, Will had been handling the sale so far, and he was Ava's designated financial power of attorney, so there was no reason for her to be there; he could sign for her.

Every time the telephone rang, Melissa's heart rate sped up. Her hands were trembling. She kept making stupid mistakes in every document she worked on. She examined the closing documents for the third time that day, just to make sure there were no errors that would embarrass her during the meeting. It all looked good.

"Hey," Sean said.

Melissa hadn't heard him come down the hallway behind her, and she was startled.

"What's wrong with you?" Sean asked. "You've been jumpy all day."

"This is my first house closing," Melissa said. "I just want everything to be perfect."

"That's why I stipulated that part of the closing costs will go to you for doing Sandy's job," Sean said. "Did Trick say when she was coming back?"

Melissa told Sean what Trick had confided in her about his wife and daughter.

"I'm going to leave it up to you," Sean said. "If you don't mind doing the work, and it doesn't interfere with our other work here, and as long as we bill him for your time ..."

"It's been a good experience for me," Melissa said. "I wouldn't want to do it full time, but then Trick doesn't have many sales these days."

"Speaking of home sales, I need to get with Patrick and Maggie about working on Mom and Dad's house," he said. "We need to make some home improvements, or they won't get anything for it."

"It will be weird not to have Bonnie in the bakery," Melissa said.

"That also reminds me," Sean said. "I need to draw up a contract for the sale of the bakery; please block out some time for me to work on that this afternoon."

Trick arrived with the B&B purchasers, a late-middle-aged couple dressed in brand new hiking gear.

"We're so excited," the woman said after everyone was introduced. "We've been dreaming about this for so long."

"It's basically turn-key," the man said. "We want to redecorate a little and change some paint colors, but other than that everything's move-in ready."

"So will you be running it as a business?" Sean asked.

"That's our dream," the woman said.

"Have you heard from Will?" Sean asked Melissa.

Melissa shook her head and had just picked up the phone to call him when Ava came in.

Sean introduced Ava to the buyers, and she proceeded to charm them. During this small talk charm offensive, Ava didn't once acknowledge

Melissa's presence; it was if she didn't exist. Melissa was actually relieved.

"I just know you'll love running a B&B," Ava said to the buyers. "It was so hard for me to let it go, but I had just got married and had a little one on the way, and my husband has very traditional ideas about marriage. Lucky for me he has enough income to support us all."

"Is Will coming?" Sean asked.

"He was called away unexpectedly," Ava said. "You'll just have to make do with me."

"His loss is our gain," Trick said, and ran his hand through his wisps of hair, giving Ava what Melissa surmised was his most smoldering look; Melissa had to struggle not to snort with laughter.

Sean invited everyone into the conference room, where Melissa served them coffee and water. Once everyone was settled, she brought in the paperwork and led them through the process of signing and initialing.

"Good gracious," the woman said, "It seems like all we do lately is sign and initial forms; first to retire, then to sell our house in Arlington, and now to buy this one."

Melissa notarized their signatures where required, using her official notary stamp.

"I didn't think felons could be notaries," Ava said.

The room went deathly quiet. Melissa could feel the blood rush to her face. All eyes turned to her, but she fixed hers on what she was doing so she wouldn't make a mistake.

"Melissa received a statement of good conduct from the West Virginia Secretary of

State," Sean said. "She's not only a notary, but she's also a certified paralegal."

"Nobody in this town thinks she did anything wrong," Trick said to the buyers. "She rescued a baby from a drug den and then brought him up as her own child."

"Which is kidnapping," Ava said. "How many years did you serve for that, Miranda? Or was that the identity you stole? Your name is actually Melissa, am I right?"

Melissa finished her part of the paperwork, scooped it up and said, "I'll be right back with copies for you."

There were tears in her eyes, and she couldn't meet anyone's gaze. Although she had left the conference room, the copier was right outside, and she could hear everything they subsequently said.

"Are we sure this is all legal?" the man asked.

"I'm feeling a little uneasy," his wife said. "I don't know if I like this."

"It's all fine," Sean said. "I don't know why Ava decided to bring this up during the closing for the sale of her property, but Melissa is my right hand in this practice. There is no one more honest or reliable than that woman. She paid the price for what she did, heroic as it was, and afterward, she put herself through school to better herself. Her son Tommy even won a full scholarship to a big ten school. They are both beloved members of this community. I'm proud to have her work beside me, and I can assure you, she was thoroughly vetted and approved by the proper state authorities. Questioning her qualifications in this setting is, frankly, Ava, pretty mean-spirited."

"It's all good, folks," Trick said. "Everything's above board and legal, nothing to worry about."

"I just wonder how advisable it is to employ her," Ava said. "It couldn't be good for public relations."

"Her story is going to be in the local paper this Sunday," Sean said. "You folks should be sure to read that, and then I think you'll be proud to know Melissa."

Melissa came back in, her face burning, gave the buyers their copies of the closing documents organized in a folder. She took the originals, plus the checks received, and returned to her desk at the front of the building.

'Don't cry. Don't cry. Don't cry,' Melissa murmured to herself as she sat there, staring upwards to keep from letting the tears fall.

She heard them all get up to leave the conference room, so she busied herself pretending to be making a call by calling her own phone, which she had muted for the meeting. She could feel it vibrating in her tote bag on the floor beneath her desk.

As Trick passed her desk, he winked and pointed his finger at her.

"We need to get together about you buying the Foxglove, jailbird," he said. "I'll call you."

As they passed, the buyers waved to her and mouthed, "thank you." They still looked worried.

Sean followed them all outside.

Ava hung back as she took her time putting on her coat, gloves, and scarf. Then she came right up beside Melissa, leaned over, and said, "I'm just getting started with you."

She lightly ran one finger down Melissa's cheek and let it trail down her neck.

"You get away from me," Melissa said.

Melissa pushed back her chair to stand up, letting the receiver of the phone clatter to the desktop. She put up her fists and waved them at Ava.

"I'm not scared of the likes of you," Melissa said. "You just say the word, lady, and you and me's gonna commence to tangling."

Ava laughed.

"If I were you, I'd find another town to live in, maybe down south with people who talk like you," Ava said. "If you really think I'm going to let you stop me from being with Patrick, you're even dumber than you look. I've got him right where I want him, and there's nothing you can do about it. You don't stand a chance, Miranda."

As soon as Ava left the office, Sean came back in, took one look at Melissa's face and said, "What happened?"

"It's a long story," Melissa said, her voice cracking with emotion. "I can't get into it right now."

As if she hadn't had enough drama for one day, Patrick came through the door.

"I need to talk to you," he said to Sean. "Right now, if that's okay."

Patrick glanced at Melissa, but she turned her head away.

"Okay," Sean said. "Hold my calls, please, Melissa."

Sean led Patrick down the hallway and closed the door to his office. Although Melissa could hear the murmur of their voices, she couldn't make out what they were saying. She longed to go down the hall and eavesdrop but didn't dare for fear of getting caught.

As Melissa picked up the receiver she had dropped on the desk, she realized she had been recording everything that had happened via her cell phone voice mail. She played it back, and Ava's threats came through loud and clear. She saved the voice mail, wondering if she'd ever have a need to use it.

While Patrick was in Sean's office, she kept herself busy organizing the closing documents and making out the deposit slip for the cashier's check.

Twenty minutes passed.

As they came down the hallway, Melissa heard Patrick say, "Keep it safe, man. It's all I've got."

"Don't worry," Sean said.

Patrick stopped at Melissa's desk.

"How are you?" he asked.

"I've been better," Melissa said.

"We need to talk," Patrick said.

"Not right now," Melissa said. "I'm working."

"Call me," he said. "I'll be at work."

The phone rang, and Melissa leaped to answer it before Sean did.

Patrick gave her a sad smile and left the office.

After she got off the phone, Sean called her back to his office. In his hand, he held a sealed, padded mailing envelope, on which he had written his name across the seal.

"Put this in our safety deposit box at the bank," he said. "And don't let it out of your hands until you do."

Melissa took the package, went back to the front, put on her coat, and gathered the things she needed to distribute, mail, and deposit. Sean followed her, and stood there, looking out the front door.

"Why don't you take the rest of the day off?" he said.

"What about the bakery sale contract?" she asked.

He shrugged.

"Let's do it tomorrow," he said. "I don't have anyone scheduled to come in the rest of the day, and I have something I need to work on with no interruptions. I'm going to lock the front door, send all calls to voicemail, and consider us closed for the day."

"Okay," Melissa said. "Listen, Sean, about what happened in there today ..."

"Don't," Sean said. "You have nothing to apologize for. Ava was way out of line."

"Thank you," Melissa said. "See you tomorrow."

As Melissa walked the few yards to the bank, she felt the padded envelope to try to ascertain what was inside. It was small, smaller than a cigarette lighter, more the size of a nail clipper. She felt it again and again and finally realized what it was: a flash drive. It had to be. What was on it? Had Patrick given it to Sean? He must have. She was dying to know what was on it, but Sean having put his name across the seal meant that no one was supposed to open it.

She considered opening the other end. Afterward, she could easily reseal that end with glue, and no one would be any the wiser. She was so tempted. But it was wrong. Sean trusted her, had stood up for her in the conference room earlier. He had done so much for her. If he had thought she should see what was on it, he would have shared it with her. No, she would put it in the safety deposit box and trust Sean to know what was best.

After her errands were finished, she went down the street to get in her car. Someone, she assumed Ava, had run a key down the side of the car, ruining the pristine paint. Melissa stood there, looking at the damage. Since it was parked on the street, Melissa assumed lack of privacy had been the only impediment to Ava knifing her tires or cutting her brake lines. She got in the car and was putting on her seatbelt when she saw someone had left a note under her windshield wiper. Her stomach rolled as she anticipated some kind of terroristic threat.

She got back in the car with it and unfolded it, her heart pounding.

"I love you," it read. "Don't give up on us. Patrick."

Carefully, she folded the note and tucked it down into her tote bag.

Her phone rang.

"When are you coming out here?" Hannah said. "Do I have to track you down like a rabbit? You're in deep trouble, little missy, and I want in on it."

"I'm on my way," Melissa said.

Hannah's farmhouse was at the end of Possum Holler, which wound around the side of the hill Rose Hill was built upon, past dilapidated houses and the cemetery. Melissa noticed that somebody had put one of those tiny houses on a previously vacant lot owned by Maggie Fitzpatrick, where a house she owned had been burned down many years before.

When she reached the farm, only one of Hanna's big dogs, the husky named Jax, ran out to greet her, followed by two little fuzzy white dogs known as Bunny and Chicken. Hanna walked out of the sun porch attached to the back of the house to meet her.

"Where's Wally?" Melissa asked her.

"Sad story," Hannah said. "The dogs went on a walkabout, and someone shot him. Jax came and got me and led me to him, but it was too late."

"That's terrible," Melissa said. "Do you know who did it?"

"Could've been anybody," Hannah said. "If we're gonna let them run wild in the woods like they do, we can hardly be surprised when some drunken idiot with a deer rifle takes a pot shot at anything that moves."

"How's Sammy taking it?"

"He's upset," Hannah said. "First his Uncle Ian and now this. He's like his dad, though, more and more. He doesn't like to talk about feelings, doesn't want to cry in front of anyone."

"He's only seven," Melissa said. "He's still a baby inside. They still need their mamas even though they like to pretend they don't."

"I don't know," Hannah said. "It seems like he's seven going on thirteen. Are they always so moody at this age?"

"I only know about raising Tommy," Melissa said. "He would go through times where he didn't want nothin' to do with me. Just wait it out, he'll come to you when he needs you. And he will."

"I hope so," Hannah said. "I miss my little punkin'."

"He's still in there," Melissa said. "They just want so badly to be big boys at that age. I remember Tommy used to act tough whenever Patrick was around, but later he'd watch Winnie the Pooh with me."

"I've got nachos in the oven," Hannah said. "Let's crack open some beers and get down to business."

An hour later, Hannah was caught up on everything Melissa knew, from the night of the accident to the mysterious flash drive in the mailing pouch. Hannah had asked questions and taken notes in a small spiral notebook that had cartoon characters on the front cover.

Melissa let Hannah listen to the voice mail.

"She's evil," Hannah said. "You need to send me that voicemail in case your phone gets stolen."

Melissa did that.

"There are two separate mysteries to solve here," Hannah said. "Number one is if Ava was there the night of the accident and the second is who was that guy that died and did he have any connection to Ava?"

"I don't see how they could be connected," Melissa said. "He was just in the wrong place at the wrong time."

"But the lack of IDs and a car really bugs me," Hannah said. "It gets my spidey senses tingling."

"Ed said they were going to publish his photo and submit his fingerprints to the FBI."

"So I need to get to Deputy Skip right away," Hannah said. "I also need to find out where the guy lived and poke my nose in there, see what I can find out."

"Maybe the guy driving the white SUV saw what happened," Melissa said.

"Could be," Hannah said. "Good thinking."

They paused while Hannah took more beers out of the fridge.

"Do you think Ava would hurt me?" Melissa said. "I mean more than just trash talk?"

Hannah nodded.

"Oh, yeah, she's a psycho," she said. "But don't worry; I'm going to do everything I can to make sure she doesn't succeed."

"I don't understand her," Melissa said. "She's got everything. Why does she have to have Patrick, too?"

"Because she can," Hannah said. "Some people are selfish that way."

"Why do people cheat?"

Hannah shrugged.

"They get off on it and think they can get away with it," she said.

"Has Sam ever cheated on you?"

"Not that I know of," Hannah said. "And he probably would get away with it. The man's an Appalachian ninja. I hope he doesn't, and if he does, I hope I don't find out. I don't want to know. I'm happier in my blissful ignorance."

"I wish I could un-know it," Melissa said. "I can't quit thinking about it, and it makes me feel so stupid that everyone knew but me."

"I admit I did hear rumors," Hannah said. "But they hid it pretty well."

"I'm not sure I can take him back," Melissa said. "I could never trust him again."

"Give it some time," Hannah said. "Let's fix Ava's wagon and then review the situation."

"She gives me the creeps."

"I'm glad you're staying with Delia," Hannah said. "Try not to be alone if you can help it, just until we get this resolved."

"Do you really think we can stop her?"

"I do, and do you want to know why? Because Ava is just one person, albeit a narcissistic sociopath, and we are legion. We use our powers for good, and that gives us an edge. Now, I've got to get out of here, because I need to pick up Sammy, take him to Delia's, and then get to work a-nose-pokin'."

As they walked outside, Hannah threw a tennis ball for the dogs to chase.

"Hey, I heard you're buying the Foxglove," she said.

"That's supposed to be a secret," Melissa said.

"If you're gonna talk on your cell phone in this town, you're gonna have your business listened in on by every granny with a scanner."

"I've heard that before, but I don't believe it," Melissa said.

"You better believe it," Hannah said. "Anytime you're in trouble, just get on the cell phone and leave me a message. Before I can check my voicemail, one of my grannies will be on the case. So, are you buying it or not?"

"Well, it's not a done deal, but close."

"What are you going to do with it?"

Melissa shrugged.

"You know what you ought to do," Hannah said. "Make it a tiny house park. Those things are selling like hotcakes. All the college kids want them. Hell, I want one."

"I saw one down the holler," Melissa said, "at Maggie's old place."

"That belongs to Hatch," Hannah said. "You should ask him about them. He knows a guy who builds them."

With nothing more to do that day, and in need of keeping busy doing something, Melissa stopped in at Fitzpatricks Service Station to talk to Hatch, Hannah's ex-high-school-boyfriend and the head mechanic.

"Hey, purdy girl," he said when she walked in the garage bay, where he was working under a pickup truck jacked up high in the air. "I'd hug ya, but I'm all covered in erl, as usual. Consider yourself hugged, though."

Melissa asked him about the tiny house.

"Ain't that something?" Hatch said. "I didn't know if I'd like it or not, but I got to tell you, I do. Me and Joshie aren't much on house cleaning, and there ain't much house to clean. It works fine for us."

"Hannah said you know a guy who builds them."

"Yes, ma'am, I certainly do. Name's Johnny Johnson. Looks like a mountain man, he does. He's an odd feller; I don't think I've ever met anyone like him. Has a peculiar way of talking. He built his cabin with his own two hands. Lives way out Pumpkin Ridge, and don't use no city water nor electric. He's got mineral rights, a wellspring, and heats it all with natural gas. He's even got a solar power hot water heater. It's the darndest thing; his whole barn roof is covered in solar panels. He runs power tools off it, too. Off the grid, they call that."

"How do I get in touch with him?"

"Dee and Levi Goldman are good friends of his," Hatch said. "They sold him the land when he came out of the military; he was a friend of their son who died. They were both pilots. Of the evenings, Levi and Johnny make music with some other fellers live out there. Mandolin and fiddle, mountain music, like. You call Dee, and she'll hook you up."

"Thanks, Hatch."

"He's odd, now. Don't let him put you off. He don't see too many people and the war done turned him funny. But he's a good man and an honest man, and if you want one of them little homes he'll fix you right up."

"How's Josh doing?' she asked. "Tommy's so fond of him and Timmy; he misses them."

"Joshie's still grievin' over losing his best friend, his half-brother," Hatch said. "I don't understand the kind of hard heart that would send a little fella away like that, and him only twelve years old. It liked to break both their hearts being parted. I'm just afraid Timmy'll come back yankified and high falutin' and won't have no time for his old friend, Joshie."

"That'll never happen," Melissa said. "Why'd Ava send him away?"

"I don't know the whole story, only what Joshie will tell me, and those two were so tight you couldn't get a blade of grass between 'em. He said Timmy found out something his mama was doing she shouldn't have been, and she done sent him away on account of that."

"That's a shame," Melissa said. "I guess he doesn't know what it was she was doing."

"Something to do with a man, near as I can tell," Hatch said. "And it weren't her rich husband, neither."

Melissa left the service station determined to find out more about the tiny houses. If it turned out she had to make a future for herself without Patrick, and if she bought the trailer park, she would have to find a way to make it produce a profit. The rent that was currently being charged would barely pay for the upkeep, but Melissa didn't want to raise it on people she knew couldn't afford it. If she could sell little houses and rent out spaces for them to be parked, she might just make some actual profit from her investment. Even if her plans changed later, it wouldn't hurt to look into it now.

Melissa called Dee Goldman, who said she would have to radio over to Johnny and see if he was in the mood to see anybody.

"He's a nice man," Dee reassured her. "He's just picky about who comes out there, and he needs to know you're coming. I'll call you back here in a minute, once I talk to him."

Sure enough, a few minutes later Dee called back to say Johnny would be willing to meet with Melissa to talk about the little houses he builds.

"If you wanna get on his good side right off," Dee said, "bring him some lemon-lime soda pop and some Mister Bee potato chips. He loves those chips."

Melissa went to the IGA, bought a 24-pack of canned lemon-lime soda and several bags of Mister Bee chips, one giant bag in every flavor.

As Melissa drove out Pine Mountain Road toward the turn off that would lead to Pumpkin Ridge Road, she kept having the weirdest feeling that she was being followed. At the top of one hill, at a wide place on the berm, just out of a sharp curve, she pulled over, and within ten seconds a white SUV passed her. She couldn't see who was driving it, but it spooked her, so she took a detour on Rabbit Run Road, and then used an even less-traveled road known as Pig Snout Hollow to get to the Goldman's.

A Mustang was not built to travel Pig Snout Hollow, and as she drove across a shallow creek, and winced as the undercarriage scraped over rocks, she wondered if she had made the best decision. She made it to the other side, and eventually, to the Goldman's farm.

The Goldmans ran an organic farm and dairy, and the metal buildings that housed their projects were scattered over several hundred acres of high-valley flatland. Sheep and cows grazed in the sunshine, and a huge flock of chickens was pecking and clucking in what looked like a giant pen on wheels, the roof covered with chicken wire to keep out hawks, foxes, and raccoons.

Dee came out to meet her, their giant, sad-looking hound dog accompanying her.

"Look at your car," Dee said. "How'd you come?"

"I took the scenic route," Melissa said.

"We'll take the ATV," Dee said. "Johnny's driveway is more creek than the road, and I don't want to get your fancy car stuck."

Dee's ATV was like a golf cart on steroids, with a camouflage-printed bonnet, a heater, and jacked up rubber tires spread wide apart, with deep treads like a tractor. Melissa loaded the bags of chips and soda into the back, while Dee instructed her dog to "stay home and guard the house."

"Will he mind you?" Melissa asked.

"Oh, yes," Dee said. "The last time he took off on his own he treed a bear, and it liked to scare him to bits, so he stays close to home. He won't mind Levi, but he'll mind me."

True to her word, the big dog, a tall redbone coonhound, trotted over to the porch and lay down like a sphinx, eyes scanning a 180-degree area.

By the time they reached the hollow that housed Johnny Johnson's farm, having bumped over what seemed like little more than a rutted deer track, Melissa felt like her internal organs had all been jolted loose, along with several tooth fillings.

The farm consisted of a tiny log cabin, maybe 600 square feet in all, and a large barn that had a concrete driveway leading up to one end and out the other. Just like Hatch had told her, the southeastern-facing roof of the barn was covered in solar panels, and he also had erected a tall windmill in a clearing at the top of the ridge. Unlike many other backwoods farms Melissa had seen, this one was neat as a pin; every foot of the fence was in good repair, there was a garden spot surrounded by tall, deer-proof fencing, and the grass had been neatly mowed. There were no parts of old cars piled up all over, no trash strewn throughout the yard. Melissa was impressed.

They could hear the whine of power tools in the barn, so they headed in that direction. A tall, broad-shouldered man with a long beard was hoisting up one end of a roof beam on a small, stick-built house frame while a skinny, tattoo-covered young man braced it with a two-by-eight. Dee put her finger to her lips, which Melissa interpreted as not wanting to surprise them while they performed such a dangerous, delicate operation.

Melissa looked around, further impressed with the neat organization of tools and supplies. There were three tiny houses in the barn, all atop flatbed metal trailers. The furthest one, closest to the opposite entrance, seemed finished; the middle one was half-finished; and this third one, the nearest one, just begun.

Once the roof beam was secured, Johnny climbed down the ladder, and they took away the two-by-eight brace. He turned and looked at the two women, his eyes met Melissa's, and she felt a jolt of energy. He seemed so familiar to her. He walked toward them, never taking his eyes off Melissa's.

"We didn't want to scare you," Dee said. "Johnny, this is Melissa Wright, the woman I told you about, who is interested in buying a tiny house."

Johnny was over six-feet tall, with broad shoulders, thick, muscular arms and thighs. His broad chest tapered to a flat stomach, and the effect all this had on Melissa was curious and disquieting. Melissa had never been attracted to any man the way she was to Patrick, and yet here was someone she had just met, who hadn't even said a word to her, and she could feel the heat of attraction spread throughout her body, so intense it made her blush, made her eyes water.

"It's a pleasure," he said and held out his hand.

Melissa put her small hand in his catcher's-mitt-size paw, and he gently but firmly shook it. At the contact of skin to skin, there was an instant shock, like a pop of electricity.

"Sorry about that," he said.

"There must be a lot of static in here," Dee said.

"Or something," Johnny said.

He smiled then, and it transformed his face from stern to mischievous. His light blue-green eyes, like sea glass, twinkled with good humor, and something else, something that seemed as if it had surprised him, too. It was mesmerizing.

Melissa couldn't seem to say anything. There was an awkward silence while she attempted to process the effect he was having on her. He took off his ball cap and ran a hand through his curly light brown hair, and then put the hat back on.

"You ladies will have to forgive me," he said. "I didn't have time to clean up before you arrived."

"Oh, you're always busy, we know that," Dee said. "Look at these houses, Melissa; aren't they cute?"

"Cute is a word often used by the women who admire my work," Johnny said. "I prefer the term efficiently-sized."

Again that mischievous grin framed by a fluffy mustache and beard.

Melissa tore her eyes away and looked at the furthermost house.

"It's beautiful," Melissa said.

"Allow me to show you around," he said. "My illustrious assistant, Mister Barlow Owsley, seems to have disappeared. He's a shy fellow, so we'll allow him his privacy. Right this way, ladies."

He led them to circle the finished house, with its board and batten siding, corrugated metal roof, and tiny metal chimney. He placed a stepladder beneath the entrance, a round-top wooden door with a round porthole and decorative iron hinges.

He climbed up inside and then offered his hand to each of them in turn. This time when he took Melissa's hand in his, she thought she was prepared for the jolt. She wasn't. She happened to catch his eye as she passed him to enter the house; she had to tilt her head way back on account of the difference in their heights.

He raised his eyebrows, made a surprised expression with his mouth, and then said quietly, so only she could hear, "That's twice, my dear. Once could be considered an accident, but twice ..."

Melissa shivered with a combination of fear and pleasure. It was disconcerting, to say the least.

He showed them around the small home. There were two sleeping lofts, one on either end, with the kitchen and bathroom tucked underneath, and a sitting area in the middle heated by a small propane stove.

"I like to have a wider separation of the kitchen and bathroom than most plans feature," he said to Dee.

"More hygienic," Dee said.

"Exactly," he said.

"I love this," Melissa said. "It's perfect."

"Too small for me," Dee said. "I've been married for a long time, and I can tell you, married people need separate bathrooms."

"My buyers backed out," Johnny said. "So it won't matter to them."

"I hope they paid a deposit," Dee said.

"I returned it," Johnny said with a shrug. "Someone will want it, and it doesn't seem right to punish young people just because their circumstances change. The young man wanted this small cottage in which to house his blushing bride, but his bride decided she'd rather blush in the large condo purchased by her doting parents."

"Happy wife, happy life," Dee said.

"My sentiments exactly, although I can't speak from personal experience," Johnny said. "Would you be interested in something like this, Melissa?"

As he said this, he reached up to rest his hands on the wood support of the sleeping loft, and leaned forward, which made his offer seem to apply to all that was on view. Melissa looked all around the small house, and then from his feet up to his eyes, considering.

He smiled at her, and it was evident to her precisely what he meant, but she wasn't about to make it easy for him.

"Where's the clothes closet?" she asked.

Johnny brought his hands back down and opened a narrow cupboard just outside the bathroom.

"If it was for me," Melissa said. "I'd need more room for clothes and shoes."

"And would your significant other like it?" Johnny asked.

"She's recently broken up," Dee said. "She only has to please herself now."

Melissa rolled her eyes, so only Johnny saw.

"That's a shame," he murmured. "So only the closet? Anything else?"

Melissa walked past him to examine the bathroom, which was fitted with smaller versions of a sink, commode, and shower. She stood in the shower and turned around. Johnny was standing in the doorway, and he lifted his hand to cover his eyes.

"I'll get you a towel," he said.

Melissa couldn't help it, she laughed.

He dropped his hand and held it out to her, steadying her as she stepped out of the shower. Again there was that spark, but this time he just raised his eyebrows.

"I need somewhere to put all my makeup," she said. "I've got a lot of hair products, too."

"I can fix that," he said.

They talked about modifications that could be made, and he had some good ideas.

They went to the kitchen end, and Melissa examined the compact, four-burner propane range.

"I could bake in this," she said. "That's amazing."

"You cook, too," he said. "It just gets better and better."

Johnny demonstrated all the places he had tucked in storage. He hadn't let a square inch go to waste.

"How many of these have you sold?" Dee asked him.

"Nine this year," he said. "I had to take a month off when I broke my finger."

He held up a crooked finger, and Melissa was impressed by its size.

"How'd that happen?" she asked him.

"Got it caught between the trailer hitch and the buyer's truck," he said. "I said 'back it up slow,' and he thought I said, 'let's go.' "

He helped them down the stairs, and when their skin contact produced yet another small shock, he murmured, "That's four."

He followed them outside, and Dee said, "It's getting onto evening, so we better get a move on."

"What do you think?" Johnny asked. "Are you interested?"

"I'd like to buy this one," she said. "I could use it as a model to sell more for you if you'd like."

"I'll make the modifications, and you can come back out to look at it," he said. "I'll have Dee call you when it's ready."

"How do you get them out of here?" Melissa said, gesturing to the thick forest all around.

"Chopper," he said with a smile. "It's a mighty peculiar thing to see."

He pointed at something Melissa had overlooked earlier. Now that he had pointed it out, she was amazed she'd missed it. Just beyond the garden plot, sitting on a concrete pad, covered in camouflage netting, was a helicopter.

"I have my own," he said.

"That's amazing," she said. "Is that what you did in the service?"

"Among other things," he said.

They walked together over to the ATV, and Melissa remembered her delivery.

"I brought you some chips and soda pop," she said.

"Good Lord, woman, your blessings are abundant," Johnny said. "You didn't have to do that, but I'm mighty obliged to you; what do I owe you?"

"We'll consider it a deposit on the house," Melissa said.

"That we'll do," he said. "You all be careful on your way back. If you get stuck, send up a flare."

Just then an enormous black bird came swooping down out of the trees and landed on Johnny's shoulder. Melissa jumped back in surprise.

"This is Edgar Allan Crow," Johnny said. "He won't harm you."

The raven nuzzled Johnny's cheek and nibbled at his ear.

"Johnny found him fallen out of the nest," Dee said. "He raised him from a chick."

"He's a rascal," Johnny said. "He'll steal anything shiny, so I often have screws and nails go missing. The upside is he brings me presents; or stolen goods, if you want to look at it that way."

Johnny didn't shake hands with her before they left and Melissa was relieved. She felt like she had run a mile, like she had climbed a mountain.

She needed a beer, she needed a cigarette; she needed ... something.

"He's a good man," Dee told her on the way back. "He had the depression something awful when he first came back, but living out here has made a world of difference. He sure took a shine to you."

"He's an excellent builder," Melissa said. "I should be able to sell several of those for him."

"I know you just broke up with Patrick," Dee said, "but you should keep Johnny in mind. He's a real good man, and he'd treat you like gold."

"I'm not clear broke up, yet," Melissa said. "I'm not looking for anybody else."

"What's keeping you hanging on?"

"I've lived with Patrick for three years," Melissa said. "We were friends for a long time before that. It seems a shame to throw it all away."

"That's a sunk-cost fallacy," Dee said.

"What does that mean?" Melissa asked.

"It means you've invested a lot in this relationship, and you don't want to believe your time and emotional energy were wasted, so instead of cutting your losses you sign on for more heartbreak."

"That makes me sound pretty stupid."

"Not stupid, honey, just human," Dee said. "My husband is a farmer because he loves to be, and an accountant because he has to be. He sees this happen all the time. People plow money into a business venture, put their heart and soul into it, and even though it's obviously failing, they continue to throw more money down the well rather than cut their losses and move one."

122

"All my investment in Patrick is from my heart," Melissa said.

"Same principle," Dee said. "You need to get out while you still have some heart left to break."

"Why do people cheat?" Melissa asked.

"Not all people cheat," Dee said. "I don't. My husband doesn't, and I know that for a fact. I know plenty of others that do, and I don't understand it any more than you do. I wouldn't stay married to a man that did, I know that for sure."

"Even if it meant losing the farm and everything you've worked so hard for?"

"Sunk-cost fallacy strikes again," Dee said. "When we make decisions, we tend to give more weight to what we might lose than what we might gain."

"But wouldn't you miss Levi?"

"Of course I would, honey," she said. "It would break my heart to leave my husband, but I could never trust him after something like that, and I'd rather be lonely than married to someone I couldn't trust."

"I don't know," Melissa said. "I've been in love with Patrick for so long I can't imagine myself any other way."

"Give yourself some time," Dee said. "If he's worth the wait, he'll be around when you come to a decision."

Melissa drove back to Rose Hill on the main roads but had trouble focusing on driving. She had made a significant commitment to buy the Foxglove Mobile Home Park and now a tiny home to put on it. She was already pretty far down a road that veered away from her path forward with Patrick and his dreams for the two of them. She wondered if their paths could cross again further along the way.

When she got to Delia's, Hannah was sitting in the kitchen talking to Claire. Delia and Sammy were in the living room with Claire's little girls, watching an animated movie. Melissa greeted them but they didn't seem to hear her, so focused were they on the television.

"Where have you been?" Hannah said. "We were starting to get worried."

Melissa told them about her trip out Pumpkin Ridge to see Johnny Johnson, but she didn't mention the instantaneous crush she had developed upon meeting him. After she was finished, Hannah leaned across the table, a grim look on her face.

"I have loads to tell you," Hannah said. "Fasten your seatbelt."

CHAPTER FIVE - THURSDAY

After Melissa left the farm, Hannah went to pick up Sammy at school. She sat in the carpool line watching for him, her 1975 Ford pickup truck standing out like a sore thumb among the shiny SUVs in front of and behind her. He walked out with Hatch's twelve-year-old nephew, Josh, whose bright red hair was easy to spot. Sammy, a good six inches shorter than Josh, had curls, but they were golden brown, blond in the summer. To Hannah's dismay, he insisted on keeping them shorn back almost to the skull, just like his father's.

Sammy stowed his backpack in the space behind the front seat of the truck and slid into the passenger seat.

"Seatbelt," Hannah said.

Sammy fastened his seatbelt.

"Tyler says that an airbag will burn your face off if you sit in the front seat."

"Lucky for us then," Hannah said, "this truck is so old it doesn't have airbags."

"Tyler's mom makes him sit in the back on a booster seat," Sammy said. "He says parents who let their kids sit up front don't care about them getting killed."

"Is that right?"

"That's what Tyler says."

"Well, you tell Tyler that we have a special seatbelt guard that makes your seat belt fit you," Hannah said, "but if his mama wants to buy us a brand new car with airbags and a booster seat, we will be glad to make you sit in it."

"I don't want to sit in a booster seat," Sammy said. "They're for babies."

"When you were little you sat in a car seat in the back of the Subaru," Hannah said. "I had to force you into it, and you screamed for a good twenty minutes before you gave in. It made taking you anywhere kind of a challenge, like big-time wrestling."

"What happened to the Subaru?"

"We drove it over three hundred thousand miles," Hannah said. "It finally died and went to car heaven."

"There's no car heaven," Sammy said. "Is there?"

"No," Hannah said.

"Is Wally in heaven?"

"Of course," Hannah said. "He's with Uncle Ian and Uncle Brian."

"I bet they like having him up there to play with."

"I bet they do."

Hannah could see her son surreptitiously wiping a tear, but she ignored it.

"Have you decided what you want to be for Halloween?"

He shrugged.

"Ninja, I guess," he said. "Or Spiderman."

"We're getting together with Claire and the girls to make our costumes tomorrow night," she said. "You need to decide so I can buy the stuff."

"Do I have to go trick-or-treating with all those girls?"

"Yep," she said. "But Josh is going, too."

"Really? For sure?"

"Hatch is going to drop him off at Delia's on Saturday afternoon," she said. "We're going to have a party and then go trick-or-treating."

"If Josh is going then that's all right," he said.

"That's what I thought," Hannah said. "Can you keep a secret?"

"Yes."

"Tommy's coming home for the kid party, to surprise his mama. Uncle Sean fixed it up."

"Awesome!" Sammy said.

"But don't you tell anybody."

"I won't," he said.

Sammy kicked at the dash as he slouched in his seat.

"Is there something wrong?" Hannah asked Sammy. "You look like you've got something on your mind."

"Tyler said you got fired from your job."

"Well, technically I'm suspended without pay pending an internal investigation," Hannah said.

"What's that mean?"

"It means that I can't work or get paid while they look for a legal reason to fire me."

"Why do they want to fire you?"

"Because my new boss wants to hire his son-in-law to take my place," Hannah said.

"That's not fair."

"Nope," Hannah said. "That's why Uncle Sean is going to sue their pants off as soon as they fire me."

"Does that mean we're poor?"

"Is that what Tyler said?"

Sammy kicked the dash a little harder and turned his face away.

"Hey," Hannah said, "Is Tyler bullying you?"

Sammy shook his head.

"Do I need to talk to your teacher about this?"

Sammy shook his head.

"We're not poor," Hannah said. "We get money from Dr. Drew, who's renting the old farm, and the new farm is paid for. I'm working at the Thorn part-time, and Daddy is doing some part-time computer stuff for the government. We're not in any danger. We won't go hungry."

Sammy just continued to kick the dash and look out the window.

"Are you worried?" she asked him.

He shook his head.

"You don't need to worry," Hannah said. "But if you ever do, just tell Daddy or me about it, okay?"

Sammy shrugged.

The truth was Hannah was the one who was worried. She and Sammy were covered by her work health insurance. Because her husband was partially but not totally disabled from his time in the armed services, he didn't qualify for the kind of veteran's insurance that covered dependents. Hannah had looked into the cost of health insurance, and the steep numbers quoted made her sick to her stomach. Right now, even though her pay was suspended she was still covered by her work policy, but she had to pay her portion of the premium out of her pocket, which was just about empty. If they fired her before or on Friday, her coverage would only last until the end of the month, which just happened to be the next day,

Saturday. Hannah put nothing that dastardly past her new boss, who just wanted her gone.

She was working four nights per week at the bar her Aunt Delia owned, where her cousin Patrick was the manager/bartender. The tips were keeping food on the table and the utilities connected, but that was about it. Her husband Sam, who worked as a full-time volunteer running a rehabilitation center for disabled veterans during the day, was at night performing network security work for the government as a contractor who did not draw any benefits. They were living hand-to-mouth, with nothing being saved. While Sam worked nights in his home office, Hannah lay awake and ran numbers in her head. They weren't talking about it, which was not unusual for them, Sam being a quiet, secretive person at the best of times, but it was creating a new tension between them that didn't help the situation.

Hannah thought Sam should quit the volunteer work and get a full-time job with health benefits to cover the whole family. She had agreed to be the primary breadwinner so that he could do what made him happy and fulfilled, and she had been glad to do it, it made things much easier in their marriage for Sam to be happy. But now, it seemed to Hannah that his labor of love was jeopardizing their future, and they needed to renegotiate that agreement.

She hadn't brought it up because she was hoping he would see what had to be done and just do it. So far, however, he was trying to do both things. It was all she could think about, but she didn't feel like she could talk to him about it. She was afraid of what might happen if she did.

Sam had a history of depression. It was, as is often the case, related to his injuries, both physical and mental, contracted during his service to the country. Both of his lower legs had been blown off by an IED while he served in Iraq. Subsequently, although he was high-functioning, and so practiced at walking on prosthetics that you could barely tell, he was still vulnerable to an interior darkness that caused him to turn away from their family when things went wrong. Hannah somehow thought if she didn't talk about how bad things were going, maybe he wouldn't go down that dark road.

Hannah dropped Sammy off at her Aunt Delia's house.

"Who are all these blond people?' Hannah asked her when they got inside.

Delia laughed.

"These are my new grandchildren," Delia said. "Aren't they beautiful?"

Although Pixie begged Sammy to play a game with her, Bluebell and Sammy took their mitts to the backyard to throw a baseball. While Pixie pouted, whined, and clung to Delia's skirt, the two older girls, Daisy and Lily, reclined on the sofa and listened to music through earbuds while they texted on their phones.

"You talked to Melissa?" Delia asked Hannah.

"Uh huh," Hannah said. "Thanks to you babysitting, I'm off to solve the crime."

"Do you think you can?"

Hannah put her hands on her hips.

"I'm the Masked Muttcatcher," she said. "I always get my dog."

Hannah went first to the fire station to talk to Fire Chief Malcolm Behr.

"Here comes trouble," he said when he saw her.

"I brought you coffee and donuts," Hannah said.

"I've given them up," he said, "on account of my blood pressure."

"More for me then," Hannah said.

"I know this isn't a social visit," he said. "What's up?"

"The night of the coal truck wreck," she said. "What happened?"

"The driver was drunk, also high, I think; his pupils were pin dots."

"And the white SUV?"

"It showed up on the fire station security camera," Malcolm said. "Twice."

"Can I see?"

"Don't see why not," Malcolm said.

He used his PC to show Hannah the footage.

A white SUV passed the camera, which was mounted above the front door of the station. There was no sound so they couldn't hear the crash; Hannah counted thirty-one seconds until the white SUV passed the camera again, going in the opposite direction. There was a long dark gash down the side of the vehicle.

"I can't make out the driver," Hannah said.

"Too dark," Malcolm said. "Can't see the license plate, either."

"So the truck driver wasn't lying about it."

"No," Malcolm said. "Plus there was white paint on the side of his truck. Lucky for him we got this; it's bound to make a difference at his trial."

"What about the stiff?"

"You'd have to ask Scott who he is," he said. "He was dead when we got to him."

"Head injury, I heard."

"Yeah," he said, but then he paused in a meaningful way.

"What?" Hannah said.

"Just something the medical examiner told me," Malcolm said. "We were just shooting the shit, you understand, yesterday; he hasn't done the official yet; he's got bodies stacked up, waiting, he says, on account of this opioid crisis, you know."

"Yeah, yeah, yeah," Hannah said. "I get it, all unofficial and off the record."

"The corpse had bruising on the throat consistent with being strangled."

"No way."

"I can't see any way he'd get that being hit by a truck, do you?"

"He landed on his back?"

"Knocked him clean off his feet," Malcolm said. "Landed on the back of his head."

"Yikes," Hannah said. "Any ideas?"

"My people didn't intubate; they used the bag and CPR, but he was gone. I can tell you without a doubt that nobody on my team touched the victim's throat with enough force to leave a bruise. Why would they?"

"Interesting."

"Patrick said he didn't see the victim until he was up in the cab checking on the driver."

"Did he check him out then?"

"Said he was trying to get the keys away from the driver so he wouldn't try to leave."

"Are there any other cameras in town that might have caught this?"

"Patrick has a camera on the outside of the Thorn," he said. "He said it wasn't on that night."

Malcolm raised his eyebrows at Hannah.

"Then it wasn't," Hannah said.

"I hope he's telling the truth."

"Why would Patrick strangle someone he didn't even know?"

"Well, we don't know who the man was, now do we?" Malcolm said. "Maybe Patrick did know him."

"My cousin is not a killer," Hannah said.

"I didn't say he was," Malcolm said. "But if Patrick didn't do it, surely he saw who did."

"You're not spreading this gossip."

"Nope," Malcolm said. "This was just the medical examiner and me talking and now you and me talking. I haven't even mentioned it to Scott. When the postmortem comes out, then we'll discuss it."

"Thanks," Hannah said. "That gives me a few weeks to work out what happened."

"When are you getting licensed?"

"I haven't had time to study for the exam," Hannah said. "Maybe next year."

"You'll be a good one," he said. "I'd hire you."

"Thanks, Behr," she said.

"Just don't you go investigating me," he said. "You gotta promise."

"You're going to have to lead a more interesting life," Hannah said. "You're too boring to do anything worth investigating."

"Afraid so," Malcolm said. "Be sure to remind my wife of that if she ever calls you."

Hannah picked up a pizza from PJs and carried it to the police station. All she knew about the accident was the brief account that had been in the Pendleton paper on Tuesday, and that was very little. She was counting on Scott's police deputy to fill in the details without realizing he was doing so.

"Oh, no," Skip said as she came in. "I don't know anything, and if I did, I couldn't tell you."

"Can't a friend just bring a pizza to another friend without all this suspicion and bad vibes you got going on in here?"

"Whatever it is, I can't, Hannah," he said. "Scott will skin me alive."

"I already know everything," Hannah said. "I'm here to give you some information; make you look good to your boss. Meanwhile, we'll eat a few slices."

"It smells delicious," Skip said. "I did miss lunch."

Hannah opened the box so that the steamy smell of garlic and oregano wafted his way.

"Is that what I think it is?" he asked.

"Extra garlic, just like you like," she said. "Feta, anchovies, olives, mushrooms, hot peppers, and onions. They call it The Stinkaroonie."

Hannah held out the box and he accepted it, closing his eyes and inhaling as he did so.

"Get some paper towels out of the break room," he said. "We have to sit out here in case Scott checks up on me."

While Hannah was in the break room, she checked to see if the filing cabinets they kept in there were locked, and unfortunately, they were. When she went back out to the main room, she brought paper plates as well. She waited until he had inhaled three pieces before she broached the subject.

"I know you took the accident victim's fingerprints and photograph," she said. "I also know that you've received information in return."

"Guy was a private investigator from Pennsylvania," he said. "You knew that, right?"

"Of course," Hannah said. "I'm way ahead of you on all this. He was legit; I checked it out."

"So you know he rented a car in Besington, Pennsylvania on Monday," Skip said.

"Sure," Hannah said. "I already talked to the guy who rented it to him."

"But did you know that car has been found?"

"Sure I did," Hannah said. "Everybody knows that."

"So don't you think it's weird that it was found at the bus station in Besington, with the guy's keys and IDs in it?"

"Totally weird," Hannah said. "And I guess you know the rest of it. Even weirder, if you ask me."

"For real," Skip said. "I don't know what that guy was investigating, but it must have been here in Rose Hill."

"I'm following up on a few leads in that direction," Hannah said. "Are you guys?"

"No crime was committed," Skip said. "She said his home office wasn't ransacked or anything."

"I knew that," Hannah said. "What else did his girlfriend say?"

"There's a girlfriend?" Skip said. "I thought it was his sister."

"That's right," Hannah said. "I meant sister."

"She called last night, said she saw it in the paper," Skip said. "She went to his apartment and said it looked as if nothing had been touched. She seemed real nice; said my voice had a real quality of authority."

"Did you get her address and phone number?"

"Sheesh, Hannah, of course, I did; I also got her to agree to come down here next week to answer some questions. She's got to work, but she's going to figure something out and call me. She said we could maybe get coffee afterward."

"Which would be entirely inappropriate."

"She's not a suspect or anything," Skip said. "I don't see why not."

"Did she tell you about the other guy?"

"If you mean his landlord, then, yeah. We called and left a message," Skip said. "He hasn't called us back."

"Somebody ought to go up there," Hannah said. "To Besington."

"It was an accident, not a murder or anything," Skip said. "I'm curious about it, but it won't bring him back, now will it?"

"That sounds like something Scott would say."

"Yeah, I wanted to go but he said I couldn't use work time to do it, 'cause our budget's so tight. I'd go myself, but I've got tests to study for."

"You've been going to school for like a hundred years. When are you graduating?"

"It's hard to go to school and work full-time," Skip said. "Especially with my hours."

"I'm not giving you a hard time," Hannah said. "It just seems like you've been working on this degree for a long time."

"I had to retake some of the classes," Skip said. "They're really hard, Hannah."

"I believe it," Hannah said. "You know, I have to go up that way to visit a friend, and I'd be glad to look in on the guy's landlord, maybe find out something for you."

"I don't know," Skip said. "Scott wouldn't like it."

"He doesn't have to know," Hannah said. "This is just to satisfy our curiosity, so we can consider the case closed."

Skip ate the last piece of crust, and wiped his hands on his uniform pants, even though there was a paper towel right in front of him. It was all Hannah could do not to treat him like Sammy, who always did the same darn thing.

"It's all the same to me," Hannah said. "I just thought if you wanted to tie up loose ends, maybe write a paper on the case for one of your classes ..."

"That would be awesome," Skip said. "You won't tell Scott?"

"Do I ever?"

He thought about it for a moment and then went back to the break room, unlocked the file cabinet, took out a file, and came back. He set the folder on the desk and opened it. Hannah leaned over his shoulder to read as much as she could while he looked through the forms and notes.

The bell on the door jangled, and Mayor Kay Pendleton walked in.

"What are you two up to?" she asked.

"Nothing," Skip said, as he shut the folder and slid it behind his back, where Hannah snagged it.

"I'll just put this away for you," Hannah said quietly.

Skip gave her a fierce look but couldn't say anything in front of the mayor. Hannah took the folder back to the break room and quickly photocopied the contents while the mayor questioned Skip about security for an upcoming gubernatorial visit, which was scheduled for the next week. As soon as Hannah was through copying, she put the file back in the cabinet, folded the copies and slid them down into the waistband of the back of her jeans, under her shirt.

She went back out into the main room, said, "I've got to run," and then quickly fled, ignoring the petulant look on Skip's face, which featured a tomato sauce stain on each corner of his mouth, just like Sammy.

Out on the street, Hannah met her cousin, Maggie, walking toward the station.

"Is my husband in there?" she asked.

"Nope," Hannah said. "Just Skip and Kay."

"What were you doing in there?"

"Just visiting with Skip," Hannah said. "What's going on with you?"

"You will never in a million years believe this, but I just got a call from Will inviting Scott and me to a surprise birthday lunch for Ava on Saturday."

"At the castle?"

"At the castle," Maggie said. "Evidently the whole Fitzpatrick family is invited. He told me to let you and Sam know, and for you to bring Sammy."

"What did you say?"

"I said I'd check with Scott and get back to him."

"We have to go," Hannah said.

"I didn't think you'd want to," Maggie said. "Why should we?"

"For our mothers," she said. "You know they are dying to get a look at the place, and if we ruin this chance for them, we will never hear the end of it."

"True," Maggie said. "Why do I think you've got something else in mind?"

"I don't know what you mean," Hannah said, "but I also don't want to give her the satisfaction of us not going."

"Where are you headed now?" Maggie asked. "I've got the rare afternoon and evening off, and I'm at loose ends. I should clean my filthy apartment, but I don't want to."

"I'm working on something," Hannah said. "You'd be bored."

"Working on what?" Maggie asked. "Something you wouldn't want Scott to know?"

"Maybe."

"Then I'm in," Maggie said. "We haven't done anything interesting in so long."

"This is top-secret stuff," Hannah said. "You may have to lie to your husband."

"What's new?" Maggie asked. "I lie to that man several times per day, and that's just in the interest of keeping my marriage and sanity intact. Men are so needy and insecure."

"Tell me about it."

"Where are we going?"

"Besington, PA."

"Why?"

"I'll fill you in on the way."

They decided to take Maggie's Jeep, which was much more reliable than Hannah's old truck. While she drove, Hannah read the case notes.

"Is this about the mystery man who got hit by the coal truck?" Maggie asked.

"Yes," Hannah said. "Let me finish this, and I'll tell you all about it."

"Are those official police records?"

"Possibly."

"Did you steal them?"

"Maybe," Hannah said. "Is copying them without permission the same thing?"

"Good job," Maggie said. "It's good to know you haven't lost your touch."

When Hannah was done reading the purloined file, she made some notes in her notebook and then told Maggie only the information she wanted her to know. Patrick being Maggie's brother made for a delicate situation.

"So you think this man was investigating Ava?"

"I'm just trying to work it out," Hannah said. "Someone said Ava was there."

"It is weird," Maggie said. "He rented a car, only to abandon it at the bus station and take the bus to Rose Hill?"

"Only he didn't take the bus," Hannah said. "According to this report, his name doesn't show up on the bus company's manifest, and the bus driver didn't recognize his photo."

"Maybe he used other IDs and a disguise," Maggie said, "and left his wallet and real IDs in the rental car."

"That seems foolish," Hannah said. "Bus stations are not known to reside in the safest neighborhoods; anybody could have broken into the car and stolen the wallet and IDs. He could have used fake IDs and still kept the real ones in his wallet, hidden in his pocket."

"He thought someone would search him?"

"Then he would have died with the fake IDs on him."

"So somebody took the fake IDs after he died?"

"If he had fake IDs and if he took the bus," Hannah said. "There's so much we don't know."

"Who are we going to see?"

"His landlord, and his sister, if I can get hold of her."

"If this is mob-related I'm out," Maggie said. "Just so you know."

"I don't think it is," Hannah said. "At least, I don't know if it is."

"Let's take Skyline Drive," Maggie said. "It's much prettier scenery."

"Suit yourself," Hannah said. "We gotta drive through somewhere, though; I'm starving."

"When aren't you?"

The address given for his apartment turned out to be the Bigelow Tavern on Main Street in Besington. It was a double-front brick building with a restaurant on one side and a bar on the other. Above the ground floor were three stories of apartments, with iron balconies and fire escapes.

"Are you coming?" Maggie asked Hannah.

"Wait a minute," Hannah said. "I'm reading the menu. I could really go for some Fries Diablo."

"You just ate thirty minutes ago," Maggie said. "Focus."

Inside, the light was dim, and it took a few moments for them to accustom their eyes to the darkness. Three men were sitting at the bar, and a couple was sitting in a booth, but no one looked up when they walked in. Hannah went up to the bar, but there was no bartender in attendance.

"He went to the can," a man said. "He had a burrito from Locos for lunch."

"That was a mistake," the second man said. "Nobody eats at Locos and lives to tell about it."

"Juan Carlos," the third man said. "They make the best burritos you can get around here."

"Casa Amigos," the woman seated in the booth said. "Theirs are the best."

"Are you crazy?" the man seated across from her said. "Rancho Del Fuego has the best burritos."

"Did you just call me crazy?" the woman said.

"Only cause you're batshit," the man said.

"There they go," the first man said.

"You shouldn't have started it," the second man said.

The woman began loudly insulting the man. He responded by doing the same to her.

"They're certainly charming," Hannah said.

"Do they always do this?" Maggie asked one of the men seated at the bar.

"Yeah," he said. "It's par for the course for those two."

The woman was now accusing the man of having sexual relations with another woman. The man responded by accusing the woman of doing the same with his best friend. The argument got more and more heated until a man came out of the back and blew an air horn at them. No one seemed startled by this but Maggie and Hannah.

"You two," the man said. "Settle down or get out."

The couple fell silent but continued glaring at each other.

"I was worried it was going to turn violent," Maggie said.

"It's just their daily drama," the bartender said. "They love to argue for an audience."

The man and woman were now making up, hands clasped across the table while weepy apologies were being exchanged. Then the woman went over to the man's side of the table, sat on his lap, and they began making out.

"People are fascinating, aren't they?" Hannah said.

"Insane is what they are," Maggie said.

"What can I get you?" the bartender asked Hannah and Maggie.

Hannah ordered a beer and Maggie said, "Make that two."

"You're not from around here," the bartender said.

"We're from Rose Hill," Hannah said.

"Across the Mason Dixon Line," Maggie said.

"We come in peace, Yankees!" Hannah announced to the bar.

The man had reached halfway across the bar with their beers but now stopped.

"You here to see me?" he asked.

"Are you the landlord?" Hannah asked, and pointed up.

"Come outside with me," he said and gestured to the front door.

He sat their beers down behind the bar, came around from behind it, and motioned to them to follow him out the front door.

As he followed them out, he called back, "Anybody touches my liquor, and they're banned for life. Howard, you're my hall monitor, and when I get back, your next one is on me."

Outside, the sun was low in the western sky, and the wind was cold.

"Make it fast," he said. "I got a business to run."

"You know why we're here?"

"I've been working here for twenty years, and in all that time no one from Rose Hill has ever asked to speak to the landlord. We have a tenant who just died under mysterious circumstances in Rose Hill, so I did the basic math."

"Why would he rent a car and then leave it at the bus station?" Hannah asked.

"He wouldn't," the man said. "He left here to drive to Rose Hill to do a surveillance job, one he'd been working on for over a year. He rented a car because his car was in the shop and I don't lend mine to anybody, no matter how good a tenant."

"Who was he surveilling?"

The man shrugged.

"He didn't give me any details; I just rent him space upstairs and sell him beers downstairs."

144

"Can we see his apartment?"

"Who are you?" he said. "You're not cops, I can tell that much."

"No," Hannah said. "The cops think it was an accident, but we don't. If we can find out who he was tailing maybe we can find out who killed him."

"I could let you up, but you probably wouldn't find anything," he said. "His sister said it looked as if nothing had been touched."

"You met his sister?"

"I've seen her around," he said. "They come in together for a drink once in a while."

"What's she like?"

"A looker," he said. "I asked him to fix me up with her, but he didn't think I was good enough, or something. I don't know."

"Can we at least look?" Hannah asked. "You can go with us, keep an eye on us."

"I gotta get back to work," he said. "My dad owns this place; I just run it for him. If he comes in and I'm gone there'll be hell to pay."

"What can we do?" Hannah asked. "Can we leave our driver's licenses with you? The keys to the Jeep? Her husband is the chief of police in Rose Hill; he would vouch for us."

Hannah ignored the look she knew Maggie was giving her.

He pretended to think about it.

"You got any dough?" he asked.

Hannah grimaced.

"I've got, like five dollars," she said. "Maggie?"

Maggie rolled her eyes, took out her wallet, and gave the man all the cash she had.

He counted it, and then looked Maggie up and down.

"You're a fine looking woman," he said. "You happily married?"

"My husband is a cop," Maggie said. "And I'm not interested."

He held up his hands and backed away.

"I didn't mean to offend you," he said. "I'll get the key."

"You owe me eighty dollars," Maggie said to Hannah

"Add it to my tab," Hannah said.

The man came back out with the key and told them to bring it back when they were done.

Through a side door and up three flights of stairs they went, and then down a hall to an apartment at the back. Inside, Hannah flipped on the lights.

"I don't know what I expected," Maggie said. "But I didn't expect this."

The apartment was traditional in the sense that there was an open concept living, dining, and kitchen area. It was unusual in that the exposed brick walls looked more like an art gallery. Every wall featured a sizable, original work of art professionally lit by industrial track lighting. Maggie looked at the paintings while Hannah found the tiny office area and tackled the files.

"These are beautiful," Maggie said.

"No laptop or PC but there's a router and cords for one," Hannah said. "Probably stolen."

"I wonder where he bought these," Maggie said.

"If he had a schedule it's gone," Hannah said. "Ditto any calendar. He probably kept it all on his phone, and they didn't find a phone."

"They're all different, but they're all the same person, I think," Maggie said.

"His files are very neat," Hannah said. "There's no 'Fitzpatrick' or 'Wooster' in here. No 'Ava' or 'Rose Hill,' either."

"It's like ten different perspectives on the same subject," Maggie said. "Impressionistic, I think. That would account for the use of light."

"This is getting us nowhere," Hannah said. "A big fat zero."

"Amazing," Maggie said.

"What is?" Hannah said.

"These," Maggie said and gestured to the paintings.

"Art isn't my thing," Hannah said. "I like comic books and Harry Potter."

"Look at them," Maggie said. "Look at the subject. What do they have in common?"

"They're all naked ladies," Hannah said.

"The same lady," Maggie said. "Don't you recognize her?"

Hannah went from one painting to the next. After the fourth one, she looked at Maggie, eyes wide.

"No way."

"It's her," Maggie said.

Hannah continued around the room until she'd studied every painting. She pointed at the bottom right-hand corner of the last one.

"He painted them."

Maggie looked at the one closest to her. The private eye's name was signed with a flourish.

"He was an artist, too."

Hannah went to the back of the apartment, into a separate room.

"Look at this," she called back to Maggie.

Hannah had flipped on the lights in this small back room, which featured a whole wall of windows from which you could see over the buildings behind it, which faced the other direction, to a park by a river. In the middle of the room there was an easel set up with a sheet over it, and on one wall art supplies were neatly organized on shelves. There were blank canvases as well as finished ones leaned against the other wall. Hannah was going through these. Maggie took the sheet off the easel.

"Hannah," she said.

"Just a minute," Hannah said. "Looks like these are all of her, too."

"Hannah," Maggie said again.

Hannah came over to look at what the sheet had been covering. This one had been sketched out, but not painted. There was a photo clipped to the side of the canvas.

"Gotcha," Hannah said.

She used the edge of the sheet to hold the photo while she unclipped it, and then said to Maggie, "Get an envelope or something for me to put this in."

Maggie went out to the office and returned with an envelope, into which Hannah dropped the photo of Ava. In the picture, she was looking off to the right and smiling. The wind was blowing her hair just like a model's in a photo shoot.

"He was in love with her," Maggie said.

"Or he was just obsessed with her," Hannah said. "Like every other mortal man we know."

"She didn't even know he was watching her," Maggie said. "It's incredibly creepy."

"Why do they all get so obsessed with her?" Hannah said.

"She's beautiful," Maggie said.

"Claire's beautiful," Hannah said. "You don't see old Ed papering the walls with her, but both Theo and this poor guy did that for Ava."

"Claire's pretty in a Rose Hill way, but Ava would be considered beautiful anywhere," Maggie said. "Besides, Theo's were just photos; this is art. He got hired to investigate her and then fell in love with her."

"We gotta talk to the sister," Hannah said. "She could probably tell us more."

"Who do you think hired him, then?"

"Will? Will's mother?" Hannah said.

"His sister might know that, too."

Hannah used her phone to take pictures of all the art pieces.

They returned the key and went back to the Jeep.

"What now?" Maggie asked.

"We gotta go to this address she gave Skip," Hannah said.

They drove to the address noted in the copy of the stolen police file, but there was a chain drugstore there in a shopping plaza. They double-checked the address inside with a clerk and then returned to the Jeep.

"She gave a fake address," Hannah said. "Let's try the phone."

After she punched in the numbers, it rang and rang, but no one answered.

"Fake, fake, fake," Hannah said.

"Why did she lie?"

"Just off the top of my head," Hannah said, "she's a crook, or she stands to gain from his death if it's not murder."

"So what do we do now?"

"What we do best," Hannah said. "Develop conspiracy theories and snoop around."

Just after they crossed the state line into West Virginia, Maggie got a call from Scott.

"I'll be home in an hour," she said and ended the call.

"You're not planning to tell him," Hannah said.

"Of course not," Maggie said. "Besides, what's to tell?"

After Maggie dropped Hannah off in town, Hannah went to Delia's to pick up Sammy and found Claire in the kitchen going through homework papers. Delia was in the living room watching a movie with all the kids.

Hannah got Claire caught up on what she and Maggie had discovered in Pennsylvania.

"It doesn't look good for Ava," Claire said. "I talked to the housekeeper today."

"Good," Hannah said. "What'd Gail say?"

"Nanny Siobhan's miserable, and she wants to quit and go home, but she's worried about leaving the children. Everyone likes Will, but he's rarely at home, and when he is, he's shut up in his office or in the bedroom wing with Ava. He sleepwalks, evidently, and although she likes him she's afraid he will accidentally scare the children in the night.

"She says Ava is very good to the small children, but she's very critical of everything

Siobhan does and warns her to stay away from Will, not to bother him with anything.

"Gail says the security guy Karl cannot be trusted. He drinks, evidently, and wanders around the property at night. Siobhan locks herself and the children in their wing after midnight and can hardly sleep for being afraid of what might happen."

"Did she mention Timmy?"

"She doesn't know why he was sent away, only that he didn't want to go, and he's terribly homesick, but Ava won't let him come home. Will's planning to take them all to England for Christmas, to see Charlotte. While they are there, Siobhan is going to be allowed to go home, and she is considering not coming back."

"That poor girl."

"Here's the juiciest bit: Gail saw Ava substitute some different pills for Will's sleeping pills."

"She drugs him so she can go out."

"To meet Patrick."

"I think so."

"Poor Melissa," Claire said. "Are you going to tell her everything?"

"I don't know," Hannah said. "I have to think this through."

"Ava has got to be stopped."

"And somebody has to talk to Patrick."

"Are you going to talk to him?"

"I don't want to," Hannah said, "but I have to."

Melissa came in the front door. Before she reached the kitchen, Claire and Hannah exchanged looks.

"I hate this for her," Claire said. "She's so crazy about Patrick."

"And he's crazy about Ava," Hannah said. "Evidently, it's contagious."

CHAPTER SIX - FRIDAY

When Melissa got to work the next morning, there was a voicemail message from Trick Rodefeffer asking her to call as soon as possible.

"What's up?" she asked him when he answered.

"Listen," he said. "Can I stop by this morning?"

"Come now," Melissa said. "Sean won't be here for another hour."

Trick showed up within minutes.

"Jailbird, we've got ourselves a doozy of a problem," he said. "I heard from the trailer park guy yesterday evening, and he's had another offer."

"From who?"

"Well, for some crazy reason, Ava has offered him twice what you did."

Melissa felt her skin turn hot.

"Don't shoot the messenger," Trick said, his hands in the air. "I don't know why Ava has her knives out for you, but evidently she means business."

"That woman's leanin' on my last nerve," Melissa said. "What can we do?"

"I told him you were a knockout; maybe flirt with him a little."

"I'm not gonna flirt with the guy, Trick," Melissa said, "but I am going to call him."

Trick helped himself to coffee while Melissa called the seller. She told him she knew he'd had a better offer, but that she thought the income from the little house project would help her keep the mobile homes that were there affordable for low-income families. He listened to her, and then said he would prefer to sell it to her, and if she could get a contract to him by the end of the day they would call it a deal. Melissa ended the call feeling triumphant.

"Sean can draw up the contract today," Melissa said. "We beat her!"

"Not so fast," he said.

"Why?"

"You're going to need the town council to approve a zoning change," Trick said. "That plot is zoned for mobile homes, but I'm not sure those tiny houses qualify."

"What do I have to do?" Melissa said. "That has to be in the contract."

"Talk to Kay," Trick said. "She's the mayor; she may be able to push it through."

"Listen," Melissa said to Trick. "I appreciate you giving me the heads up on Ava's offer; I know your commission would have been more with that sale."

"Money's not everything," Trick said.

He leaned against her desk and gave her what she knew he thought was a sexy look. It was kind of sad, really.

"I'm not interested," she said.

Trick stood up straight and lifted his hands in the air.

"It was worth a try," he said. "I'm only a man."

"I'll tell you what I will do," Melissa said. "You help me sell the tiny houses, and I'll give you a commission on those."

"Deal," he said, and they shook on it.

"And another thing," Melissa said.

"Anything for you, darlin'," he said.

"You call me 'jailbird' one more time, and I'm gonna kick your paw-paws right up into the top of your tree."

Around noon a tall, dark-haired woman came into the office. She looked familiar to Melissa, but she couldn't place her. She was dressed in a navy blue pantsuit, a white blouse, and sensible navy blue shoes.

"Teresa Reyes," she said. "I have an appointment with Mr. Fitzpatrick."

Melissa's heart rate sped up, and she could feel her face flush. The appointment wasn't on Sean's calendar. How could she have screwed that up?

The woman's face bore a neutral expression that Melissa could not read.

"Is Mr. Fitzpatrick in?" the woman asked.

"He is," Melissa said. "I'll get him for you."

Instead of calling his office she hurried down the hallway and entered without knocking.

"Teresa Reyes is here," Melissa said. "I'm sorry I didn't have her on the calendar."

Sean didn't seem surprised. He calmly rose and went down the hall, where he shook the woman's hand and invited her back to the conference room. Melissa, who had every intention of listening at the door, was then dismayed when Sean turned to her.

"Melissa, remember that package I had you put in the safety deposit box?"

Melissa nodded.

"Would you mind to get it back out for me? There's something in it I want Ms. Reyes to have a look at. And lock the front door when you leave. I don't want to be disturbed."

Melissa, heart pounding and nerves jangling, hurried to do as he asked. When the bank employee gave her a pen to sign the safety deposit box log, her hand trembled as she signed. She brought the padded envelope back to the office, knocked on the conference room door, and when Sean opened it, Melissa noticed his laptop on the table.

"Thank you," he said. "Now, if you don't mind, I'd like you to take a nice long lunch, and don't come back until 2:00. You can put the phones direct to voicemail and lock up as you leave."

And then he whispered "and don't worry."

Melissa didn't know what to do with herself. She was too nervous to eat and didn't want to see anyone she knew. She went to the IGA, bought a bottle of soda, and took it to the park to drink. No sooner had she sat down on a bench than Ava's nanny arrived with Olivia, who was throwing a tantrum. The nanny handled it well, and within seconds had redirected Olivia to bossing around the other kids in the sandbox.

The nanny sat down on the same bench as Melissa, gave her a rueful look, and rolled her eyes.

"She's a handful," Melissa said.

"She's a narky snapper and a pain in my arse, but I'm mad for her," the woman said. "My name's Siobhan, pleased to meet you."

She held out her hand, and Melissa shook it.

"I'm Melissa," she said in turn.

"One of these yours?"

"No," Melissa said. "Mine's in college."

"You don't look old enough for that."

"Thanks," Melissa said. "Where are you from?"

"Kinsale, County Cork, Ireland," Siobhan said. "And in 45 days, Lord willing, I'll be back there to stay."

"How long have you been away?"

"Since this one was born two years ago," she said, gesturing to Olivia. "It will break my heart to leave her, but if I stay here much longer, I'll lose my feckin' mind."

"Why's that?"

"Her mother, her majesty, is a feckin' slapper," she said.

"What's that mean?"

"I'm sorry," Siobhan said. "I'm supposed to talk like an American around the children, but I'm sick and tired of trying to be someone I'm not."

"I hear ya," Melissa said. "I concentrate so hard on grammar sometimes it gives me a headache."

"Where are you from?"

"Tennessee," Melissa said. "It doesn't even matter where you're from, it only matters to these folks that you're not from here."

Siobhan held out her hand, and they shook on that.

"A slapper's a slut, by the way," Siobhan said.

"I know what that means."

"You would think the woman would be satisfied with that hunk of a husband she's got. He's mad for her, all right."

"But she's not."

"Off her nut, if you ask me," Siobhan said. "Got it made, she does. Feckin' eejit."

"She cheats."

"Yes, she cheats, that pile of shite."

"She's that obvious about it?"

"To me it is, and to everyone else it is, but she's got himself so twisted around her little finger he's blind in one eye, and the other one's not seein' too well."

"So he doesn't know."

"He doesn't want to know," Siobhan said. "He's worried she's going to leave him any minute; always racing around, trying to please her. Ungrateful skank that she is, she treats him like a plonker when really, he's a bit of a dream."

"Is she a good mother?"

Siobhan snorted.

"For show, she is. When himself is around or someone she wants to impress."

"Do you think she'd leave him?"

"Not a chance," Siobhan said. "He's covered up in cash, that one is. Filthy with it."

"What would he do if he caught her cheating?"

"He'd think it was his fault," Siobhan said. "He'd be begging her to forgive him for driving her to it."

"That's sad."

"It's driving me right round the bend, I tell you," Siobhan said. "I don't know how I'll last another month and a half."

"But you'll miss the kids."

"I'll miss this one, that's for sure. Livvie's a right little devil, but she's a good 'un, not like her mam."

"What will you do for work at home?"

"My mam has a café in Kinsale, right in the middle of the touristy bit," Siobhan said. "Nothing sounds finer to me than working in the caf all day, getting pissed with my friends at night, and bangin' me some lads. I'm too young to live like a feckin' nun."

"Will you go to school?"

Siobhan shrugged.

"I might, yeah," Siobhan said. "I just need to blow off some steam, you know?"

"I do know," Melissa said. "Can I give you some advice, though?"

Siobhan shrugged.

"Imagine yourself at your mother's age, and how you want to be living. Do you want to still be working in a cafe, feet hurting, tired all the time, serving tourists, and living on tips?"

"I've got lots of time to figure that out."

"I know it seems like it," Melissa said. "I wish I'd looked out for myself instead of worrying about what some guy wanted, or if he did or didn't love me."

"No worries here. Men are full of shite, like," Siobhan said. "They can't keep it in their pants, none of them. Still and all, there's nothing like a good, hot snog to cheer a girl up."

"Why do men cheat, do you think?"

"It's not their fault, like," Siobhan said. "They've got that willy, yeah? Leads them around like a dog, doesn't it? And dogs don't half like to roll in shite."

Melissa laughed.

"I heard that same answer just the other day," she said.

They watched Olivia bossing the other children around, and Melissa reckoned she came by it naturally. Charlotte had been just like that, charming and sweet when it suited her, but mean and demanding when that didn't work.

"Do you ever see Charlotte?" she asked.

Siobhan shook her head.

"She's not allowed back here," she said. "I don't know what she did, but it must have been bad."

Melissa saw Will's security man, Karl, get out of his car and walk toward them. There was something about that man that made the hair rise up on the back of her neck.

"I've got to go," Melissa said. "It was so nice to meet you, and I hope you'll be happier back in Kinsale."

"Mind yourself," Siobhan said. "I'll see you around."

When Melissa got back to work, the woman had gone, and Sean was sitting at the front desk, talking on the phone. He hung up just as she came in.

"There you are," he said. "Nice lunch?"

"I can't eat. I'm too wound up," Melissa said. "Was that lady here because of Patrick?"

"Melissa, relax," Sean said. "I know you've had a rough time lately, but I think you're getting a bit paranoid."

"When someone's out to get you it's not paranoid," Melissa said. "It's watching your back for an excellent reason."

"It's going to be okay; will you trust me on that?"

"What's going on, Sean? What was in the envelope?"

"I can't tell you," he said. "Just know that our family has your back, and we're going to do everything we can to protect you."

"I appreciate that, I do," Melissa said. "She looked familiar, that lady."

"She's worked in Rose Hill before. That's all I'm going to say about her," Sean said. "Let's do some work."

Later in the afternoon, Sean and Melissa were going over the trailer park sale contract when Ava came in. The color was high in her beautiful face, and her nostrils were flaring.

"You just made a huge mistake," she said, pointing her finger at Sean.

"Why is that?" Sean asked in a calm voice.

"She," Ava said, now pointing at Melissa, "ruined a deal I wanted to make, and that's a serious conflict of interest."

"The way I understand it, it's you who wants to ruin things for Melissa," Sean said.

"As soon as I tell my husband about this, you'll be fired as our attorney," Ava said. "And he may sue you for what she did."

Sean had been sitting on the edge of Melissa's desk, but now he stood up and faced Ava.

"I look forward to meeting you in court," he said. "The results of the discovery process alone should provide the judge with a very entertaining picture of you and the kinds of things you've been doing lately. I somehow don't think you'd like your husband to know what you've been up to, so I suggest you give more thought to the consequences of this temper tantrum you're throwing. Now, if that's all, Ava, we have work to do."

"I don't understand," Ava said. "Why are you protecting her? I'm family."

"She's my friend," Sean said. "And come to think of it, she's family, too."

"She just cost you a high-paying client," Ava said. "And by the time we're through with you, I can assure you that more will follow us out the door."

"I have plenty of clients," Sean said, "and to a one, they are all more pleasant to deal with than you. You can save your vitriol, Ava, because I'm firing you as a client."

Ava turned and stormed off in a huff.

"I'm sorry," Melissa said.

"Don't be," Sean said. "There are few things I hate more than being bullied."

"I guess you know what's going on."

"I know a lot, that's true," he said. "I'm sorry for what you're going through, and I wish I could assure you that my brother has more good sense than he's shown lately. If there's anything I can do to help, I hope you'll let me."

"There is something," Melissa said and told him about the zoning approval she needed.

Fifteen minutes later, Sean and Melissa were in Mayor Kay Templeton's office.

"The council meets next week," Kay said. "We have a full agenda, but I'm sure I could shoehorn this matter into the schedule."

"How do you think they'll vote?" Sean asked.

Kay thought about it.

"Three against and seven for," she said. "I have three people who would no doubt love nothing more than to raze the ground those trailers sit upon and put up a row of high-priced condos, and six individuals who will rubber stamp anything I want to be passed."

"What about the seventh person?"

"That's Hannah," she said. "You have nothing to worry about."

Hannah came in just before the end of the workday.

"Is he in?" she asked as she pointed to the back.

Melissa nodded and called Sean. He came up to the front to greet Hannah.

"Well, I'm officially sacked," she said. "I got the call a little while ago. They're offering me six months' severance if I sign a paper promising not to sue them, but if I don't sign, I get nothing."

"So we sue," Sean said.

"The thing is I need that money now," Hannah said. "My health insurance is kaput as of Saturday, and we can't get anything else on this short of notice, even if we could afford it."

"Let me call Anthony," Sean said. "He can get you a policy, and I can pay for it. We'll put it on your tab and take it out of the settlement."

"What if we don't win?"

"Let me lay it out for you: you are a woman over forty who has never had a poor performance review in twenty years of faithful service employed by the county. This new boss of yours has let it be known he wants to hire his unqualified twenty-year-old son-in-law and pay him probably twice as much as you. I know every judge in this part of the state, and they all know I only bring cases before them I know I can win. I don't know what your idiot boss thinks will happen, but the county will settle fast and for a lot more than six months' severance, and then they'll probably fire him. You on board?"

"I'm scared, Sean," Hannah said. "Are you sure?"

"It's a slam dunk," Sean said. "What's their official cause for firing you?"

"I took too many days off in July," Hannah said. "That was when Sammy was so sick, and we thought he might have meningitis."

"That thrills me no end," Sean said. "The jury will eat that up. Working mother punished for caring for her child. I can't believe they dared try that on."

"Here's the thing," Hannah said. "I love my job. I don't want to stop. I'd miss it."

"False cost sunkenness," Melissa said.

Hannah looked at Melissa as if she had lost her mind.

"I think you mean 'sunk-cost fallacy,'" Sean said.

"Yeah, that," Melissa said. "It means you stay with the crappy thing because you're so used to crappiness and afraid of making a change."

"Basically, yes," Sean said. "I could probably get your job back for you, Hannah, but he'd always be looking for another reason to fire you, just for revenge. Eventually, it would change how you felt about your job, and you'd be miserable. I recommend you cut your losses and sue their asses off."

"You always wanted to run a no-kill shelter," Melissa said. "If Sean got you enough money you could start one."

"I'm thinking mid-six figures," Sean said. "I'm very confident about this, Hannah. Please trust me. Do you want to talk to Sam about it first?"

"He's the one who told me to speak to you," Hannah said. "He said it was up to me."

"What's it gonna be?"

Hannah chewed her lip and blinked fast.

"Hell, let's do it," she said. "Let's sue their asses."

"High dollar! High dollar!" Melissa chanted as she clapped her hands.

"I'll call the county and announce your intentions," Sean said. "Melissa, you take Hannah down to Anthony's office. We need to get you and Sammy covered by health insurance today."

When Hannah and Melissa got to Delia's house later that evening, they found Bonnie and Claire there with Hannah's son Sammy, Hatch's nephew Josh, Claire's four girls, Ava's daughter Olivia and son, Ernie. The women were working on Halloween costumes.

Little Pixie and Oliva were fairy princesses, Bluebell was Rey from Star Wars, and Sammy was Spiderman.

Ernie had to explain his costume, as he was the Sith cat Kuro from a manga anime series. Joshie, wearing a black wig and a small business suit, explained he was Dr. Sōsuke Banba from a Japanese anime television series titled Kagewani.

Bonnie rolled her eyes.

"When my kids were little you got to be one of three things: a hobo, a pirate, or a ghost."

The two older girls wanted to be mermaids, so Claire was applying temporary rainbow color streaks to their long blonde hair.

Ed and Patrick came through the front door with pizzas, and Sam followed behind with grocery bags of chips and soft drinks.

"I hope it's okay I came," Patrick said to Melissa.

"I don't mind," she said.

Olivia came over to Patrick and reached up for him to pick her up. He did so, saying, "It's Princess Olivia! Look, Melissa, it's her royal highness. Isn't she pretty?"

Melissa had a close view of the two of them together, and the likeness was striking. She fled to the kitchen to escape all the uncomfortable feelings this produced.

"I told you," Bonnie said to her as she followed close behind. "Didn't I tell you? The spitting image. Look at her hands if you get the chance. That's my granddaughter."

Melissa did her best to avoid Patrick, although she was keenly aware of his proximity at all times. Hannah's parents Curtis and Alice arrived, soon followed by Hatch, Maggie, and Scott. The party got louder, the children more shrill as they were plied with carbohydrates and carbonated sugar water.

In every room she tried to escape to, Melissa saw something that made her want to disappear: Claire and Ed embracing in the kitchen, Patrick cuddling Olivia in the living room.

Finally, Melissa fled to the backyard. There she found Sam sitting on the picnic table.

"Hey," she said. "Scoot over."

He made room for her, and she sat next to him.

"It got to be a little too much in there," he said. "Nice out here, though."

"I love them all, but it was giving me a headache," Melissa said.

"It's kind of cold," he said and offered her his jacket.

She shook her head.

"Feels good," she said. "I like the smell of wood smoke, too; it smells like fall."

"Smells more like something else burning," he said, as he raised his head and looked all around.

"Over there," he said, and stood up.

He pointed in the distance, where Melissa could see an orange glow reflected off the trailers in the mobile home park that was soon to be hers.

"What's doing that?" she asked, but Sam was already running to the house.

And then she knew.

By the time she got there, many other park residents had gathered outside their trailers. Bruce had trained his garden hose on the conflagration, but it had no effect. The sirens from the fire station began going off, and engine sirens were deafening as both turned down Peony Street. Melissa stood amongst her neighbors and watched as the trailer she had called home went up in flames.

It was mesmerizing. It was horrifying.

All of Tommy's school papers. His little league trophies. His baby clothes. His birth certificate. His adoption papers. Their photo albums. Every gift Patrick had ever given her.

The flames were hot on her face. It reminded her of the fire down in Florida, the one that changed everyone's lives forever; the one that made Tommy her son.

Patrick came up behind her and put his arms around her, but she felt nothing.

"There's nothing we can do," he said. "Let me take you back to Delia's."

Melissa turned and looked up at him.

"This is Ava's doing," she said.

He let go.

"You can deny it if you want to," she said. "You can defend the precious love of your life all you want, but you and I both know it's true. She's poisoned the well, and now we all have to drink from it. This is on you, Patrick. You brought this down on my head, the woman you were supposed to love and protect. You betrayed me, but now I'm the one that's sufferin' for your sins."

He started to speak, but she held up her hand.

"I know you're well and truly sorry, but I'm done with you. I want you to feel it, know it, and go."

Patrick backed away and then turned, disappeared in the crowd.

Claire came up and put an arm around her, followed by Hannah and Maggie. They didn't say anything, just stood there at her side until the flames were doused, the crowd had dispersed, and nothing remained but the blackened wreckage of her former home.

"This takes me back to when Theo burned my house down," Maggie said. "You never get over something like that."

"Your book burned up," Melissa said to Maggie. "I'll pay you for it."

"Don't worry about that," Maggie said. "Did you like it?"

"I hated it," Melissa said. "Catherine and Heathcliff were horrible, selfish people who didn't care who they hurt."

"I guess that's one way to look at it," Maggie said.

"Let's go," Claire said. "I'm freezing."

Melissa turned to Hannah.

"I talked to Bruce," Hannah said. "He couldn't swear it was Ava he saw the night of the accident."

"She did this," she said.

"I know," Hannah said.

"I want her punished," Melissa said. "I want her to suffer for what she's done."

"It will be my pleasure," Hannah said.

When Hannah got home the kitchen sink was empty, the counters and table had been wiped clean, and the dishwasher was running. She looked in the laundry room and found two baskets full of clean, folded laundry where there had been a tall, dirty pile when she left the house. The floor still needed to be swept and mopped, and there were still dust cobwebs dangling from the corners of the ceiling, but for their house, this was clean.

She found her husband and son in the family room. Sammy was asleep on the couch, the two little white dogs curled up next to him, the husky lying on the floor in front of them. Sam was watching a blacksmith competition on television, his son's head on his lap.

"Who's winning?" she asked.

"The young guy," Sam said. "The underdog."

Hannah squeezed in beside him at the end of the couch, and he put his arm around her.

"You cleaned," she said.

"Yep," Sam said.

"Are you in trouble or something?"

"Sammy and I were just trying to help out," he said. "We also cleaned the bathrooms and put toys away."

"Wow," Hannah said. "Thanks."

She looked at Sammy.

"Look how long he's gotten," she said.

"He'll be taller than you in a couple years," Sam said.

"I'll have to stand on a stump just to look him in the eye when I ground him."

"How's Melissa?" he asked.

"Gutted," Hannah said.

He nodded.

"Sammy and I are on health insurance now, thanks to Sean and Anthony."

"So I heard," Sam said. "I also heard we're going to be rich litigants."

"So he says."

"I got an offer for a teaching position at Quantico."

She turned and looked at him.

"When did this happen?"

"Today," Sam said. "A few days ago I told Tony I was looking for work and his old C.O. got back to me today. He's at the academy now."

"Tony-from-Kuwait Tony?"

He nodded.

"What did you tell him?"

"That I'd have to talk to you."

"Hah, right."

"I did. I am."

"Do you want to do it?"

"Partly."

"Which part?"

"I'd be good at it," he said. "I might like it."

"Be a long commute."

He turned and gave her a look that said, 'very funny.'

"I can't see you leaving your wounded warriors," she said.

"I said a part of me wants to do it, not all of me."

"Is it a good offer?"

He rubbed the thumb and fingers of one hand together.

Hannah whistled.

"That much?"

He nodded.

"Full benefits package," he said. "Relocation expenses."

"We'd have to move."

"Naturally."

Hannah looked over at the other side of the living room, where a striped tabby cat was curled up in an armchair.

"Whose cat is that?" she asked.

"I thought it was ours," he said. "It wanted in."

"I guess it's ours now," she said.

"Watch what this guy does," he said, gesturing at the television. "He's just about to win the whole thing, and at the last minute, his blade breaks in two."

"You've seen this one before."

"A couple times."

"The thing is," Hannah said, "I don't want to leave. This is our home. Sammy has friends here, our family's here. My folks are getting older; they're gonna need us more."

"I could go, come home on the weekends."

"No," Hannah said. "I want you here for Sammy."

"Just Sammy."

"You know what I mean."

Sam pulled her close and kissed the top of her head.

"I know," he said.

"Plus, we're going to be rich," she said. "All our problems will be solved."

"Could take a while," he said. "Probably shouldn't count on it."

"We'll be okay," Hannah said. "Either way."

"Most likely," he said. "You feel like fooling around?"

"I gotta feed the pony."

"I already did."

"Good man," she said.

"I bought you some donuts."

"I definitely feel like fooling around with a man who buys me donuts."

"That was the plan."

Sam turned the television off.

"I'll take him up and meet you in five," he said.

"I can probably eat ten donuts in five minutes."

"I hid them."

"Oh, I get it," Hannah said. "I get the donuts afterward."

"You got that right," he said. "I want you hungry and motivated."

Afterward, lying in bed, Hannah licked donut glaze off her fingers.

"These are highway donuts," she said.

"Only the best for you."

"I've got a problem I need you to help me solve," she said. "It's kind of a delicate situation."

"Tell me about it."

"It involves Ava."

"That one I know about," Sam said.

"Care to share?"

"Classified."

"Okay," Hannah said. "So you know Ava has turned into a murderous banshee who won't rest until Melissa's tits up in Rose Hill Cemetery."

"I think you're exaggerating."

"I'm not," Hannah said.

She told him all the evidence she had plus her theory.

"Did you know all that?" she asked.

"Not all of it," he said.

"What do you think?"

"You need hard evidence."

"Would Patrick testify against her?"

He shrugged.

"Let's say it was me Ava was after," Hannah said. "She wanted you, and I was in the way. She shot the dogs, poisoned the cats, got Sammy taken away by children's services, and burnt our house down. What would you do?"

"I'd get hard evidence, turn it over to the police, and let them take care of it."

"No, you wouldn't."

"Nah, I'd probably make her wish she'd never been born."

"That's more like it."

"What exactly do you want me to do, Hannah?"

"Help us," she said. "Every one of us has a small piece of evidence, but it's just our word against hers. Melissa has an audio of her threats, and I think Patrick has video evidence that he's turned over to Sean, but I haven't talked to him about it yet."

"I can neither confirm nor deny that."

"Going all Glomar on me now, huh?" Hannah said. "That's okay, I've got my ways. I'll find out."

"What's your endgame?" he asked. "Do you want her to go to jail? Do you want her kids to lose their mother?"

"I want her stopped," she said. "I want her to be profoundly afraid to do one more thing to anyone I love. And if she was forced to move away from here that would be the dark chocolate icing on the devil's food cake of what I want."

"Let me think about it," he said. "Are you going over there tomorrow?"

"Yep."

"Be careful," he said. "Ava won't like you snooping around in her life."

"What? Lil ole me?"

"Just be careful."

"I'm so good at this I could be a professional," she said. "Bonnie's going to glue herself to Ava's side and keep her distracted while I snoop."

"They have a security guy."

"He's a drunk," Hannah said. "Maggie's going to get him liquored up."

"Are there any donuts left?"

"Just one," Hannah said. "But I don't think you've earned it."

"What more can I do?"

"I don't know if you can do more," she said. "I may need a younger man for this. An underdog."

"I can promise you my blade will not break."

Sam pounced, Hannah squealed, the donut was squished, but neither of them much cared.

Melissa lay in bed, unable to sleep. She still felt numb and exhausted, but her mind was restless. When her phone made a noise, she pounced on it.

It was Tommy.

"Patrick called me," he texted. "Do you want me to come home?"

"No," she texted back. "I'm fine. You stay in school."

They exchanged some chit chat and told each other they loved each other.

Afterward, she felt better. At least she felt something other than helpless grief. Ava could take everything she had, but she couldn't come between her and Tommy. That thought made her wonder if Ava would be tempted to try something on Tommy.

"I'd kill her," Melissa said out loud.

Her phone made another noise, and it was Patrick this time. She ignored it and then deleted it. She looked at the time; he was just about to leave work at the Thorn. On impulse, she got out of bed, put on some clothes and shoes, turned off the alarm, and let herself out of Delia's house, locking it behind her.

It was clear and cold; bound to be a hard frost before morning. All the stars in the sky sparkled, and the moon was just a sideways smile in the dark sky. She walked to the end of Iris Avenue and stood at the corner, behind an oak tree. She watched the part-time waitress leave the bar. Then the light went off above the side entrance.

There was a movement in the alley behind the bar.

She blinked and squinted to try to make out what moved out of the darkness. It was a person, a slim form, dressed in a black hoodie and dark pants. Melissa's heart thumped as this person went up the wheelchair ramp to the side door, the door opened, and the person slid inside, closing the door behind.

Melissa started to move, walking faster and faster, not thinking about what she was doing. She marched up the ramp, reached the side door of the bar, and pulled on the handle; it was locked. Thinking fast, she took out her keys and searched through them until she found the one she used to use on this door. It still fit. She unlocked it and pulled it open, trying not to make any noise.

The back room was dark, with only a shaft light from the front to illuminate a sliver of it. Melissa could hear Patrick in the front room doing closing chores. She looked around but could not see where the other person had gone. She stepped forward, toward the pull-down stairs to the attic, and her foot kicked against something that was on the floor. She picked the pieces up– a hoodie, a pair of leggings, and small hiking boots, too small to be a man's.

Melissa looked up toward the top of the ladder, where she could see candlelight flickering against the slanted ceiling.

So this was what they did and where they did it.

What they were still doing.

She considered her options.

She balled up the clothes, clutched them and the shoes to her chest, and left the way she came in, locking up behind her. She went back to the alley and tossed the bundle in the dumpster.

Then she made a call.

Melissa waited, concealed up in the branches of the oak tree until she saw the revolving, colorful lights of a county sheriff's car coming up Rose Hill Avenue. It was followed by two more. Melissa grimaced; she didn't realize there'd be more than one squad car responding to a suspected burglary.

Three county cops exited their cars and converged on the corner next to the bar; then one disappeared around to the front, and another came back to the side door. The third stayed at the corner. Melissa could hear the cop at the front, pounding on the door. Then the cop nearest to her did the same on the side door. He drew his gun as the door opened and Patrick came out with his hands up.

At least he was dressed.

He talked to the side door cop while the other two came around the side of the building;

their guns were drawn. Patrick turned around, placed his hands against the wall, and was patted down. He pulled out Patrick's wallet, removed his ID, and examined it by flashlight. They allowed Patrick to turn around, talked to him some more, and then stood around for a while, as one of the cops spoke into the radio handset stuck to his shoulder.

Eventually, someone came down the sidewalk toward them, and when he reached the streetlight, Melissa could see it was Scott. Scott showed them his badge and ID, talked to them for a bit, they all shook hands, and the county cops left. Patrick spoke to Scott for a little while and then Scott left.

Patrick went back inside.

Melissa was chilled to the bone, her teeth chattering, but still, she waited. After about fifteen minutes, the smaller person left the bar via the side door, wearing clothes and shoes that were much too big, and disappeared down the alley. Melissa dropped out of the tree and ran down Iris Avenue, staying close to the apartment buildings on the east side of the street. When she reached the end of the street, she hid in the vestibule of the next to last building and watched as the slim person walked down Pine Mountain Road, got in a white SUV, and drove away.

A few minutes later, Melissa was treated to the sight of Patrick, dressed in his socks with a tablecloth wrapped around his waist, walking home to his mother's house. Melissa had to clasp her hand to her mouth to keep from laughing out loud.

Melissa left the vestibule and walked back down Iris Avenue. As she crossed the street toward Delia's house, headlights illuminated her, and with the roar of an engine, a vehicle bore down on her. Melissa was momentarily stunned, transfixed by the bright lights, but was able to gather her wits fast enough to scramble out of its path as it flew by.

Melissa whirled around fast enough to see the back of the white SUV as it reached the corner, then turned left with a squeal of tires. She could hear it do the same at the corner of Pine Mountain Road and Rose Hill Avenue. Melissa began to run, fearing it would circle around to try again, but as she reached Delia's front porch, she could hear the SUV roaring northward as it left town.

Her heart was pounding as she fumbled with her keys and let herself in the house. She reset the alarm and crept down the hallway, back into her room, out of her clothes, and into bed.

Too keyed up to sleep, her eyes flickered back and forth as she replayed in her mind what had just happened.

Ava knew what she had done or at the very least, had seen her afterward.

And had tried to kill her.

Her phone made a noise, and she checked it.

Patrick was texting her.

"Thinking about you. Missing you."

Melissa deleted the text with a furious punch of the finger.

She had sunk her last cost on that fallacy.

CHAPTER SEVEN - SATURDAY

Saturday morning, bright and early, Hannah, Sam, and Sammy arrived at Bonnie's house to do some work. Uncle Fitz was stretched out in his recliner, watching golf on a sports channel. Aunt Bonnie was kneading dough at the kitchen counter. Sammy hugged Bonnie from the side, and she turned to kiss the top of his head.

"Whatcha making?" Hannah asked her.

"Cinnamon rolls for the Halloween party tonight."

"Yum," Hannah said.

Patrick was sitting at the table, dark circles under his eyes, drinking black coffee. His beagle Banjo was asleep on his feet. Sean was sitting with him at the table, going through their father's toolbox.

"We're going to need new everything," Sean said. "Most of this stuff is either broken, rusted, or both. Plus we need scrapers, exterior house paint, caulk, rollers, and brushes."

"And new boards for the front porch," Sam said. "A tape measure, nails, a hammer, and a saw."

"I'll paint the trim if you do the rest, Sean," Patrick said. "Let's get one of those spray guns. It'll go so much faster."

"I wanna spray the gun," Sammy said. "Can I spray the gun? Please?"

"No way," Sam said. "You're my helper today, and we're on porch duty."

'You probably shouldn't be up on a ladder, considering the state of you," Sam said to Patrick.

"You're in charge of the circular saw," Patrick said to Sam. "I'd probably saw off all my fingers."

"Painter's tape, drop cloths, and a circular saw," Sean said, as he made a list on his phone. "It might be cheaper to burn it down."

"Sonny's store is open," Bonnie said. "I can give you some money."

"Not necessary," Sean said.

"Don't worry, Ma, we've got this," Patrick said. "I'm poor but strong, Sean's rich and generous, and Sam's smart and partly bionic."

"I'll cook you something good for lunch, but I can't stay," Bonnie said. "How do chili and cornbread sound?"

"Delicious," Hannah said. "I'm going to be working mostly in a supervisory capacity, but I'll be certain to work up an appetite."

"I'm off to the hardware store," Sean said.

"I'll go with you," Sam said.

Bonnie poured oil into an enormous ceramic bowl and rubbed it all over the interior. She then balled up the dough and plopped it down into the bowl, covered it with a wet dish towel, and set it on top of the gas range to rise.

Hannah poured herself half a cup of coffee, topped it off with half-and-half and several spoons full of sugar, and then sat down across from Patrick.

"You look like you sorted wildcats before breakfast," she said.

"Something like that," he said.

"I'm going to go to the IGA to get some groceries," Bonnie said, as she took off her apron. "Are you going to Ava's later?"

"I am," Hannah said.

"Are you going to change clothes?" Bonnie asked.

"I will," Hannah said.

"Are you planning to wear a bra?" Bonnie asked.

"And makeup," Hannah said. "Just like church."

"C'mon Sammy," Bonnie said to Hannah's son. "You can push the buggy and pick out one treat."

"I want ice cream, and candy, and a soda pop," he said.

"You'll get what you get, and you won't throw a fit," Bonnie said.

When Hannah heard the door close behind them, she rooted around in the cabinets until she found a bakery box full of leftover sticky buns and sat it on the table. When Patrick reached over to help himself, she smacked his hand, and he stuck out his tongue at her.

Hannah closed the door between the kitchen and the front room. Her Uncle Fitz was sawing logs in his chair, but she didn't want to take a chance he would overhear. She cut off a couple of rolls for Patrick, put them on a plate and set them down in front of him. Then she got a fork out of the drawer and sat down with the rest in the box.

"All right, dick-for-brains, what in the hell is going on with you and Ava?"

"Don't start, Hannah."

"I'm gonna start, and then I'm gonna keep on going until you confess," Hannah said.

"Nothing can stop me. I'm tenacious, you know that. You might as well spill it."

"It's complicated."

"I can guarantee it's not," Hannah said. "You've been boning Ava for years now, right? I know she's beautiful, any idiot can see that, but it must be real love to have gone on for that long. You could have married her after Brian died, your mother be damned. Why didn't you?"

"She didn't want to," Patrick said. "One condition of Theo's bequest was she not get married again."

"I didn't know that. What a weasel. And Theo was a jerk, too."

"I can understand it; what have I got to offer her? That money rescued her business, paid all her bills, and would pay for the kids' college tuition. It just made sense to collect the money and still see each other in secret. That way Ava got the money and my mom stayed off my back."

"Sounds reasonable," Hannah said. "Also very convenient for Ava. What about Melissa? Why drag her into it?"

"Melissa loves me, she always has. We were tight, man, she was always a good friend to me, and Tommy was my little buddy. When she took up with Ed, I realized how much I loved her. And then when she went to prison I had to be there for her.

"I didn't intend for the thing with Ava to go on after Melissa got out of prison," he said. "But I couldn't stay away from her. Then she got pregnant, and I'm pretty sure I'm Olivia's father."

"Anyone with two good eyes can see that," Hannah said. "You should have come clean with Melissa and married Ava then."

"Yeah, but Will had all that money, and Charlotte was in trouble. Ava couldn't pay for boarding school in Switzerland like Will could, and I certainly couldn't. Ava knew if she married him she'd lose Theo's trust fund, but she would never have to worry about what happened to her kids."

"Did Charlotte kill Professor Richmond?"

"If she did he deserved it," Patrick said. "Bastard molested her."

"Did Ava kill him?"

"No way," Patrick said. "There were some other kids involved; Ava thinks it was probably one of them."

"I don't know about that," Hannah said. "I think Ava's got it in her, and Charlotte does, too. I think whoever gave Ava up for adoption probably did time for being a serial killer. You're just blind to her faults."

"I'm not," Patrick said. "I just love her in spite of them."

"So you know she's not perfect?"

He nodded.

"Let's just say I recently had my eyes opened."

"Tell it all to your little cousin, sweet potato," she said. "Contrary to what my husband says, I can keep a secret, at least for a couple of hours."

He shook his head.

"C'mon," she said. "I can help. Let me help."

"No one can help," Patrick said. "It's all going to hell, and no one can stop it."

"Please, you're so pitiful," Hannah said. "Listen, you may have lost Melissa, I don't know.

She's pretty fed up, and I don't blame her. But I'm not gonna let Ava destroy her or you. I'm just not. I'm sick and tired of Ava getting away with murder."

Patrick's head popped up.

"Sam told you."

"Yeah, of course, he did," Hannah said, and then willed her face to maintain a poker player's lack of expression.

Patrick took a deep breath and sighed as he slumped into his chair.

"I couldn't believe my eyes," he said. "It's in the video, though, and there's no denying it. Ava killed that guy."

"The guy who was investigating her."

"Yeah, I guess," Patrick said. "She thinks maybe Will's mother hired him. There were photos of her on his camera from pretty far back."

"Did she confess to you when you told her you knew?"

He nodded.

"Last night," he said. "I've been avoiding her since I saw the video, but I let her come to the bar last night. I told her I knew what happened and she didn't deny it. She said she did it for me, for us."

"Ava only ever does anything for herself," Hannah said.

"Maybe," Patrick said. "If she goes to jail, Hannah, what happens to her kids?"

"I guess Will doesn't know about Olivia."

He shook his head.

"I'd have to take them to court to get custody, get a DNA test, all of it, and then how is that best for Olivia? She likes me, I'm her Uncle

Patrick, but Will is her father, the only one she's ever known. It's effed up."

"You can't let her get away with murder. She tried to kill Melissa."

"She knew Melissa wasn't staying there," he said. "She just wanted to send her a message. It's still bad, I know."

His voice was filled with anguish and his eyes filled with tears.

"She's got you excusing attempted murder as some kind of a teenage lark," Hannah said. "That's what's effed up, Patrick."

"I can't believe this is happening."

"Pull yourself together, ya big dumb punkin' head," Hannah said.

"I loved her," he said. "I still love her. How could I do that to her?"

"Melissa will be all right."

"I meant Ava," Patrick said. "How can I be the reason she goes to prison?"

"Murdering that man will be the reason she goes to prison," Hannah said. "How could you live with yourself if you don't? She might kill somebody else."

"What's wrong with her? Why does she do these things? Is it just money?"

"Money, status, vanity, pride, self-preservation," Hannah said. "Take your pick."

"I know she loves me," he said. "The way she explained it, it was just more practical to do it the way she did. She gets all the material things she needs from Will, but she still has me. I know you don't understand, but we have something that's bigger than anything else. I can't help it, I just love her."

"Ava only really loves herself," Hannah said. "I'm not saying that because I'm jealous she's so beautiful and all you men fall at her feet like fools. Ava does everything she does because she adores herself, first and foremost. She loves her kids when they're tiny reflections of her, and to keep up the perfect mother image that's so important to her. When they become individuals apart from her and embarrass her, talk back to her, or do something to make her look bad, she's done with them.

"Ava loves how you make her feel. She loves that star-crossed lover's story she tells herself, but it's financial security and status that matter to her, and as hot as you Fitzpatrick boys are, you're none of you rich enough. After Brian died, she used Scott to fight her battles for her until Theo's money came, and then she was done with him. Were you seeing her while she was with Scott?"

He nodded.

"They never slept together," he said.

Hannah snorted.

"Like she'd tell you if they did," Hannah said. "I get how in love you are with Ava. I can even understand you continuing to sleep with her while you were shacked up with Melissa. The heart wants what the heart wants, and all that stupid crap. But now that you know what she really is, now that you know there is nothing she wouldn't do, including murder, how can you continue to have anything to do with her?"

"I haven't had sex with her since that night," he said. "I looked at the video after the accident, and from then on, I couldn't do it."

"But you saw her last night."

"I let her come thinking we would do what we usually did, but instead, I made her talk about what happened that night."

"And she expects you to keep her secret, I guess," Hannah said. "Did she ask for the video? Or does she think you destroyed it?"

He shook his head.

"I can't talk about the video," he said. "Don't ask me why. I just can't."

"Okay, okay," Hannah said. "What's supposed to happen next?"

He shrugged.

"It's over. I'm not going to see Ava anymore."

"But you want to?"

"Of course I do," he said. "When you feel like we do it's hard to let go."

"And Melissa?"

"She's done with me. I think she called the sheriff last night. Three cops showed up at the bar, and then someone stole Ava's clothes. It seems kinda funny now. It almost gave me a heart attack last night. I thought they had come for Ava."

"It sounds like something I would do," Hannah said. "Good for Melissa."

"Hannah, I just don't know what I'm going to do without her."

"Without Ava."

"No, without Melissa. She's always been there for me. She's the one who cheers me up and says I can do anything and makes me laugh. No matter what happens, she's always on my side. I miss that."

"Who wouldn't?" Hannah said. "It must be exhausting being your one-woman cheerleading squad, though, don't you think?"

"She loves me," Patrick said. "Or at least she used to. What can I do, Hannah? What can I do to get her to forgive me and take me back?"

"I don't know, buddy," she said. "If I were Melissa I wouldn't be too quick to forgive you. It may take a while."

"I hope not too long," he said. "A man needs sex, Hannah."

"Don't I know it," Hannah said. "You shouldn't have any trouble finding someone for that."

"I don't want to start over with someone new or bang a bunch of skanks. They create so much drama; it's exhausting. I'm even honest with them; I tell them this leads to nothing. They say just sex is fine with them, but they never mean it. Then they cry and call and hang around, and I'm getting too old for that. I want Melissa. I know her, and she knows me. It's easy with her. She gets me. I want back what we had."

"Of course you do," Hannah said. "Here's your problem, though."

"What's that?"

"You're kind of a prick," Hannah said. "I don't know whether to hug you or kick your ass."

Maggie and Scott arrived, and Patrick went upstairs to take a shower, Banjo following behind. Scott sat down in the living room to talk to the now semi-alert Fitz while Maggie started a new pot of coffee.

"Where is everyone?" Maggie said. "What's going on?"

Hannah tried to look innocent.

"What's the matter?" Maggie asked. "Cat got your tongue?"

"My husband kept me up late last night," Hannah said. "I'm exhausted."

"You two," Maggie said and rolled her eyes. "It's unnatural to be married as long as you have and still be having so much sex."

"What can I tell you?" Hannah said. "He brought me donuts."

"You're easy," Maggie said.

"And cheap," Hannah said. "What would Scott have to bring you?"

"Jason Momoa," Maggie said.

"What's going on in here?" Scott asked as he entered the room.

"Nothing," Maggie said. "Just girl talk."

"Ew," he said. "Spare me from that. Where is everybody?"

When Hannah and Maggie, along with Sammy, arrived at Ava's, Claire met them in the courtyard.

"Where have you been?" Claire said. "Will's freaking out. Everything's ready, but Ava's missing, and the kids are eating all the cupcakes."

"We'll just see about that," Hannah said. "If there are no cupcakes left when I get inside there are going to be some legendary time-outs at this party."

"Is it all girls in there?" Sammy asked.

"Ernie's in there," Claire said. "But you like Bluebell, don't you?"

"She's all right," Sammy said. "But Ernie likes Pokemon and Bluebell doesn't.

"All of you like to play guns, though," Hannah said.

"Ernie doesn't have any toy guns," Claire said. "Ava won't allow it."

"That's okay," Sammy said. "I brought mine."

While Sammy retrieved his arsenal from Maggie's Jeep, Claire lowered her voice and said, "Ava is missing, for real. Will says she forgot to take her phone with her so he can't track her. She was going to run some errands, but that was hours ago."

"Well, we know she's not with Patrick because we spent all morning with him at Bonnie's," Hannah said.

"Will tracks her through her phone?" Maggie said. "That's pretty controlling."

Sammy returned with his arms full of plastic firearms, and they went inside.

Delia, Bonnie, and Ava's housekeeper Gail were gathered in the kitchen, gossiping. Nanny Siobhan and Ava's husband, Will, were in the grand foyer, trying to interest the smaller children in a game, but they were already wild, with sugar coursing through their veins, hitting each other with balloons. The cousins skirted the melee and went to the kitchen.

Hannah poked Maggie and pointed upwards.

"Go on," Maggie said.

"Where's she going?" Claire asked.

"Snooping," Maggie said.

Hannah casually walked around the grand entryway, ostensibly looking at artwork and architecture, keeping her eye on Will and the nanny. She made her way over to the north wing stairway, and as soon as they were not looking, she darted up to the second floor.

She poked her head into rooms until she found Ava's dressing room and bathroom. She slipped a pair of latex gloves out of her back pocket and put them on.

She looked in all the drawers of the dressing room, feeling underneath the contents to find anything hidden. She thoroughly searched every drawer but found nothing out of the ordinary.

In the bathroom, she found a bottle of pills with a prescription label made out to Will. Underneath the sink, in a tampon box, she found another bottle of pills with a prescription label made out to Ava. Ava's prescription was for an opioid painkiller Hannah had heard of people getting addicted to. Hannah tipped out one of the pills and compared it to one of Will's; they were identical. She took out her phone and photographed both labels and both pills before she put them back where she found them.

In the bathroom garbage, Hannah found three pregnancy tests, all positive.

"Oh my," she said to herself. "I wonder whose this one is."

Back in the dressing room, Hannah opened the door to the huge walk-in closet and flipped on the light. It was as big as Hannah's bedroom at home, and every inch was taken up with clothing, handbags, and shoes.

"Great gobbly goobers," she said. "How could one woman need so many clothes?"

A thorough search of the closet finally yielded a camera and a cell phone with a cracked screen hidden in a leather tote bag with a scarf covering the contents. Hannah picked up the camera, and water trickled out of it. She removed the memory card and had just slid the card down into her jeans pocket when she heard a sound out in the dressing room. Quickly, she stowed the loot just the way she'd found it, slid her small body behind a hanging wardrobe bag big enough to hold a wedding dress, and held her breath.

From her hiding place, she watched as Ava came in, went directly to the tote bag, removed the contents, wrapped them in the scarf, and put them in a garbage bag. She then randomly pulled clothing off hangers and stuffed them in the bag until it was full. She tied the top and carried it away.

Hannah waited until she was sure Ava was gone, and then she quietly left her hiding place. She peeled off the latex gloves and stuffed them in her back pocket.

From the top of the stairs, she could hear the kid's party seemed to have moved out of the foyer to another room. She tiptoed down to the bottom of the stairs and was turning the corner when she ran into a man.

He looked to be in his mid-fifties, with a graying military brush cut, wearing a suit and tie.

"What were you doing up there?" he asked her.

His tone was authoritative, accusing, and hostile.

Hannah put her hands up.

"You caught me! I was snooping," Hannah said. "This may be the only chance I get to see the place and I wanted to have a good look. They're sure loaded, aren't they? Ava's certainly done well for herself. The first baby daddy was my cousin, Brian, and he was as poor as a dirt farmer. She's traded up a couple times since then."

He stared hard at her for a few moments and then relaxed his mouth into a smile.

"You must be Sam's wife," he said.

"Guilty as charged," she said. "How do you know my husband?"

"Through mutual friends," he said. "He's a good man."

"He has his moments," Hannah said. "What friends do you both know?"

"You better go on," he said. "The party's starting in the formal dining room."

Hannah was trembling, the stolen memory card seeming to burn a hole in her pocket. When she entered the dining room, Ava was standing at the head of the table with Will's arm around her.

"Oh good, Karl," Ava said, and Hannah realized the man who had busted her was standing right behind her.

"I brought down a bag of clothing I want to donate, and I left it by the door to the garage," Ava said. "Do you mind to put it in my car? I'm going to the church later to help them set up the rummage sale, and I want to take it with me."

Karl went off to do her bidding, and Will cleared his throat.

"Even though my wife swears she hates surprises, I knew she would enjoy this one. You must forgive us for taking so long to invite you here to our house, but we wanted to have it completely finished and looking its best before you saw it.

"Ava doesn't like a fuss made over her birthdays, but I say if anyone deserves a fuss it's her. She takes care of the children and me and this house, plus she's been essential in assisting me in taking over my father's business concerns. I don't know what I would do without her.

"You've had the privilege of knowing Ava her whole life, and I've only had a little over four years. I'm jealous of you, but I'm grateful for how much you've loved and supported her over the years before we got together. So it's only fitting that you be here for this milestone birthday, her fortieth."

Hannah caught Maggie's eye, and Maggie rolled her eyes. They both knew Ava's fortieth birthday had been two years ago.

"I'm lucky, and I know it," Will continued. "I look in the mirror every day and ask myself what did I do to deserve this beautiful, brilliant woman. I know it's not my looks, for obvious reasons, or my money, because she had plenty of that when I met her. So I can only conclude that it must be love. Raise your glasses, everyone. Happy birthday to the love of my life, the mother of my child, and my reason for living. I love you, honey."

Hannah didn't have a glass in her hand, so she just watched as everyone else raised theirs to Ava. Ava looked around the room with a broad, fake smile and trepidation in her eyes, seeming not to want to meet any critical glances. Her focus flitted over Hannah, stopped, and then returned. Their eyes met. Hannah felt the memory card in her pocket and smiled.

'I've got you, my pretty,' she thought to herself.

Ava refocused on the flaming-candle-covered cake Gail brought from the kitchen, and everyone sang the birthday song. At the end, Hannah sang "for she's a great gob of green Jello," but no one seemed to notice.

After the cake was eaten and the children were bundled up and turned outside to run off some of the sugar, Maggie sidled up to Hannah.

"What's the word?" she asked.

"Good job with the security guard," Hannah said. "I got busted at the bottom of the stairs."

"The first time I saw him was when he came in behind you," Maggie said. "How'd you fare?"

"Good, I think," Hannah said. "But first, somebody needs to get down to the church and snag the bag Ava drops off."

"We're way ahead of you," Maggie said. "Claire's mother is going straight there from here."

Hannah spied Ava as Will assisted her in putting on her coat.

"She doesn't know what she's up against," Hannah said.

"Nope," Maggie said. "But she soon will."

As the party guests assembled in the driveway in preparation to depart, Hannah noticed a pallet of construction supplies, including cinder blocks and deck boards, on the north terrace.

"Whatcha building?" she asked Will.

"A covered boat dock," he said.

"Nice," Hannah said.

"It was supposed to be completed for Ava's birthday," he said, "but we've been so busy I couldn't get to it in time."

"Where was she?" Hannah asked.

Will gave Hannah a look that was equal parts fear and surprise.

"What do you mean?" he said.

"Today," Hannah said. "Where was she earlier when you couldn't find her?"

"Oh, that," he said, with a look of relief. "Ava took my Rover to get some work done on it. While she was waiting she fell in love with the new model, so she ended up trading it instead."

He gestured to a brand new white Land Rover parked on the far side of the wide driveway.

"It's her birthday, but she bought me a gift," Will said. "That's just the kind of woman she is."

"Yes, very thoughtful," Hannah said.

"Kind to a fault," he said. "Ava's always thinking about other people."

"Oh, there's no question about that," Hannah said. "Ava always knows what other people are thinking, and acts accordingly."

The weather on Halloween was always cold in Rose Hill, and sometimes the children had to traipse through deep snow to get from house to house. This year featured a beautiful, clear night with temperatures in the low fifties.

The Fitzpatrick families had gathered at Delia's house for a Halloween party before the kids went trick-or-treating. Everyone, that is, except Delia, who hadn't returned from the rummage sale set up at her church.

"Do you think we should check on her?" Claire asked.

"She'll be here any minute, I'm sure," Bonnie said. "Those Methodists are so disorganized. Everyone wants to be the boss, but no one wants to work. They don't have Sister Mary Margrethe to keep them in line."

"Do you think this is enough candy?" Claire asked.

"If Hannah would quit eating it," Maggie said.

"I am not," Hannah said, through a mouth full of candy.

Bonnie and Claire were making last minute adjustments to the costumes. Ed, Scott, and Sam were watching football on TV in the living room.

"Just what these children need is more candy," Maggie said.

"I think they should all go to Aunt Maggie's house for a slumber party afterward," Claire said.

"I will not be at home," Maggie said. "I can assure you of that."

Melissa came in the front door and shrugged off her coat. It was not until she entered the kitchen that they realized her son Tommy was right behind her.

"Look what the cat done dragged in!" Melissa said.

Everyone hugged Tommy, and then Hannah jumped on his back and rode him around the kitchen table a few times, but eventually, they released him to join the men in the living room.

"That must have been a surprise," Claire said.

"Sean arranged it," Melissa said. "I didn't know nothing about it. He just turned up around noon and surprised me. He's flying right back tomorrow."

"That was sweet of Sean," Bonnie said. "He's a good boy."

"It did my heart good to see him," Melissa said. "I didn't know how much I missed him until he came through the door. I cried like a baby."

Her eyes teared up again at the memory.

"He's a good boy, too," Bonnie said as she hugged Melissa. "He has a good mama."

"She never hugs me," Hannah said.

"Me, neither, and I'm her daughter," Maggie said, and then evaded the pinch her mother aimed in her direction.

"How was the party?" Melissa asked.

Hannah gave the thumbs up, her mouth full of caramel corn.

Quietly, Maggie got Melissa caught up on what had happened.

"We either wait until Mom gets back with the camera, or we need to find a camera the memory card will fit in," Claire said.

"A real camera," Maggie said. "One with different lenses like everyone used to use before cell phones."

"Sean has one of those," Melissa said. "It's at the office."

"Let's go get it!" Claire said.

Melissa and Claire left to get the camera and soon after, Delia came in, carrying a garbage bag.

"Did you get it?" Hannah asked her. "Is that it?"

Delia took off her coat and sat the bag on the table.

"It wasn't easy," Delia said. "I was waiting in the vestibule when she got there, and I tried to take it from her there, but she held onto it. Fortunately, she had Olivia with her. The little precious ran up the aisle in the sanctuary and Ava dropped the bag to chase her. I snagged it, took it downstairs, and hid it in the cloakroom behind some folding tables.

"When she came down to the basement, she asked me what I did with it, and I told her I put it on the pile with the others in the fellowship hall. She spent the next hour frantically going through each bag, pretending to be sorting. She made a huge mess, but no one wanted to offend her. I thought she'd never leave. I had to wait until she was gone to retrieve it from the cloakroom. I was a nervous wreck the whole time."

Hannah untied the bag, pulled the clothes out by the hands full and flung them on the floor.

"Hannah, those are expensive clothes," Delia said, as she picked them up.

"Clothes of the enemy," Hannah said.

When she reached the bottom of the bag, she looked perplexed.

"It's not here."

"What's not there?" Bonnie asked.

"The camera and the phone," Hannah said. "I saw her wrap them up in a scarf and put them in here."

She shook the empty bag.

"She must have ditched them somewhere on her way to the church," Maggie said.

"Probably threw them in the river as she crossed the bridge north of here," Bonnie said.

"I'm so sorry," Delia said.

"Nothing's your fault," Hannah said.

"If she ditched them, then why was she so frantic to find the bag?" Delia asked.

"Because these clothes were in it," Maggie said. "She never intended to donate them. They're expensive."

"No, you should have seen her," Delia said. "She was frightened, panicked."

"And no one saw you put the bag in the cloakroom?" Hannah asked.

"I don't think so."

"Someone must have gotten to it before you left," Hannah said.

"I can't imagine who," Delia said.

"Oh well," Maggie said. "All the evidence is gone."

Claire and Melissa came in with the camera.

"Someone broke into the office," Melissa said.

"What?" Scott said as he jumped up.

"Sean's there now," Claire said. "He got a call the alarm had gone off. Skip's with him."

"They didn't steal the computers or petty cash," Melissa said. "It looked like they went through all the drawers and tried to pry open the safe."

"Looking for something," Sam said and met Hannah's eye.

"I'll run up there," Scott said, and Ed made to follow.

"Stop right there," Claire said to Ed. "You're on trick-or-treat duty this evening."

"I'll call you later," Scott said and left.

"Does anybody want to go trick-or-treating?" Hannah asked.

All the children responded with shouting and screaming. It was deafening.

"It's after six o'clock," Delia said. "I had no idea it was that late."

They sent the children off with Sam and Ed, and Delia heated up the chicken and dumplings she had made earlier in the day.

"My favorite!" Hannah said.

While Delia and Bonnie tended to dinner, Hannah removed Sean's memory card from his camera and inserted the stolen one. There was a delay while new batteries were procured for the camera. Once it was working, they scrolled through the photos. The most recent ones were of Ava, arriving at the bar or leaving.

"That's a kick in the pants," Melissa said, and Claire hugged her.

Scrolling back further, they came upon pictures of Ava posing, seemingly deliberately, for the camera.

"Hannah, look at the brick walls," Maggie said.

"I know," Hannah said. "That's the private investigator's apartment."

It was evident Ava was enjoying posing for the photographer. Some of the photographs were intimate and revealing.

"Ugh, I can't look at anymore," Melissa said, and left the room, with Claire following.

There was one the photographer had taken as a selfie, while Ava slept naked next to him. There was also one taken in the bar downstairs from his apartment.

They scrolled to the end, where there were more surreptitious photos of her, again taken outside the Rose and Thorn. The date of the earliest one was almost nine months previously, and the last one was the night of the accident.

"They all get obsessed with her," Hannah said.

"So he was surveilling her, fell in love, somehow contrived to meet her, and they had an affair," Maggie said.

"No. Ava found out the PI was spying on her," Hannah said. "She seduced him to control the situation."

"And now that he's dead, she thinks she's in the clear," Delia said.

"She robbed a dead man's body," Bonnie said. "What kind of monster does that?"

Hannah held her tongue. Ava was far more monstrous than the rest of them knew.

"You know what this means, don't you?" she said to Maggie.

"We're going back to Pennsylvania," Maggie said.

"Now?" Bonnie asked.

"We have to," Hannah said. "But we'll eat first."

They showed the bartender the photo of Ava that they had printed and brought with them.

"That's her," he said. "That's his sister, Angela."

Maggie and Hannah looked at each other.

"You're sure?" Hannah said.

"Her I would not forget," he said. "Gorgeous."

"How long had his sister been coming in here with him?"

"I've known this guy for five years, maybe," he said. "He's been bringing her in here for the past six months. I guess maybe they weren't close before then."

After interviewing the bar owner's son, they drove to the address the "sister" had given the police, the drugstore in a strip mall. Outside in Maggie's Jeep, Hannah and Maggie sat talking.

"Recap," Maggie said. "I need to think this through."

"Ava was at the scene of the accident," Hannah said. "She took his keys, wallet, camera, and phone."

"She took his car, brought it here, and stole anything out of his apartment that could implicate her," Maggie said. "Then what?"

"She called the Rose Hill police station from Besington so it would show up on the station caller ID; she said she was his sister, saw it in the paper, what could she do to help? They weren't close, but she knows some things. She tells them where his apartment is, and that his landlord owns the bar downstairs. That way if anybody does look into it everything checks out, and they find all his other case files but not hers."

"When did she call?"

"Wednesday night," Hannah said, after referring to the file.

"She would have to have called from a burner phone or a payphone," Maggie said.

Hannah pointed to one outside the drugstore. They both got out of the Jeep, and as they walked toward the pay phone, Hannah dialed the number from the police file. The pay phone rang until Hannah picked up the receiver.

"She called from here, and she gave them this number," Hannah said, pointing to the number engraved on the pay phone's metal housing.

"So she might have gone in there," Maggie said, referring to the drugstore. "She used their address."

"There's no address posted on the building, though," Hannah said. "So where did she get it?"

"It would be on their receipts. She must have bought something."

"We'll show them the photo," Hannah said.

The first three employees they showed the picture to did not recognize Ava. The last one did.

"Oh yeah, she was like, movie star good-looking," the man behind the photo counter said. "I followed her around just to get a better look at her. She asked me if I thought she was stealing, but she was just kidding."

"What did she buy?"

"I remember it well," he said. "She needed lighter fluid for her grill, but that summer stuff was all gone a long time ago, I told her. She said she just needed something to light the coals with so I told her rubbing alcohol would work. She bought a big bottle of that and one of those stick lighters, you know, butane."

When Hannah wrote down his name, and the time of Ava's visit, he got worried.

"Did she like, go missing or something?"

"No, she's just fine," Hannah said. "We just needed to verify her story. Nothing to worry about."

"I'm glad. She was so nice," he said. "She's the hottest woman I ever met in real life. Tell her I said hi."

Hannah and Maggie got back in the Jeep and sat there for a few moments, looking straight ahead, lost in their thoughts.

"What did she need the lighter fluid for?" Maggie asked.

"To burn up the files and the hard drive from his PC or laptop," Hannah said. "We could look in every trash can from this county to ours, but I'm not going to."

"She's there when the guy dies, right? Or just after," Maggie says.

Hannah hesitated but found she just couldn't break Patrick's confidence. Not yet.

"She realizes she knows him," Hannah said.

"She panics," Maggie says.

"No, not her. She's cool as a cucumber," Hannah said. "She takes his wallet with his IDs, his phone, and his camera."

"And his keys," Maggie says. "She finds his car by clicking the lock button on the key fob."

"So she takes the car, hides it somewhere, and brought it back here Wednesday night."

"Where could she hide it?"

"Melissa ran into her outside the garage apartment behind the B&B," Hannah said.

"So she hid his car in the B&B garage," Maggie said, "until she could deal with it."

Hannah reminded Maggie about the boat with Ava's coat in it found at the bottom of the dam.

"So that's how she was getting back and forth to Rose Hill," Maggie said.

"I thought she was in the white SUV," Hannah said. "But the security camera at the fire station showed only about a minute between the white SUV coming and going, and that's not long enough to do all that. She took the boat. I don't know what happened to her on the way back, but the boat with her coat in it ended up on the other side of the dam."

"Then what did she do?"

"On Wednesday she brought his car back to Besington," Hannah said.

"She could hide her own car in the B&B garage while she drove his car up here."

"What was her excuse to be gone long enough to do everything she did here and somehow get back to Rose Hill?"

"We'll have to ask someone close to her," Hannah said. "There's something else. Something I haven't told you."

"Don't hold back now," Maggie said. "I'm already in this up to my elbows."

Hannah told Maggie what the coroner had told Malcolm. She demonstrated strangling Maggie, putting both thumbs across her windpipe.

"So you think Ava killed the guy?" Maggie asked.

Hannah nodded, but she didn't elaborate.

"But why kill him?" Maggie said. "If he were that crazy about her he wouldn't want to hurt her."

"Except maybe she wasn't crazy about him," Hannah said. "She was handling him the best way she knew how, to keep him under her control, but he was an inconvenience, a threat. He may have been pressuring her to leave Will, to stop seeing Patrick. Maybe he threatened blackmail. She wouldn't leave Will, certainly not for some PI with an apartment over a bar in Besington. If she left Will for anybody, it would be Patrick."

"She was just covering her tracks."

"Eliminating a complication."

"What are you going to do?" Maggie asked.

"I don't know," Hannah said. "Let's tie up all the loose ends here and then regroup. I want to go to the bus station and show some people her photo."

Of course, they remembered her. She was so beautiful. Her purse had been stolen, so she didn't have any ID. Such a lovely lady. So anxious to get home to Rose Hill. She paid with cash. The name she gave was also fake. Yes, it was on Wednesday.

"That's how she got home," Maggie said.

"After she dumped his car here," Hannah said.

They sat in the parking lot of the bus station, their thoughts on all that must have happened on Wednesday night. The moon was high in the sky now, and Maggie said they should think about heading home.

They didn't speak again until they crossed the state line.

"You think we should tell Scott," Hannah said.

"Of course not," Maggie said. "But what are we going to do?"

"What have we got?" Hannah said. "We've got one guy says he sold her rubbing alcohol and a lighter in the drugstore, which is connected to the phone and address the fake sister gave. We've got the bartender landlord who thought she was the guy's sister. The bus station staff could ID her. We've got the photos of her in his apartment, which we illegally removed from the stolen camera, which has now disappeared, so that's tricky. We know those paintings are all of her, but could you convince a jury of that beyond a reasonable doubt?"

"Why didn't she take the paintings?"

"Too big, too many, doing so would attract too much attention," Maggie said. "Or she was so confident no one would investigate that there'd be no one who would connect her to them. I don't know, Hannah. It's still all circumstantial."

"Okay," Hannah said. "I wasn't going to break his confidence, but here it is: Patrick has video from the Thorn security camera that showed Ava was at the scene of the accident."

"I thought he said it was turned off."

"It wasn't."

"Great," Maggie said. "That will show Ava stealing the man's stuff."

"Except it also showed her killing him."

"What?"

"She strangled him and then stole his stuff."

"How do you know this?"

"Patrick told me this morning."

"What's he going to do?"

"He won't say. Sam, Sean, and Patrick are all up to something, but he wouldn't tell me what."

"What do we do?"

"Well, I'm of a mind to turn all this over to Sam, and trust him," Hannah said. "He said he would help us."

"Lord, when Scott finds out, we're all in big trouble."

"Mostly you, though," Hannah said. "I'm going to tell him it was all your idea."

Back in Rose Hill, at Delia's house, the kids were zoned out in front of a movie in the living room. Pixie and Olivia were asleep on the couch between Ed and Sam. Tommy was seated on the floor with Sammy and the other kids. Hannah waved at her husband as she passed through, and he winked at her.

In the kitchen, Claire was painting Delia's nails, and Melissa was putting a load of towels in the washer. Claire's little Boston Terrier, Mackie Pea, was curled up sleeping with Delia's black cat, Dinah, in a basket of clean, folded laundry sitting next to the washer and dryer. The kitchen smelled like coffee and cinnamon rolls; it was warm and cozy.

"Are Ava and Will going to pick up their kids?" Hannah asked Delia.

"Nope," Melissa said.

"They're staying the night with Ed and Claire," Delia said.

"That should be a circus," Maggie said.

"What's two more?" Claire said. "We'll just throw them in there with the rest; it will toughen them up."

"You look like you don't have good news," Delia said.

Hannah and Maggie quietly got them caught up on what they had found out in Besington. They did not mention what Patrick saw on the video.

"This has gotten out of hand," Delia said. "We need to tell Scott and let the police handle it."

"I'm going to hand it all over to Sam," Hannah said. "We all trust him, right?"

Everyone nodded.

"What's going to happen to her kids?" Claire asked.

"If she goes to jail," Delia said, "Will has custody of Olivia, but I don't think he's adopted the other three. Bonnie would have thrown a fit if he had."

"Charlotte's old enough to take care of herself," Maggie said, "but she would always have a home with one of us."

"Not me, thank you very much," Claire said.

"We don't know for sure that Charlotte killed Professor Richmond," Delia said.

"I know what I know," Claire said. "There's no doubt in my mind. Why do you think they whisked her out of the country when they did?"

"Boy trouble is what they told Bonnie," Delia said.

"Do you think Will would continue to pay for her school?" Hannah asked.

"Or Timmy's?" Claire said.

"Hard to tell," Maggie said. "You couldn't blame him if he didn't."

"Do you think there's any chance Charlotte is Theo's daughter?" Hannah asked.

"Every chance," Delia said.

"You've thought this before?" Hannah asked.

Delia nodded.

"I can't prove Ava had an affair with Theo, but it wouldn't surprise me."

"With a sociopath and a psycho-narcissist for parents, how could she go wrong?" Claire said.

"His biological sister's still alive for the DNA test," Maggie said. "I'd love to be a fly on the wall when Gwyneth gets that subpoena."

"Then Charlotte would be owed that sweet, sweet Eldridge money," Hannah said.

"What about Timmy?" Maggie said.

"I guess Bonnie would get custody of Timmy and Ernie," Hannah said. "She's the next of kin."

"But they're not in any shape to raise children," Maggie said. "They can barely get around, themselves. That leaves Scott and me. Oh, Lord. We'll have to move to a bigger place."

"It was a shock at first," Claire said. "But now I can't imagine living without our girls."

Melissa had been so quiet that when she finally spoke, it startled them.

"I know what you're all thinking," Melissa said. "Olivia is Patrick's, and he should get her."

"Poor Will," Delia said. "He'll lose everybody."

"Here's something else to consider," Hannah said. "I think Ava's pregnant again."

She told them about the pregnancy tests she'd found in Ava's bathroom.

"This one might be Will's," Maggie said.

"Or Patrick's," Melissa said.

"Or the private investigator's," Hannah said.

Hannah waited until Sam put Sammy to bed and came back downstairs to the kitchen. Hannah told him about the snooping expedition at Ava's and all they had discovered on their trip to Pennsylvania. While she spoke, he leaned back in his chair, his arms crossed over his chest, and scowled. She showed him the photos on Sean's camera and gave him the copy of the police file notes. He removed the memory card and put it in his back pocket.

"Burn these," he said about the file copies after he read through them. "Tonight."

"So that's everything," Hannah said. "We know Ava killed the guy, but we don't know what happened to his stuff. Delia is convinced Ava thought it was still in the bag she brought to the rummage sale."

"I'll take it from here," Sam said.

"What will you do?" she asked.

He shook his head.

"You don't trust me," she said.

He raised his eyebrows at her.

"I know, I know," she said. "I can't keep a secret, and I have a loud mouth. I just can't stand not knowing."

He leaned over and kissed her forehead.

"Try to stay out of trouble," he said. "And keep an eye on Melissa. I don't think Ava's done."

"Whattaya mean Ava's not done?" Hannah said. "What's she gonna do?"

"If she doesn't think she's trapped, maybe nothing," he said. "But I wouldn't want to corner her right now if I were you."

"Why kill Melissa?" Hannah asked. "Ava's won, for all she knows. Melissa is not going to take Patrick back. Nor should she, if you ask me."

"But Patrick still loves Melissa," Sam said. "That makes her an obstacle. We all know what Ava does to obstacles."

Hannah's phone rang at 3:00 a.m.

"There's somebody outside messin' with my car," Melissa said. "I'm too scared to go out there."

Hannah relayed this information to Sam.

"Tell her to call the police," Sam said. "I'm on my way."

Hannah stayed on the phone with Melissa while she used Delia's landline to call the police, and until Scott arrived.

"Sam pulled up right behind him," Melissa said.

"Call me later," Hannah said. "I'll be up."

Sam returned home about an hour later.

"What happened?" Hannah asked.

"Somebody tried to cut her brake lines," he said. "Someone who didn't know what the hell they were doing; they just cut every line under there. That car wouldn't even have started."

"Ava," Hannah said.

He shrugged.

"Scott took a statement, but when he asked if she knew who might have done it, Melissa looked at me, and I shook my head, so she said she didn't know."

"Did you tell Scott?"

He shook his head.

"Nah, I don't think that's the way to approach this. Scott's a good man, but this needs more finesse."

"Any idea how long this finesse wagon's gonna take to show up?"

"Not much longer now," Sam said. "Trust me."

Sam went to his office, and Hannah went back to bed but had trouble going back to sleep. When the phone rang, she assumed it was Melissa, but the number was not one she recognized.

"Aunt Hannah," the voice said.

"Timmy?"

"Yeah, could you come get me?"

"Where are you?"

"At the bus station."

"In Rose Hill?"

"Yeah," he said. "I'm cold."

Hannah was getting dressed as Sam came out of his office. She caught him up as she ran past him.

"You have to contact Ava," Sam said. "If you don't she can claim you're kidnapping him."

"Oh, shut up," Hannah said.

Timmy was standing out of the wind, under the awning of the Dairy Chef. When he saw Hannah's truck, he came running. When he got in on the passenger side, Hannah could see he was trembling with cold, his eyes were red from crying, and snot was running out of his nose.

"Charlotte said she'd be here, but she didn't show up," he said. "I didn't know what to do."

He dissolved into tears, and Hannah reached over to hug him. She fished behind the seat until she found a sweatshirt, and gave it to him to put on. She found a fast food paper napkin in the glove box and wiped his face with it, made him blow his nose. Once she had him buckled up, she pulled out of the parking lot.

She hated to think he had come all this way by himself; she didn't want to think about all that could have happened to a skinny twelve-year-old boy on his own. What was Charlotte thinking standing him up like that? And where was she?

Hannah could hear his teeth chattering with cold.

216

"Where's your coat?" she asked him.

"Somebody at the bus station stole it," he said. "I sold my phone to a guy to pay for the bus ticket, and when I came back from buying it, somebody had taken my backpack and my coat."

"Why did you run away?"

"I hate it," he said. "I can't take it anymore. If they make me go back, I'll kill myself."

He broke down in tears and Hannah patted his shoulder while she made the turn onto Possum Holler.

"We'll fix it," she said. "Whatever it is, we'll fix it. You never have to do anything that drastic, do you understand? Nothing is ever so bad that you can't call me and I'll fix it for you. Do you hear me? You must never think anything is so bad that you have to do anything like that. You have so many people here who love you, and we'll all work together to figure this out."

"If you call my mom she'll send me back," he said, between hiccupping sobs. "I can't go back."

"You trust me, buddy, right?" she said.

He nodded.

"I'm gonna fix it," she said. "I don't care who I have to fight, whether it's bare knuckles or through your Uncle Sean in court, but you will not be going back."

Hannah had tears in her eyes as the boy sobbed his heart out. By the time they got to the farm, he was still hiccupping. She led him into the kitchen, where Sam was sitting at the table. Timmy went straight into his arms and cried some more. Hannah watched her husband's steely façade soften as he wrapped his arms around the boy.

"Don't worry," he told Timmy. "Whatever it is we'll fix it."

It was now Hannah's turn to raise an eyebrow at her husband.

"We're fixing it," he said to Hannah.

CHAPTER EIGHT - SUNDAY

Melissa woke up when she heard Delia leave for church. She lay in bed and went over recent events in her mind. If it weren't for Tommy sleeping in the room across the hall, she might have put her head under the covers and refused to come out.

She took a shower, got dressed, and then peeked in at him. His limbs were flung in every direction, his blankets tangled up around him. He had always been a rowdy sleeper; as a little boy, he was known to kick and punch and end up each morning at the opposite end of the bed from where he started. He was trying to grow a beard; it was coming in sparse and patchy. She leaned against the door jamb and let her eyes drink him in.

Her phone rang in the other room, and she hurried to get it before it woke him up. It was Dee Goldman.

"Johnny's bringing your house this morning," she said.

"By helicopter?" Melissa asked.

"He's dropping it in Hannah's pasture, and Curtis is going to tow it to the trailer park," Dee said. "Levi and I are leaving now; we'll be there in a half hour or so."

Melissa woke Tommy and told him to get dressed.

"My house is coming!" she said.

"What?" he said, still groggy with sleep.

"My gull-dern house is coming!" she said. "We gotta get over there and clean the lot."

Delia had left her copy of the Sunday Sentinel on the kitchen table. Melissa had completely forgotten about the story Ed had interviewed her for, but now she sat down to read it while Tommy showered and got dressed with what felt like torturous slowness.

Even though she had agreed to have it published, her face burned with embarrassment imagining all the city's subscribers sitting at their breakfast tables, reading about the most traumatizing events of her life.

When Tommy came into the kitchen, she handed him the page with her story on it, and he hugged her.

"I knew," he said. "Ed sent it to me a couple days ago."

"Should I have let him do it?"

"I think you should have," he said. "Sam told me about a therapy they use for vets with PTSD; the counselor has the vet repeat the story of the traumatic incident over and over in a safe environment until they are desensitized to the memories that used to trigger overwhelming emotions. It gives them a sense of control over it. You're not only telling your story here, but you're also confronting one of your biggest fears: how people will react when they know your story. By doing this, you controlled the narrative, and now it's out there; it's not just gossip and rumors; it's your truth."

"Then why do I still feel so ashamed?"

"You need to tell it some more times," Tommy said. "It might be a good idea to get a counselor to help guide you through it."

"How'd you get so smart?"

"I had a great group of people who brought me up," he said.

They bundled up, left a note for Delia, and walked briskly down the street, their breath a frozen vapor trail left behind them as they went.

Tommy hadn't yet seen the remnants of their burned trailer. They stopped at the edge of their property, and she put her arm around her son.

"I can't believe it's gone," he said. "Have you looked to see if there's anything left?"

She shook her head.

"I can't," she said. "But you go on if you want to. Just be careful of all the broken glass."

As Tommy gingerly made his way through the rubble, Melissa took a deep breath. She didn't have time to wallow in the past, even the recent past. She took the weed eater she had borrowed from Delia's house and tackled the overgrown, vacant trailer space to the right of her burned-out mess.

By the time she had the space cleared, had identified where the water connects and the sewage drain were, Maggie, Scott, Claire and Ed had arrived.

"Where're the kids?" Melissa asked.

"They're with my mom," Claire said. "Ava and Will decided to go out of town for a few days, and we're keeping them."

"Where to?" Melissa asked.

"Canada," Claire said.

"She's running away," Melissa said.

Maggie shook her head at Melissa and then gestured at Scott.

"It's just a quick vacation," Ed said. "Will said he had this planned as a birthday surprise."

"If he had this planned then why didn't he have childcare lined up before this morning?" Claire asked.

"They have a nanny," Melissa said.

"What are you talking about?" Scott asked.

"Nothing," Maggie said. "Never mind."

"You know, this jealousy you all have of Ava is ridiculous," Scott said. "I don't understand why you can't let it go."

"You're right, honey," Maggie said. "We need to just let it go. Let it go, Melissa."

"You go first," Melissa said. "Then you, Claire."

"When my husband tells me I should do something, I do it right away," Maggie said. "Consider it let go."

"Me, too," Claire said. "If I had a husband, that is."

"Very funny," Scott said to Ed. "What's going on?"

Ed shrugged, and the cousins joined Tommy in the search through the trailer rubble.

"You doing okay?" Ed asked Melissa.

"No," she said. "But I'm breathing, I'm on my feet, and I'm moving forward."

"That's good," he said.

"How are you doing with all them kids?"

"It's crazy and hectic and nonstop," he said. "But I love it."

Someone shouted and pointed up toward Peony Street, where Hannah's dad's wrecker was towing the trailer with Melissa's little house down the hill, with Hannah following in her truck. Johnny Johnson and Barlow Owsley were sitting on the edge of the truck bed, and Johnny waved at Melissa.

222

"Who is that?" Ed asked her.

"My hero," Melissa said and ran toward the truck.

Johnny supervised as Curtis backed the little house onto the spot Melissa had chosen. Barlow stood off to the side, his arms crossed; a scowl on his face that Melissa could tell meant he didn't want anyone to talk to him.

It didn't stop her.

"You've done such a great job," Melissa said to him. "I sure do appreciate you all gettin' this ready on such short notice."

Barlow nodded but did not make eye contact.

"I figure I can sell these things as fast as you can make them," she said.

He nodded again.

"Barlow!" Johnny called, and the young man jumped and ran.

They detached the trailer from the truck, and Curtis pulled the wrecker away to park it. Johnny sent Barlow underneath the trailer with a tape measure, and Barlow called out numbers that Johnny wrote on a scrap of paper. Melissa walked up to him.

"My esteemed colleague is giving me the measurements for the PVC we need to buy," Johnny said. "If your local hardware establishment is open today we should be able to get the water and waste pipes connected. I brought some propane for the stove. You'll probably have to wait until tomorrow to get the electric company to send someone out. Do they meter everyone separately here?"

"They do," Melissa said.

"Nice place you have here," he said. "Who are all these people?"

Melissa looked around, at the friends and neighbors who had gathered, all offering to help. Maggie was handing out go-cups of coffee from the bookstore, and Bonnie was offering everyone pastries from bakery boxes. Dee and Levi Goldman were conversing with Bruce and Gloria; Tommy was showing Sammy something on his phone that was making them both laugh.

"Family, friends, and neighbors," she said.

"You certainly are blessed," Johnny said.

"I am," Melissa said.

By dinner time, the water and waste pipes were connected and working, and the little propane heater was quickly heating up the interior. Everyone had taken the little house tour, and Johnny was the recipient of many questions and compliments.

"Everybody is invited to the bakery for supper," Bonnie told them. "It will be pieced together, but nobody will go home hungry."

The crowd broke up, and Melissa looked for Johnny, who was talking to Sam. Tommy and Barlow Owsley were playing ball with Sammy, using a piece of wood and a pine cone.

"Hey," Hannah said, as she approached Melissa. "Nice house."

"Thank you," Melissa said. "I can hardly believe it's mine."

"Nice house builder, too," Hannah said. "Claire, Maggie, and I all agree when we say hubba hubba."

"Stop," Melissa said. "It's not like that."

"Patrick wanted to come, but I told him not to," Hannah said. "He might be at the dinner, though."

"Thanks," Melissa said. "You know, I must be getting over it, 'cause I hadn't thought of him once today."

"Not even once?"

"Well, maybe a little," Melissa said. "But nothing like I would have before."

"Sam's over there recruiting your boyfriend for the vet rehab program," Hannah said.

When Melissa approached, she could hear Sam telling Johnny about a new therapy.

"Hey," Melissa said. "Y'all going to come eat or what?'

"Sorry," Sam said to Johnny. "I get carried away talking about it. If you ever want to check it out, come on down to the community center. I'd love to show you around."

"Thank you," Johnny said and shook Sam's hand. "It sounds like you're doing a great job. I'm not much of a joiner, as they say, and I'm not comfortable with crowds of people, but I'll definitely come and see it sometime."

Hannah grabbed Sam by the hand and pretended to drag him away.

"I'm starving," she said. "I wanna get there before all the good stuff is gone."

Melissa stood with Johnny and watched as they left.

"Are you comin' to dinner?" she asked him.

"No, I don't believe I will," he said. "It's not that I don't appreciate the invitation, or that I'm averse to spending more time in your lovely company. I just get fidgety around so many people, and Mr. Owsley is ten times worse."

Melissa looked over at Barlow, who was laughing and horsing around with Sammy and Tommy.

"He's doing all right," Melissa said. "Come and eat supper with me. You don't have to stay long, but I want you to come."

"You're swaying me," he said.

"If you get scared I'll hold your hand," she said.

"That's certainly the best incentive," he said. "Just please don't expect me to remember anyone's name."

"Just mine," she said.

"That, I'm not likely to forget," he said.

"Tell me something," she said. "Don't you miss people, living out there in the woods like you do?"

"Up until now I haven't," he said. "But I have a feeling I might start."

He grinned at Melissa, his big smile framed by his woolly beard and mustache.

Melissa smiled back at him, and a warmth spread throughout her body that, rather than scaring her, made her feel happy and safe. She used to get that feeling when she stood next to Patrick, but that seemed like a long time ago.

Johnny locked up the little house and called to Barlow. Tommy and Sammy followed him over, and they all got in the Goldman's SUV. Tommy was crushed in next to Johnny.

"Nice house," Tommy said.

"Thank you," Johnny said.

"I'd like to do a story on your work for my school paper," he said.

"I would be glad to accommodate you," Johnny said. "I am a bit hard to get hold of, however, on account of I don't have a computer, a phone, or mail delivery."

"Are you Amish?" Tommy asked.

Johnny chuckled.

"No, just shy."

Patrick was not at the bakery, and Melissa was relieved. She spent that time listening to Tommy interview Johnny and pushing more food on Barlow. Sammy asked Barlow about his tattoos and was treated to a spoken word tour of the most visible ones.

"That's the most I've heard him talk since I've known him," Johnny whispered to Melissa.

"He just needs to get out more," Melissa said.

"Do you have this effect on everyone you meet?" Johnny asked.

"What effect?"

"Drawing people out, making them feel welcome and at home."

"I'm just nice, I guess," Melissa said. "I like people, mostly."

Melissa looked up as Patrick walked in and made a beeline to her table. A hush fell over the assembled.

"I need to talk to you," Patrick said.

"I'm busy," Melissa said.

"It's urgent," Patrick said.

"Not now, Patrick," Melissa said.

Johnny Johnson stood up to his full height and held out his hand. He was a little taller than Patrick, but they were matched for size.

"I don't believe we've met," he said to Patrick. "The name's Johnny Johnson."

Patrick looked irritated, but he shook Johnny's hand.

The handshake lasted a little longer than it should have, and when Johnny released Patrick's hand, Patrick winced.

"I've been enjoying the company of your friends and family," Johnny said. "Won't you join us?"

"Look, pal," Patrick started, but his mother intervened.

"Son, you are not using the manners I raised you to have," she said. "Now, go get yourself a plate of food, sit down, and eat."

Patrick did as he was told, and Bonnie looked at Johnny with a raised eyebrow.

"I apologize for my son, Mr. Johnson," she said. "He wasn't raised to act like that."

"No offense taken," Johnny said and bowed to Bonnie. "I have to tell you I have never eaten as good of food as that of which I have partaken this evening. This has definitely spoiled me for my own cooking."

Bonnie smiled, but her eyes were still narrowed.

"I'm glad you could join us," she said.

She looked at Melissa, who felt a little scorched by her gaze.

Dee and Levi were ready to call it an evening, so Johnny said goodbye and thanked everyone, while Patrick glowered in a corner. Melissa walked them outside and thanked him again.

"It was my pleasure," Johnny said.

"Sorry about that business," Melissa said and gestured to the bakery.

"It's always good to size up the competition," Johnny said. "Proximity is on his side, of course, but you're going to go to sleep each night in a house I built for you."

Melissa laughed.

"Come back and see us," she said.

She hugged Barlow, and he blushed bright red. Tommy shook his hand and said, "I'll send you my playlist."

As she watched them drive away, Tommy put his arm around her.

"You did good," she said to him. "You're a good boy."

"Only because you were such a good mom," he said and kissed her on top of her head.

"Tommy, we've got to go if you're going to make your flight," Sean said.

Melissa grabbed her son tighter.

"It wasn't near long enough!" she said. "But I know you got to go."

"I almost forgot," he said, and took something out of his pocket. "I found this."

It was a tiny green plastic soldier from a set Ian had given Tommy when he was little.

"It's only a little melted," he said. "I'm going to take it with me."

She tried to hold back the tears, but it was no use. She waved as they drove away in Sean's car. Hannah came up and put an arm around her.

"I can't believe he's in college already," Hannah said.

"It won't be long before you're crying about Sammy going off to school," Melissa said.

"This kid?" Hannah said and grabbed Sammy to pull him into a hug while he squirmed to get away.

"Mom!" Sammy said. "Stop it."

"Oh, but I love you," Hannah said, and tried to kiss him. "Let your mama cuddle you a little, why don't ya?"

"Yuck," Sammy said, and pulled away.

"Tommy used to do that, too," Melissa said. "Everything changes, you'll see."

Melissa stood outside until everyone left and Patrick was alone in the bakery dining room. Then she went back in and sat down across from him in the booth.

"Who the hell was that guy?" he asked her.

"He's making tiny houses I'm gonna sell at the trailer park," she said.

"I don't like the way he looks at you," Patrick said.

"That ain't none of your business anymore," Melissa said.

"I still care about you," Patrick said. "That will never change, no matter what happens."

"Then why did you cheat on me all that time?" she asked. "And don't bother to deny it, everyone's done told me about it."

"Look," Patrick said. "I don't know what to say except I'm sorry. I know I'm the bad guy, and everybody hates me for it, but I can't change the past, nobody can. What matters is the future. All I care about is if you love me enough to forgive me and let me come home."

"I'm still too mad about it," Melissa said. "I don't know if I'll ever get over it. It's bad enough you lied to me and messed around with Ava all that time, but you also made me look like a fool, and that stings something awful. The worst part is it turns out you weren't the good friend I thought you were. I didn't really know you at all. I was just a fool for your good looks and what we did in bed. I thought we had some great love, but it turns out it wasn't that great, and it probably wasn't love."

"You miss me," he said. "You can't say you don't."

"Course I do," she said. "But why would I lay down with someone who stuck a knife in my back? Love doesn't work like that. Leastways not for me."

"No one will ever love you like I do."

"Maybe not," Melissa said. "But right now having no man at all is still better than you."

When Melissa arrived at Delia's house, she was surprised to find Timmy and Joshie playing a card game with the older two of Claire's girls.

"I could hug you to bits!" Melissa said to Timmy but settled for ruffling his hair and kissing the top of his head.

She looked around. Pixie and Olivia were playing with Claire's old Barbies, Ernie and Sammy were building a blanket fort, and Hannah's mother Alice was reclining on the couch with an ice pack on her head.

"What's wrong with her?" Melissa asked Hannah.

Hannah rolled her eyes.

"What's ever wrong with her?" she replied. "She's allergic to fun, for one thing. Happiness gives her a headache."

"Where's Delia?" Melissa asked the kids in the kitchen.

"She's out back talking to some lady," Timmy said.

Melissa looked out the kitchen window and saw Delia sitting at the picnic table in what seemed like a serious conversation with the woman, Terese, who had come to see Sean the other day.

Hannah walked up beside her.

"Who is that?" Hannah asked. "She looks familiar to me."

"I don't know," Melissa said. "But she was in our office the other day, talking to Sean."

"Probably somebody Ian knew," Hannah said. "I'll ask her later."

They turned back to look at the kids playing cards.

"Does Ava know Timmy's home?" Melissa asked.

"Delia made me call Will," Hannah said. "Ava and Will are in Canada, of all places. Will said they're combining a weekend getaway with some work he needs to do up there this week, something to do with his father's business. They asked Delia to keep the kids."

"Doesn't the sudden trip seem fishy to you?" Melissa asked. "Or are we just suspicious?"

"No, it's ten kinds of shady," Hannah said. "According to the housekeeper, Gail, Ava and the nanny had a knock down drag out fight last night, and this morning the nanny flew the coop; left a note saying she was going home and by the way, she quit. So what does Will do? Spirits Ava out of the country. Maybe he knows more than we think he does."

"Did you talk to Ava?"

"No, he said she was napping. When have you ever known that she-devil to take a nap?"

"I wish we could talk to the nanny," Melissa said. "What did Will say about Timmy?"

"I told him how depressed he was, that I was afraid if they made him go back he might do something terrible to himself," Hannah said. "Will said Timmy was always overly dramatic; they would let him have this week as a vacation and then deal with it when they got home. He was going to call the school."

"Poor little fella," Melissa said.

"I can tell you one thing," Hannah said. "That boy's not leaving Rose Hill again while Bonnie Fitzpatrick draws breath. Sean's already working on it."

Delia came in the back door.

"It's getting colder," she said.

"Who was that woman?" Hannah asked her.

"Just an old friend," Delia said. "She stopped by to tell me how sorry she was to hear about Ian."

"How was Timmy today?"

"Subdued until Joshie got here," Delia said. "He's back to his old self now."

"Are you staying in your new house tonight?" Hannah asked Melissa.

"I guess I'd be chicken not to," Melissa said.

"If it would help, I could stay with you," Hannah said. "We could have a slumber party."

"I could use your help here, with the kids," Delia said to Melissa. "If you don't mind."

"I don't mind at all," Melissa said.

"Claire's coming to get hers, but that still leaves Olivia and Ernie."

"I'll take Timmy and Sammy home with me," Hannah said. "Hatch is letting us have Joshie."

Ed arrived to pick up his brood, and the party broke up. Delia gave Olivia a bath while Melissa played checkers with Ernie, who was pouting about not getting to go to Hannah's with Timmy.

"It's not fair," he said.

"I'm sorry, partner," Melissa said. "Your mommy left Delia in charge of you, and you have to be where your mama says."

"Mommy hates me."

"She doesn't hate you."

"She does," he said. "I heard them talking about me. They're gonna take Livvie when they move to London and send me away."

"You're all going on vacation to London, to see Charlotte," Melissa said. "At Christmas time."

"No, we're not," Ernie said. "Will bought a house in England, and they're moving there. Except they're leaving Timmy at sleep-away school and they're looking for a sleep-away school for me, too."

"Are you sure?"

"Nanny Siobhan and Mommy had a big fight about it, and Mommy made Nanny Siobhan cry. 'They're not your children!' Mommy said. 'It's none of your business!' Then Nanny Siobhan packed her suitcase and Karl took her to the airport."

"How terrible for you to see that," Melissa said. "I'm so sorry."

"They didn't know I was there," he said. "I was hiding behind the curtains."

"Maybe you misheard," Melissa said. "Sometimes when grownups are angry they say things they don't mean."

"I'm not lying!" Ernie said and flipped up the checkerboard so that all the checkers fell onto the floor. "I'm not lying! She made Nanny Siobhan cry and then she left us. They're going to send me away like they did Timmy. Mommy and Will hate me!"

"What's going on in here?" Delia said from the doorway, where she held Olivia wrapped up in a towel.

"Ernie bad," Olivia said. "Ernie bad, bad, bad!"

"Ernie is not bad," Delia said and handed Olivia to Melissa so she could get down on her knees and hug the crying boy.

"You stinky," Olivia said to Melissa, and then laughed. "Stinky, stinky, stinky."

Melissa looked into Olivia's blue eyes, the mirror image of Patrick's. The child's dark hair and facial features were all Ava, except for the eyes. Melissa held out Olivia's little hand and looked at her pointer finger, which was longer than the middle finger.

"Bunny!" Olivia demanded, and Melissa retrieved her bunny from the living room floor.

Olivia tucked the bunny under her chin, stuck her thumb in her mouth, closed her eyes, and rested her head on Melissa's shoulder.

Ernie was sobbing in Delia's arms, crying so hard he couldn't talk. Melissa wondered if he would throw up, he was so upset.

"What happened?" Delia asked Melissa.

"Nanny Siobhan went back to Ireland. Ernie says Ava and Will are moving to London and taking Olivia with them. He heard them say they were looking for a sleep-away school for him."

"Oh, my goodness," Delia said and embraced the little boy that much closer. "I hope that's not true."

'Where's their wonderful mother now?' Melissa thought to herself.

It took a while to get Ernie calmed down enough to get his bath and go to bed. Delia and Melissa stayed with the children until they both were asleep, and then they reconvened in the kitchen.

"Thank you for staying," Delia said. "I don't know what I would have done."

"The truth is I'm afraid to stay in the little house," Melissa said.

"But Ava's in Canada," Delia said.

"So who sabotaged my car last night?" Melissa asked.

"I hadn't thought of that," Delia said. "Who in the world would have done that?"

"I can't think of anyone else," Melissa said. "But I'm glad my car's locked up at the gas station, and you have an alarm system."

"This is all so crazy," Delia said. "I wish Ian were still alive; well, the Ian that once was. He'd know what to do."

"You said he never liked Ava," Melissa said.

"He didn't," Delia said. "He knew way before the rest of us."

"Since Brian is dead, and Will hasn't adopted Timmy and Ernie, what happens to them if Ava goes to jail?"

"Bonnie and Fitz are their next of kin, being Brian's mother and father. Charlotte's not old enough to take them; at least I can't imagine the court allowing that."

"I was worried about what would happen to them if she was arrested," Melissa said. "Now I think they might all be better off."

"Except Olivia."

"Yes, there's Olivia," Melissa said. "She's Patrick's; there's no doubt in my mind."

"Ava's got a heart made of ice," Delia said. "But I used to believe she made an exception where her children were concerned."

"I wonder what she would do," Melissa said, "if she had to choose between them and herself."

"I don't know," Delia said. "Let's hope we don't have to find out."

CHAPTER NINE - MONDAY

Hannah woke up as Sam came to bed.

"What time is it?" she asked him.

He paused, seated on the edge of the bed, in the process of removing his lower leg prosthesis.

"It's two a.m.," he said. "Are you awake or talking in your sleep?"

Hannah sat up.

"Why? What's going on?"

He turned and looked at her.

"I've got some homework for you to do tomorrow."

"Really?" she asked. "You're gonna let me help?"

"I want you to find out which businesses or houses in town have security video cameras anywhere near the scene of the crime, and see if they'll let you look at the footage."

"On the night of the wreck?"

He nodded.

"Also the night Melissa's trailer was burned, the night she was almost run over, and the night her car was sabotaged."

"Why didn't I think of that?" Hannah asked.

"You would have," Sam said. "I have faith in your nosy nature."

"The bank for sure," she said. "Amy's husband is the security guard, so that's a cinch."

"Don't tell anyone any more than you have to," Sam said. "And if you find something, make a copy on a flash drive and bring it to me. Ask them not to destroy their copies; they may be evidence in the commission of a crime."

"Why hasn't Scott done any of this?"

"Until the post-mortem report comes back, there's no reason for him to think a crime was committed," Sam said. "Right now he's constrained by official rules and regulations that we don't want to ask him to circumvent."

"We're keeping Scott out of it, then," Hannah said. "But what if we do discover a crime has been committed? Do we tell him then?"

"This may be too big for him," he said.

"Do tell."

"Not right now," he said. "But do me a favor, and don't be alone with Ava. And keep an eye on Melissa; I don't like the direction this thing is headed."

"Don't worry," Hannah said. "Got it and got it."

"Let me ask you something else."

"Anything, boss man," she said. "I'm working for you now."

"Did you ever hear any gossip about Ava's daughter and that professor who died a few years ago?"

"Only that Claire thinks Charlotte killed him because he drugged and molested her, and that Ava covered it up," Hannah said. "Ava and Will shipped her off to boarding school in Europe right afterward. It's nothing Claire could prove, just circumstantial evidence, but she's convinced."

"Does Scott know about that?"

"I don't know," Hannah said. "Why do you ask?"

"If you can find out anything more about that, without kicking a hornet's nest, I mean, I could use that information."

"Aye aye, sir," Hannah said. "Any chance you could tell me more."

"None whatsoever," he said. "First let's see how trustworthy you are with what I just gave you."

"I'll never go to sleep now," Hannah said. "My mind is working flat out; I need food."

She started to get up out of bed, but he caught her around the waist.

"Wait a minute," he said. "I've got an idea how you can burn off some that energy."

"I'm sure you do, honey," she said, as she pushed him over onto his back. "I'm sure you do."

Later that morning, Hannah dropped Sammy off at school, and although she tried not to make eye contact, she was not successful in evading Tucker's mother, Sue-Lynne, who blocked her exit. Hannah rolled down her window.

"Good morning, Hannah," Sue-Lynne said. "Do you have a minute?"

Hannah put her truck in park, got out, and said, "Sure, what's up?"

Sue-Lynn gave Hannah an open up-and-down look of disapproval, her eyes sweeping Hannah's sweatpants, hiking boots, and Sam's puffy down jacket.

Hannah crossed her arms and waited.

"I'm chair of the field trip committee," Sue-Lynne said. "Next month Tucker and Sammy's class is scheduled to go to DC for a day trip."

"That permission slip is on the bulletin board in my kitchen," Hannah said. "I'm sorry I haven't remembered to bring it in."

"I was talking to some of the other members of the committee, and we wondered if maybe the amount we are asking parents to cover was going to be too big of a stretch for you and Sam right now."

"I don't remember how much it is, but there's no problem," Hannah said. "I just have a lot going on right now and forgot to bring it in."

"You don't have to pretend with me, Hannah. I know you just lost your job and that while the work Sam is doing with the injured veterans is laudable, we are aware he doesn't make any money. If you can't afford the trip fee, the committee thoroughly understands, and we would be glad to take up a collection on your behalf. No one has to know who it's for. I wanted to also suggest that you apply to the IWS to have Sammy's school lunches covered by their charity fund."

Hannah felt the heat rise in her face, and her body trembled, representing the fight part of the fight-or-flight response being activated.

"I appreciate your offer," Hannah said, "but Sam and I are fine. We can pay for Sammy's lunches and the field trip fee. I'll bring the money and the permission slip when I pick Sammy up this afternoon."

"I can tell you're offended," Sue-Lynn said. "We have only the best intentions, I can assure you. It must be humiliating having to struggle to make ends meet. It's only by the grace of God that any of us aren't in the same boat, I'm sure. Please don't be mad."

Hannah could feel the hairs rise up on the back of her neck. Her heart rate sped up, and her fingers felt twitchy like they were independently compelled to flick Sue-Lynn on the forehead.

"For me to be offended," Hannah said. "I would have to give a rat's ass what you and your concern troll committee think of my family and me. I'm not offended, Sue-Lynne; I'm just tired of it. Tired of you all talking about what losers you think we are, and tired of your son sharing your low opinion of us with my son. If you really want to help my family, Sue-Lynn, you could do that by not gossiping about us to your friends or trashing us in front of your son, and then maybe he wouldn't report every nasty thing you say to Sammy. That would really help a lot."

Hannah could feel the heat and pressure building in her chest. She knew she was on the verge of a complete meltdown, and as good as it would feel at the moment to wrestle Sue-Lynn to the ground, hold her arm behind her back and make her cry "Uncle," she could not do that and still live in this town. There were already several other mothers listening while pretending not to.

Sue-Lynne held her hand to her chest.

"Hannah," Sue-Lynne said. "I don't know what you're talking about. I would never do something like that. I'm just not that kind of person."

"Then there's nothing to worry about, is there?" Hannah said.

Angry tears stung behind her eyes, but she would be damned if she would let this woman see them. She had to get away before she did something she would regret.

"Clearly, I've upset you ..." Sue-Lynne began, as she stepped forward and reached out toward Hannah as if she were about to put her hand on her arm.

Hannah stepped back and reached for the truck door handle.

"I'll bring in the permission slip and money this afternoon," Hannah said. "I'll bring cash, and I'll want a receipt. Are we done here?"

Sue-Lynne let her mask of concern drop and lowered her voice.

"I don't know why you're acting so ugly to me," Sue-Lynn said. "We're only trying to help. Our intentions are only good."

"Oh, I think you accomplished what you set out to do," Hannah said. "Now you can go back and report what I said. Be sure to convey to the committee how petty I think you all are, and how little I care what you think of my husband or me. The next time, however, my son reports to me some mean thing your kid heard you say, I'm coming straight for you, and there will be no doubt about my intentions."

"Are you threatening me?"

"I'm defending my family," Hannah said. "There's a world of difference."

Hannah got back in her truck and made sure to double check the way was clear before she pulled away from the curb. She didn't want to actually murder any of these nasty witches, even though she felt like it.

Hannah drove straight to the bank but sat parked outside in her truck, still trembling from her encounter with Sue-Lynn. Thinking about the many years that lay ahead, dealing with Sue-Lynn and all the ones like her while she and Sam tried to get Sammy raised and educated without sacrificing every shred of self-esteem he had, made her weary to the bone. It was hard enough going through hard times without a chorus of pretty women dressed in yoga pants reminding you that you didn't fit in, that you'd failed at some contest you never signed up for.

For herself, she could brush it off, but for Sammy, it wasn't tolerable.

She. Would. Not. Tolerate. It.

Even if by some miracle she won that lawsuit and they used the money to move into one of those new houses in that subdivision with the gated access. Even if she got a nose job, wore tons of makeup, bought all new clothes and uncomfortable shoes. Even if she carried gigantic purses that cost the same as six months' worth of groceries. Even if Sam could get along with all the barbecuing husbands, who golfed while their wives played tennis and met for brunch. Even if all that was possible, Hannah knew there would always be something about her that would not fit in, would refuse to, even.

And she didn't need to fit in, didn't want to be like them, she just wanted to be treated with respect. Hannah was okay with how she looked and how they lived. Why couldn't everyone else mind their own business and leave her family alone?

The tears that stung her eyes spilled over, and she rested her forehead against the steering wheel while they dripped off her nose.

There was a tap on the passenger side window. Hannah wiped her face before she looked over. It was Melissa.

"I'm gettin' in," Melissa said as she opened the door and climbed in. "What's wrong? What happened? Whoever did this better watch out, 'cause I'm about to pop open a can of Chattanooga whoop-ass."

Hannah told Melissa about her exchange with Tucker's mother.

"That low-life window-licker," Melissa said. "We had one of them boys in Tommy's class, too, by the name of Braxton or Brixton, I forget which. What was his mother's name? Bree Anne? Briar Anne? See? You will eventually forget their stupid names. What a booger out of the old snot-nosed hag that boy was. Tommy never wore the right shoes or had the right labels on his clothes, and old whatsisname never let him forget it."

"What did you do?"

"I taught my son that you deserve to be proud of what you accomplish and how you treat people, not how much your stuff cost," she said. "I taught him that if that was all them stupid losers had to be proud of, he should feel sorry for them. He was full of love and goodness when all them kids had was dollar signs where their hearts should be."

"You're an awesome mom," Hannah said. "I gotta try to remember all that."

"I also used my tips to buy him some shoes that cost as much as a week's worth of groceries," Melissa said. "I had a weak moment."

"You're the best."

"Delia and Ian taught me how to be a good mom," Melissa said. "They raised me right alongside Tommy. I'll never be able to repay them."

"We're lucky," Hannah said. "If it weren't for Sean covering our health insurance payments, and Delia letting me work at the Thorn, we would be in dire straits right now. We have no savings, no retirement plan, and the rent Drew pays on the farm out on the ridge is just enough to pay the property taxes and insurance."

"Would he buy it do you think?"

"I don't know," Hannah said. "We own the place where we live now, but honestly, Melissa, unless we win that lawsuit I don't know how we'll afford to keep it. And if we sell this farm, then where would we live? With my parents? Fat chance. Besides, Sam can't live in town; he'd go nuts."

"We'll figure something out," Melissa said. "Don't worry."

"I haven't told anybody else, but Sam got offered a job in Virginia, and as much as I don't want to leave, we might have to."

"I sure hope not."

"It might be nice to live like other people, with a husband who goes to work and a house that doesn't need a million repairs. Sammy could go to a good school and I could ... Well, I guess I could do something."

"You don't really wanna leave Rose Hill," Melissa said. "This is your home."

"I'm just tired of being the butt of everyone's jokes," Hannah said. "I'm sick of living in this fishbowl with all the friggin' piranhas."

"Listen, I been looked down on my whole life," Melissa said. "It's hard to be proud of yourself when everybody's telling you nothing you do is good enough. I figured once I went to prison, I couldn't get no lower on the social pole. When I got out, I had to make a choice. I could hide from everybody, afraid of what they might say, or I could decide what the hell, those em-effers are gonna point and whisper anyway, I might as well make something of myself. I can spit in their eye if they don't like it."

"You're braver than me."

"Nobody's braver than you," Melissa said. "You're the Masked Mutt-catcher, for gosh-sakes. At some time or another, you've helped every person in this gull-dern town, whether or not they had a pot to pee in. Sue-Lynne hasn't got the guts you've got; she hasn't got the heart you've got; she's just got money. She may be a big fish in this pond, but come on, lady, this ain't much more than a mud puddle, anyway."

Hannah teared up again.

"Quit being so nice," she said, "or I'll never stop crying."

"What are you doing today?" Melissa asked her. "How can I help?"

Hannah explained what her assignment was, following up by saying, "You can't tell anybody."

Melissa rolled her eyes.

"I'm the best at keeping a secret," she said. "Don't you know that by now?"

At the bank, her old friend Amy was only too happy to help Hannah. Her husband, Roger, the lone security guard at this small town bank, took Hannah to his office, showed her how to use the video monitoring software on his desktop PC, and left her to it.

Hannah scanned back to the night of the accident. The camera that was pointed in the direction closest to the crash had a view of the crossroads of Pine Mountain Road and Rose Hill Avenue. Because of the camera angle, she couldn't see the actual accident site. The camera did pick up the coal truck making a right onto Rose Hill Avenue, heading north, and a few seconds later, the white SUV coming to a stop on the sidewalk in front of Fitzpatrick's Service Station.

Under the glare of a nearby street light, she could make out Will in the passenger seat and someone else in the driver's seat. That person, a large man, got out of the driver's side of the SUV, looked at the side of the vehicle, then got back in, closed the door, and made a U-turn before driving back the way they came.

Hannah backed the video up and replayed it several times. She counted the seconds between when the SUV appeared and then disappeared; it seemed to corroborate with the time recorded by the fire station video camera. There would have been no time to stop at the accident scene on the way out of town.

She went back and stopped on a frame that most clearly showed the man who got out of the SUV. She zoomed in on his face, but the video picture was grainy black and white. She squinted. She got close to the screen. She stood up and backed away from the display to look. She looked away and then quickly looked back. She zoomed the view back out.

There was no doubt in her mind; the driver was Karl, Will and Ava's security man.

Hannah was fast forwarding the video when she saw something that made her back it up and hit replay. She watched someone exit the alley behind the service station, cross Rose Hill Avenue at a fast walk, and then run down Pine Mountain Road toward the river.

A slight figure, this person wore a dark parka with the hood pulled over the top of their face. As soon as this person passed the newspaper office, he or she was lost in the darkness of the alley. Hannah waited, but no car or SUV appeared, white or otherwise.

Fast forwarding to the night that Ava almost ran over Melissa, Hannah was twice able to see the white SUV approach the intersection and turn north. She zoomed in on the license plate both times and was able to see the letters and numbers. She wrote those down in her notebook.

On the night Melissa's car was sabotaged, she saw someone dressed in dark clothing leave the alley behind her family's service station and several minutes later, return the same way. She could not get a good look at this person's face. The figure was slim; could be male or female.

Hannah copied all the relevant sections of the video and saved the files to a flash drive she kept on her keychain. On her way out she thanked Amy and Roger and told him it had been beneficial.

"You don't erase any of those, do you?" she asked.

"At the end of the quarter," he said. "I was gonna do it this evening."

"Please don't," she said. "We may need it."

Hannah crossed the street and was passing the diner when someone inside caught her eye. She passed the door, but then slid up next to the building and peeked back through the window. It was Karl, Ava and Will's security person, sitting in a booth with the woman Terese, whom Delia had been talking to in her backyard. They were intent in conversation, and it looked intense. Now why would those two know each other and what could they be talking about?

Hannah casually entered the diner, turning her head as if she were interested in the specials printed on a chalkboard.

"Sit anywhere," said a bearded young man with wire-rim glasses who was wearing a three-piece wool suit that looked as if it were sewn in 1879.

Hannah walked oh so casually over to the booth behind the one Terese and Karl were sitting in. Karl had his back to her, and Terese didn't know her, so although she looked at Hannah, she didn't seem to recognize her as anyone she knew. When Hannah sat down in the booth, her head was only about six inches from Karl's. They spoke in low voices, but Hannah's hearing was excellent.

"We're so close," Terese said. "When will they be back?"

"He says they're playing it by ear," Karl said. "They may want me to bring the children up to meet them in New York so they can fly straight from there to the UK. I'm stalling over Olivia's passport."

"We can't let her take the children out of the country."

"I think I can talk them into leaving Ernie and Timmy with their grandmother here in town," he said. "But Ava won't go without Olivia."

"And the nanny?"

"She's already back in Ireland," he said. "She wants nothing more to do with them. She's scared, and I don't blame her."

"And our Oxford student?"

"I don't know," he said. "She left school a week ago, and no one has heard from her."

"Is her mother worried?"

"Not very," he said. "She's got her own problems right now."

"Hello, my name is Atticus, and I'll be serving you today," the bearded man said to Hannah. "Our hot drink special is a spiced pumpkin latte served with ginger-infused organic whipped cream. Our iced drink special is an East African cold brew slow-steeped in cool water for 24 hours, served with goat milk froth sweetened with clover honey."

"Just coffee," Hannah said.

"Light roast, medium roast, dark roast or Americano?"

"Medium."

"Skim milk, whole milk, half-and-half, cream, almond milk, or soy?"

"Whole milk."

"Organic cane sugar, honey, Agave, Rice Syrup, Tevia, or black?"

"Cane sugar."

"Our lunch special is a roasted portabella vegan patty melt served with spicy beet frittes."

"No thanks."

"Today's dessert special is a kiwi and mixed berry torte topped with dragon fruit salsa spiked with lime and honey."

"Just the coffee, buddy, thanks."

It was all Hannah could do not to kick the guy. She was missing what they were saying. He walked away while giving her the side eye, no doubt assuming the amount of her tip would correspond to the dollar value of her outfit.

"Let me know," Terese was saying. "I won't pull the trigger until she's in range."

Hannah's eyes almost bugged out of her head. Her heart pound in her chest and her hands shook. Was the woman using a metaphor or was she seriously talking about shooting Ava?

Terese and Karl stood up to leave, so Hannah kept her head down and pretended to be furiously texting on her phone. She waited until they had exited the diner to look up, and then watched them go in opposite directions.

She stood up just as the waiter returned.

"Your coffee," he said.

"Make it to go, please," Hannah said.

He sighed.

Hannah fished in her pocket and came back out with a crumpled five dollar bill.

"Here," she said. "You drink it and keep the change."

Her next stop was Anthony Delvecchio's insurance agency on the corner of Iris Avenue, the street where Delia's house was, and Pine Mountain Road, which ended at the river.

Anthony was glad to help. He had one camera that pointed north up Iris Avenue, and

Delia's driveway was in the shot. They backed the video to the night Melissa thought Ava tried to run over her. They watched Melissa creep down Iris Avenue and hide in the vestibule of the apartment building behind Anthony's building. They then saw Patrick, covered in only a tablecloth wrapped around him, walking home. After that, it clearly showed Melissa walking down the street, the headlights of white SUV, and Melissa jumping out of the way.

He switched to the video from his other camera, which highlighted the sidewalk and street in front of his office. They were able to watch a clearly identifiable Ava, dressed in Patrick's clothes, as she walked past the insurance office and went down the street to where Melissa said she had parked her SUV. A few moments later the SUV passed the camera going east on Pine Mountain Road.

Anthony zoomed in on the license plate, and Hannah checked it against the number she had written down. It was different than the one on the night of the murder.

He fast-forwarded to the same SUV flying past the office after it had almost hit Melissa and paused it long enough for Hannah to verify the same license plate number.

"We've got her," Hannah said. 'Two video confirmations should be good enough for any jury."

"I had no idea," Anthony said. "This opens up a big can of worms for me."

"Why's that?" Hannah asked.

"Ava came in a few weeks ago and took out a substantial insurance policy on her husband," he said. "You didn't hear that from me."

"Who's the beneficiary?"

"Ava is the primary and Olivia is the contingent."

"Just the one kid?"

He nodded.

Hannah wrote that down in her notebook.

"She's a piece of work, that one," Hannah said. "Let's look at the night of the accident."

Hannah surmised that if Ava drove to Rose Hill that evening, she would probably have parked in the same place.

At about the time Patrick would be leaving work, they could see a hooded figure walk up the hill, past the office, and turn into the alley. Hannah fast-forwarded until they saw Ava again, only this time she was running down the sidewalk from Rose Hill Avenue. When she reached the alley, she took something out of her pocket and threw it in the dumpster next to the antique store. She then rushed passed the office, headed down the hill toward the river.

"When does the trash get picked up?" Hannah asked.

"Today," Anthony said, and they both jumped up and ran for the door.

When they reached the dumpster, they could hear the garbage truck making its way down the alley toward them. Anthony boosted Hannah up over the edge and shown the flashlight from his phone down at what she was doing.

"What are we looking for?" he asked her.

"I don't know," Hannah said.

She tossed out all the closed bags of garbage and directed him where to shine the light.

"Score!" she called out. "Get me a large envelope."

Anthony ran back inside the office, and when he returned, Hannah was standing in the dumpster, talking to the men walking alongside the garbage truck, making them laugh. They collected the bagged trash she had thrown out and then rolled on across Pine Mountain Road into the next alley.

Anthony handed Hannah a large envelope and some rubber gloves his cleaning lady kept in the office kitchenette.

"Good thinking," she said as she put them on.

"The only things that were not in bags were these," she said.

She put the man's winter gloves and a rag she had found in the envelope, and then Anthony helped her out of the dumpster.

"I'm relieved this isn't a restaurant dumpster," Hannah said. "No food, no critters."

Back in Anthony's office, they forwarded the video to the night Melissa's car was sabotaged. The assailant passed Anthony's building, went down Iris Avenue, crawled under Melissa's car, and then eventually crawled back out and walked up the street toward Anthony's camera. Under the streetlight at the corner of Iris Avenue and Pine Mountain Road, they could clearly see that person's face.

"I thought she was in England," Anthony said.

The nearest video camera to the trailer park was owned by Spurlock's Feed and Seed. Landis Spurlock left Hannah to look at the footage while he waited on customers.

"I keep that to deter the mulch thieves," he said. "Beats hauling them heavy bags back in every night."

Hannah was disappointed not to have a clear shot of the trailer park.

"Anybody else around here have a security camera?" she asked.

He thought about it.

"The bicycle factory," he said.

Hannah walked down to the bicycle factory, racking her brain trying to think of some plausible reason she could ask to see their video footage. It didn't end up mattering, however, because the assembly foreman told her that Will's security man had removed the whole security system days ago.

"Why," Hannah asked.

The man shrugged as he replied, "He didn't say."

"Have you had a break in?"

"Not that I know of, and I would know."

Hannah retrieved her car from in front of the bank. She drove slowly down Rose Hill Avenue, looking for video cameras. Machalvie Funeral Home, diagonally across the street from the Rose and Thorn, had the best view of the crime scene and a video camera pointed right at it.

Unfortunately, owner Peg Machalvie hated Hannah.

She drove up Peony Street and parked outside the community center. In the basement of what used to be Rose Hill High School, Sam was

257

spotting a young man who was bench pressing a barbell loaded down with weights. He signaled for Hannah to wait, and then called someone else over to take his place.

Behind the community center, on the concrete porch that faced the old bus barn, Hannah laid out what she had learned. Sam listened with an impassive face, one she was used to seeing when his business was network security for the government.

"So," she finished, "I didn't think Peg would let me in the door of the funeral home, never mind look at their security video footage. They probably have a video of the whole thing, though. It's a straight shot to the PJ's Pizza parking lot."

"Who's friends with Peg?" Sam asked.

"Marigold, I guess," Hannah said. "She hates me too, though. Actually, anyone awful enough to be friends with Peg is bound to hate me for some reason."

"Some reason?"

"I've got a big mouth," Hannah said. "I say what I think. So sue me."

"Not my wife," Sam said. "My wife is on the city council; she's beloved by all two and four-legged creatures in this county."

"She sounds nice," Hannah said. "Too bad for you this wife got caught nailing a garlic braid and a crucifix over the back door of the funeral home."

"Why did you do that?"

"Well, first of all, Peg's obviously a creature of the night, I mean, just look at her," Hannah said. "Plus I'd had a few beers and Maggie double-dog-dared me."

"Patrick said all the electric was out on that side of the street due to the wreck," Sam said. "You think the funeral home's video camera would still have been on?"

"They would have to have a backup generator," Hannah said. "Can't have any bodies thawing out, now can we?"

"Anybody have a funeral scheduled today?"

Hannah's mouth dropped open.

"Samuel Harold Campbell, are you asking me to infiltrate the funeral home under the guise of being a mourner, brazenly enter an office marked 'staff only,' illegally access the videotape from their security camera, and then surreptitiously make a copy of said tape?"

Sam narrowed his eyes at her but then smiled.

"Piece of cake," Hannah said.

The deceased was the scion of a large Mennonite family from Fleurmania, so every room of the funeral home was packed with all the many members of their immediate family, extended family, church family, and neighbors. Luckily for Hannah, one of the sons of the departed had, along with all his sons, built the barn at Hannah's family's farm out on Hollyhock Ridge, and he was touched that Hannah had thought to come and pay her respects.

Hannah's confederate in this scheme, Bonnie Fitzpatrick, the idea for whose participation Hannah considered a brilliant stroke of genius on her own part, had trapped Peg Machalvie in the entrance alcove and was inquiring about prepaying for deluxe funeral plans. Bonnie Fitzpatrick was one of the few people Peg feared, and besides, Peg would never ignore an inquiry about deluxe prepayments.

Hannah had already noted the emergency generator behind the funeral home, so she knew they had power after the electric pole fell over on the night of the murder. Hannah's stealthy reconnaissance inside revealed Peg's sons, Hugh and Louis, were stationed in the viewing room on either end of the casket. She peeked into a prep room and saw a woman busy applying makeup to a corpse. Seeing the coast was clear, Hannah entered Peg's office and helped herself to her PC.

"No password," she said as she easily gained access to her desktop. "Amateurs."

Instead of taking the time to look at the video files, she copied all the files from the "South View" camera for October onto her flash drive. She had 95% of the last one downloaded when she heard voices in the hallway.

It was Stuart Machalvie, Peg's husband.

"This way, milady," he said, as opened the door to the office. "We won't be disturbed in here for a little while."

He looked pleased with himself as he ushered a pretty woman into the office. Hannah recognized her as the young lady who had been down the hall applying makeup to a corpse.

Stuart had his hand on the woman's backside when he saw Hannah. He froze, and out of the corner of her eye, Hannah watched the download reach 97%.

"Mrs. Campbell," Stuart yelped and then drew his hand back as if the woman's rear was hotter than a lit stove. "What are you doing in here?"

"Hold on a minute," Hannah said.

She held up a finger while she watched the screen.

98%

99%

100%

Hannah removed the flash drive attached to her key ring and put it in her pocket. She saluted the startled woman.

"Greetings, corpse painter," she said. "As you were. Carry on."

"Hannah, I can explain," Stuart began.

Hannah put a finger to her lips and said, "Shush Stuart. I didn't see you, and you didn't see me. Are we good?"

Stuart chuckled.

"It was nice not seeing you, Hannah."

After making her way through the crush of the black-garbed mourners, Hannah grabbed Bonnie by the arm as Peg shot her a hateful look.

"We gotta go," Hannah said.

"Well, I'll be in touch," Bonnie said to Peg as she backed away. "Thank you for your time."

"I'll drop off some brochures at the bakery," Peg said.

"You do that," Bonnie said. "Bye now."

Peg narrowed her eyes at Hannah, who crossed herself and hissed before being pulled away by her aunt. They crossed Rose Hill Avenue and walked down the sidewalk together.

"Did you get it? Did you get it?" Bonnie wanted to know.

"Oh, I got it," Hannah said. "Thanks to you."

"I love doing this spy stuff," Bonnie said. "You've got to let me help you more."

"You're like a secret weapon," Hannah said. "I can only deploy you when nothing else will work."

Back at home, in Sam's office, she and her husband viewed the purloined video footage together. It featured a hooded figure, obviously the same one she had watched on the bank's video, the one who crossed Rose Hill Avenue, the one she watched on Anthony's video, who tossed the gloves and rag in the dumpster next to the antique store.

This person walked directly to the man on the ground and shone a flashlight on his face. He or she knelt next to him, searched his clothing, took out his wallet, and looked at his IDs. He or she walked around the crime scene and picked up objects. He or she knelt once more beside the prone man, placed the thumbs of both hands on the throat of the victim, left them there long enough to strangle him to death, and then calmly checked the victim's pulse before standing and sprinting toward the alley.

The EMTs arrived in the ambulance moments later.

Afterward, Hannah didn't feel the satisfaction she thought she would. She felt sick at her stomach.

"You can't see her face," Sam said.

"But Patrick was there," Hannah said. "He knows who it was. Between his eyewitness testimony and all the video evidence, we've got her."

"Not necessarily," Sam said. "She will claim Patrick's lying. It's her word against his, and she can afford the best attorneys."

"What now?" she asked Sam.

"I'll take it from here," he said. "You keep an eye on Melissa and stay away from Ava. I'm not kidding around about that."

"Shouldn't I be looking for our car vandal?"

"I don't think that's a good idea, either," he said. "Where's Timmy?"

"He's with Delia."

"Try to keep everybody together," he said. "There's safety in numbers."

Arriving at Delia's house after the city council meeting, Hannah found several members of her extended family. The atmosphere was jubilant.

She pulled Delia aside.

"What's going on?" she asked. "Why are you having a party and didn't invite me?"

"Jess's parents signed the custody agreement," Delia told her. "They will still have visitation, but Claire and Ed can start the adoption process with their blessing."

"Do the girls know?"

Delia shook her head.

"Claire and Ed have been shielding them from all that," she said. "We're just calling this a Halloween candy swap party."

"I need to talk to you in private," Hannah said. "Let's go outside."

Delia grabbed a jacket, and they went out back to sit at the picnic table.

"I saw Ava's security guy having lunch with your friend, Terese," Hannah said. "I overheard some things that worry me. What's that about?"

Delia shrugged.

"C'mon," Hannah said. "Today I watched a video of Ava killing a guy."

"Bonnie told me about your adventure at the funeral home," Delia said. "Is there any doubt about what you saw?"

"None," Hannah said. "It was cold-blooded murder."

"Those poor children," Delia said. "What will happen to them?"

"Have you heard from Charlotte?" Hannah asked.

"No, why?"

"I think she's around here somewhere," Hannah said, and then told her about the video of her sabotaging Melissa's car.

"Why would Charlotte want to hurt Melissa?" Delia asked.

"Think about it," Hannah said. "Patrick was the only father she knew from the time her own father bugged out until she got shipped off to Europe as a teenager. She wouldn't want anyone to get in the way if she thought Patrick and Ava were going to finally be together. She probably thinks Will is in the way, too, poor guy."

"I know what Claire thinks," Delia said. "I don't want to believe Charlotte could have murdered Professor Richmond, although I could easily believe Ava would."

"Evidently, the poison apple didn't fall far from the arsenic tree," Hannah said. "We need to keep an eye out for Charlotte. She may try to get in touch with Timmy."

"Those poor little souls," Delia said. "Bonnie and Fitz are in no shape to raise them, and I can't see Maggie doing it."

"Don't forget Patrick is Olivia's father."

"Some father he'd be," Delia said. "I love my nephew, but he's just like his father, who was just like his father."

"Do tell."

"Oh, you've heard the gossip."

"And you've seen proof?"

"I've seen enough, and I've heard enough," she said. "I don't think men like that can change."

"My dad was not like that."

"No, and neither was my husband," Delia said. "I don't know what makes one brother like that but not the rest."

"Sean could raise them."

"I hadn't thought of Sean," Deli said.

"He loves kids, he's a good person, and he can afford to do it. We could help him."

"Well, she has to be arrested and tried first," Delia said. "Can you imagine growing up in this town after that?"

"Yes," Hannah said. "And we'll raise them to hold their heads up high and be proud to be a Fitzpatrick. Anyone who says otherwise gets an eye full of spit."

Delia patted Hannah.

"You're right," she said. "I just get tired thinking about all they'll have to go through."

"We've got this," Hannah said. "Sam and I can help."

"I'm so thankful for you girls," Delia said. "I don't know what I'd do without you."

"Now, about Terese," Hannah said.

"Hannah, honey, I made a promise I have to keep. I cannot tell you anything about Terese except to say, anyone she trusts, you should trust. She's good, and she's on our side."

Melissa came outside.

"C'mon, you guys," she said. "Pizza's here."

"Did you order my favorite?" Hannah asked.

"Yes, and you have one all to yourself," Melissa said. "But you hafta hurry."

Hannah was just finishing her pizza when she received a call from Patrick.

"Can you cover for me later tonight?"

"Where's your waitress?"

"She called in sick," he said. "I need to leave for a while; will you tend bar?"

"Where are you going?"

"To see a man about a horse," he said.

"I remember what that means," Hannah said. "Who is she?"

"Do you want the money or not?" Patrick asked.

"I'll be there by eight," Hannah said.

When Hannah got to the Rose and Thorn, Patrick was leaning over the bar whispering in the ear of a young blonde woman. When he saw Hannah, he stood up straight and began polishing clean highball glasses.

Hannah looked the blonde over as she passed her. College girl, by the looks of her, and pretty drunk. When she walked around behind the bar, she gestured toward her.

"She legal?"

"She has an ID that says she is," Patrick said.

Patrick took his jacket off the hook on the wall and slipped his arms in.

"Can I ask you something?" Hannah said.

"Can I stop you?" Patrick answered.

"Do you even want Melissa back?"

He shrugged.

"If she'd have me," he said. "Meanwhile, a man's gotta do what a man's gotta do."

"Are you coming back?"

"Around ten," he said. "Or I'll call."

Hannah sorted out the mess Patrick always left in the till, cleaned off the bar top, and served customers. Around ten o'clock her husband came in and sat down at the end of the bar, where her Uncle Ian used to sit.

"What'll you have?" she asked him.

"Whatever's on draft," he answered.

Hannah brought him his beer and leaned on the bar.

"So tell me," she said. "Why can't Patrick be faithful?"

"He is faithful," Sam said. "In here."

He pointed to his heart.

"But what about south of there?" she asked him. "Why can't he control himself?"

"He can," Sam says. "He chooses not to."

"Well, there you have it," Hannah said. "What about you?"

"You know me," Sam said.

"I do," Hannah said. "Sometimes I feel like I have to work overtime to keep you faithful."

"It's nice work if you can get it."

"What if I ever can't, though?" Hannah asked him. "Is that all I am to you?"

"You know better than that."

"I wonder," Hannah said. "Where's our son?"

"Beats me," he said, but then smiled.

"Safety in numbers, you said."

"They're all staying at Delia's tonight."

"So what you're saying is, we have the house to ourselves tonight."

Sam waggled his eyebrows.

"What time do you get off?" he asked.

"As soon as Patrick gets back," Hannah said. "Although if I remember correctly, he always had a way of being later than he thinks he will be."

"College girls are high maintenance," Sam said. "They like to cuddle afterward."

"How do you know it's a college girl?"

"It's a day that ends in y, isn't it?" he said. "Like shooting fish in a barrel for Patrick."

"He'll eventually be too old for them," Hannah said. "What then?"

"There's always somebody," Sam said. "You know that."

A group of young people entered the bar, and Hannah sighed.

"You need me to help out?" he asked.

"You tend bar, and I'll waitress," Hannah said.

"Split your tips?" he asked.

"I'll make it worth your while," Hannah said. "Don't you worry."

Pumpkin Ridge by Pamela Grandstaff

CHAPTER TEN - MONDAY

Earlier that morning, when Melissa checked her email, she saw the attorney for the four little girls' grandparents had responded with an attachment.

"Sean!" she called out. "It's here!"

Sean came up the hall and waited while Melissa opened the attachment and printed it. He went to the printer, picked up the pages as they printed, and scanned each one for notes from their attorney.

"No notes," he called out.

"No way," Melissa said, as she came down the hallway.

By the time the last page printed out, the one with the grandparents' notarized signatures, Sean was shaking his head in disbelief.

"No changes and they signed it," he said. "I can't believe it."

"Should I call Claire?"

"Go ahead," he said. "They'll be so relieved."

When Melissa told her the news, Claire screamed and then cried.

"Oh, honey," Melissa said. "Don't cry."

"I had convinced myself they weren't going to allow it," Claire said. "I didn't want to hope for it to work out."

"You call Ed," Melissa said. "I'll start on the adoption application."

Just after noon, the couple who had purchased the bed and breakfast from Ava came in the office. They didn't look happy.

"I need to talk to that lawyer," the man said, and pointed toward the back.

The man had a bandage on his forehead and a black eye beneath it.

Melissa called Sean and then told them they could go back.

"You go on," the woman told her husband. "I'll wait here."

Melissa got the woman some coffee and then sat down with her in the waiting area.

"Are you all right?" she asked her.

"No," the woman said. "We're not all right. We're quite a long way from all right."

"Oh no," Melissa said. "Why?"

"We've had enough," the woman said. "We're not going to stay."

"What happened?"

"We discovered someone has been living in the apartment over the garage," she said. "We changed the locks yesterday, but last night they broke a window and were in there again."

"Did you see who it was?"

She shook her head.

"Probably drug addicts," the woman said. "We heard that was a problem here."

"That's a problem everywhere," Melissa said, but the woman rolled her eyes and clutched her purse a little tighter to her body as if Melissa might snatch it.

"Harvey ordered an alarm system and cameras from the hardware store, but they won't be here until next week sometime. We couldn't get anyone to come any sooner. I can't believe the number of things you can't get done here, no matter how much you're willing to pay."

"I'm sorry for you," Melissa said. "What was it you wanted Sean to do?"

"We want out of the deal," she said. "Before we have any of our stuff moved here we need to find out if we can get the contract canceled."

"Have you had anyone make reservations?" Melissa said.

"Our first guests showed up the night of the closing," she said. "We told them we weren't ready for customers, but they seemed like a nice couple, said they were here to visit their son at Eldridge and couldn't find any accommodations anywhere nearby. They begged us, offered to pay double the rate. So we took pity on them and let them stay."

"That was kind of you."

"They carried on all night. From ten in the evening until two in the morning they went at it. And the language! I wanted to call the police, but Harvey said we didn't need that kind of bad publicity right off the bat. He was too afraid to go up there and tell them to keep it down; who knows what they might have done."

"That's scary," Melissa said.

"Also there were ... other noises," the woman said. "You know."

Melissa thought she did know.

"Well, it is a hotel," she said. "You're gonna get those kinds of noises."

"It's a bed and breakfast, not a brothel!" the woman said. "What if there had been a family with kids staying with us, too?"

"I guess you can't pick and choose your customers in business."

"When they left the next morning, they didn't even seem embarrassed."

"Maybe they didn't know you could hear them."

"If that was all that happened we could write it off as a fluke," she said. "But then the other noises started."

"More noises?"

"Moaning," she said. "With no one in the house but Harvey and me. Moaning like the house was haunted."

"Was it on Halloween?" Melissa asked. "Maybe it was a prank?"

"No, this started Friday night," she said. "We couldn't find where it was coming from; it seemed to come through the air vents."

"That's scary."

"So no sleep for the first three nights, and then on Halloween night after trick-or-treating was over, Harvey heard noises out back. He found several empty beer bottles under the pine trees out back. He looked up at the tree and could see someone's feet dangling there. He yelled at them to come out of the tree, and they dropped a beer bottle on him."

"Oh my goodness," Melissa said. "Then what happened?"

"He came inside with his head bleeding, and his eye swelled up, so I called the police. By the time the deputy got there, the trespasser was gone, and he helped us search the property. That's when we discovered someone had been living in the apartment over the garage. Whoever it was had left a sleeping bag and food there. The old van which the former owner had left in the driveway is gone, so we think they stole it. The deputy called the man who owns the hardware store ..."

"Sonny Delvecchio."

"Yes, Mr. Delvecchio, and he came and changed the locks for us the next morning, on Sunday. So this morning we get up and find the window broken at the top of the apartment stairs, and the sleeping bag and food are gone."

"So at least whoever it was has gone."

"We don't care," she said. "We've had enough."

"It hasn't even been a week," Melissa said. "It's awful bad luck, but I'm sure it will get better if you give it time."

"We've made a huge mistake," she said. "We had this idea of how it would be, and it's not like that at all. I guess we didn't know what we were getting into."

The phone rang, and Melissa dealt with that call while Sean walked Harvey up to the front.

"I can ask them," Sean said. "They have no legal obligation to allow you to back out, but I can ask. I'll let you know what they say."

"We'll gladly give up the deposit," Harvey said. "Otherwise, I think we'll have to sue to get out of the contract. We've got to get out of this godforsaken town."

"No offense," his wife said.

After they left, Melissa and Sean discussed the situation, both agreeing it was unlikely that Will and Ava would allow the buyers to back out of the sales agreement.

"Those checks are deposited," Sean said.

"What about disclosure?" Melissa asked. "Can they say the sellers didn't disclose the place was haunted?"

Sean rolled his eyes.

"I'd love to see that argued in court, but I'd never try it," he said. "They can't say Ava should have disclosed that running a B&B is hard and customers can be rude; that's on them. It was just unrealistic expectations and bad luck, that's all."

"I wonder who was staying in the apartment," Melissa said.

"Some homeless person," Sean said.

"I wonder," Melissa said.

Melissa worked on the adoption application for Claire and Ed, but her mind kept wandering. Early in the morning, she had awakened from a pretty steamy dream; so real, in fact, that if she'd been a smoker, she would have lit up afterward. It had been Patrick, of course, and in the dream, she had been more than a willing participant; she'd been the aggressor. Flashes of this dream kept bubbling up in her mind, making it difficult to think about anything else.

She was amazed to find that the shock and anger she felt as a result of Patrick's betrayal was lessening in intensity, and in its place was a physical longing for him so intense she felt like she needed to grip the desk lest her body go running off looking for him.

Although she fought her emotions, her mind was flooded with memories of the many times they had fooled around. She could remember when their desire for each other was so strong they'd enter the trailer tearing their clothes off and spend the next hour knocking over furniture and crashing into walls while they satisfied that passion.

It could easily have been Patrick and Melissa shocking the B&B owners.

Over the years, they had shared tender mornings, stolen afternoons, and hot, sultry nights. They'd broken in the Mustang, front seat and back. They'd done it in every room of the Rose and Thorn, possibly on every surface. Patrick's body, with its strong, muscular arms, broad shoulders and chest; the way he could actually pick her up and put her where he wanted her; and then his relentless pursuit of her pleasure; it was all like a drug to Melissa, and she was now in withdrawal.

Melissa craved it, she missed it, and she felt like she might lose her mind over it. Thinking she would never have that again was causing her actual physical pain and mental anguish.

She wondered if she could sue Ava for alienation of affection. She looked it up online to see if that was still possible in West Virginia. It was! She tried to imagine that court proceeding and pictured the entire town lined up around the block to get in to see it.

She allowed herself to consider her actual options. She could take Patrick back and have all the good sex again, but at what cost? Everyone knew what had happened; she'd look like a fool. She could almost ignore what anyone else thought of her, but what about what Tommy thought of her, and what she thought of herself?

She considered the idea of having sex with him one more time, just to stave off this piercing loneliness and physical longing, but she knew that would only prolong the suffering. The thought of him and Ava together hurt in her chest, like she was having a heart attack. Her heart had been attacked. Could someone actually die of heartbreak?

The phone rang, and it was Mayor Templeton.

"Good news," Kay said. "The zoning change was approved today, and you even get to pick the new name for your property."

"What do you mean, the new name?"

"It's on the official town map as Hollyhock Mobile Home Park, and you can keep that, of course, but you could also change it to anything you like."

"I don't know what to change it to," Melissa said. "Can I think about it?"

"Of course, dear. The council will have to approve whatever you choose, but that shouldn't be a problem. You just let me know."

Melissa doodled some names on a legal pad. Her mind wandered as she did so.

Hollyhock Gardens.

Hollyhock Terrace.

Hollyhock Circle.

Heartbreak Tiny Home Park.

Lyin' Ass Cheater's Home for Peckerheads.

A stray notion, one that had been playing around the edges of her consciousness, ran in front of her train of thought.

"Sean!" she yelled.

He came hurrying down the hall.

"What?" he said. "You scared me to death."

"I know who was living in the apartment behind the B&B," she said.

She outlined her theory, and Sean seemed to consider it.

"That would account for the haunting noises as well," he said. "I'll call Sam."

As Melissa was leaving work, she got a text from Patrick.

"Left something for you with Delia."

When Melissa arrived at Delia's the house was full of kids and noise. Delia hugged her and said, "Isn't it wonderful?"

Melissa did indeed think it was wonderful, but she wasn't in the mood to celebrate. Selfishly, she just wanted to hide somewhere and have a self-pity party.

There was an old cigar box on the kitchen table; she took it down the hall to her room and sat on the bed with it. Patrick knew she had a weakness for old cigar boxes, just like the one she had kept her treasures in when she was a little girl. Treasures to her back then would have been trash to anyone else, but she didn't get presents, and on Christmas, she might get one thing if her aunt could find it cheap enough at a rummage sale.

Something rattled in the box, so she opened it. Inside was a tiny metal replica of her blue Mustang, a Matchbox car that Patrick had treasured as a boy. He must have been cleaning out his room at his mother's house and found it.

Patrick had always wanted a vintage blue Mustang and had been more excited than Melissa about finding one for her and fixing it up. She wasn't dumb; she knew he had picked that particular car to give to her because that meant he could have it. But she loved him so much, it was natural to want him to have something he dreamed of having.

There was no note.

As she held the little car, noticing the edges where the paint had been worn off by the little boy version of Patrick, tears formed in her eyes and spilled over. She allowed herself to acknowledge the deep longing she felt, the loneliness that was tormenting her. She missed him so much. He knew her so well. How could she go through life without those arms around her, that strong, protective embrace where she felt cared for, where she belonged?

Right now, the fact of Ava didn't seem to matter as much.

She had known for years that Patrick was in love with Ava. Even after he knew what Ava was capable of; how easily she took advantage of Scott and Maggie's breakup to snag Scott for herself in order to shore up her reputation; how content she was to keep her relationship with Patrick a secret; and how willing she was to marry someone else just for his money; still, Patrick remained devoted.

Apparently, he could forgive her anything.

He loved Melissa, too, she knew, just in a different compartment in his heart—a smaller one, no doubt, under the stairs with Harry Potter. If she could bring herself to share him with Ava, if she could find a way to accept that flaw in him, to look the other way, could she then be sure to always have him?

Right now, as lonely as she felt, as much as she longed for him, it didn't seem like that big of a deal. Other women did it. They just didn't talk about it. If she took him back, she would be right back in the heart of his family where they all loved her and hated Ava.

It felt safe there.

She deserved to be a part of that family. She had earned his devotion. She was good for him, and he fulfilled her needs: to be accepted, cared for, to belong. It had always been Patrick for her; but could she accept him for the flawed man that he was?

She felt a small flame of hope flare up, just thinking about taking him back. Maybe all this hurt and embarrassment could be put aside. Maybe she just needed to expand her belief in what a relationship should be. She just had to overlook this one flaw in an otherwise perfectly good man.

She would marry him. Maybe they'd have a child right away. Ava would never be able to take him away from a family. She would make him a family. She would get him to stay.

Melissa heard Hannah arrive. She didn't want to talk to anybody about her decision, least of all Hannah or Claire, whom she knew would look at her with pity. Feeling ashamed and foolish, she slipped out the bedroom window and made her way to the little house at the trailer park. She wanted to be alone with her thoughts, which felt fragile and vulnerable. If she was going to talk herself into doing something dangerous, and possibly doomed, she couldn't afford to have anyone interrupt that process.

At the little house, she was surprised to find the door lock pried open, and even more surprised to find Ava's daughter, Charlotte, sitting inside.

"Sorry," she said when Melissa gasped. "I didn't have anywhere else to go, and I don't want my mom to know I'm home."

Melissa's heart raced, and to her surprise, she felt almost as afraid as she had been when she ran into Ava behind the B&B. It was probably because Charlotte, at nineteen, was the spitting image of her beautiful mother, causing suspicion and fear to prick Melissa like a million tiny needles.

"What are you doing here?" Melissa asked her.

She stayed in the doorway with the door open, not willing to be alone with Charlotte or without an escape route.

"Close the door," Charlotte said. "It's freezing."

"I don't think so," Melissa said. "This is my house, and you broke and entered. That ain't right. That's against the law."

Charlotte rolled her eyes.

"Don't get your panties in a bunch," Charlotte said. "I just needed a place to crash until my mom leaves for Europe. After that I can stay at Will's place; the cleaning lady will let me in."

"Were you staying in the garage apartment behind the B&B?" Melissa asked her.

"You heard about that, huh?" Charlotte said. "I dropped a bottle right on that fat old man's bald head, scared him to death. I made them think the place was haunted."

"Getting those folks to move out won't put everything back the way you want it," Melissa said. "Ain't no way your mom's leaving Will and moving back in there."

"We were happy there before Will came," Charlotte said. "He ruined everything."

"You're grown up now," Melissa said. "It's time for you to make your own life the way you want it, and let your mother have what she wants."

"What she wants is Patrick," Charlotte said, and then smiled slyly at Melissa.

"Then that's between her and Patrick," Melissa said.

"Except you want him, too, right?" Charlotte said. "He might feel sorry for you, and he might be fooled by your sweet lil ole honey chile way of talking, but you will never hold a candle to my mother. They have something you will never have."

"That's between Patrick and me," Melissa said. "That ain't none of your business."

Charlotte had been sitting with her hands under the small kitchen table, but now she drew them out from underneath to reveal the knife she was holding. She pointed it at Melissa.

"Oh, I think it is," Charlotte said. "You know I killed that old guy, right? What makes you think I wouldn't kill you, too?"

Melissa turned quickly to leave and leaped right into Johnny Johnson's arms.

"Woah, there," he said. "What's your hurry?"

Melissa's heart was thumping. She turned back and pointed at the little house just as Charlotte appeared in the doorway, a backpack slung over her shoulder.

"I'm leaving now," she said to Melissa. "Thanks, y'all, for the southern hospitality."

She said this in an exaggerated southern accent, obviously making fun of Melissa.

"You clear on out of here," Melissa said. "If I ever see you near my home again I'll take a ball bat to you, I don't care who you are."

"Does Patrick know about him?" Charlotte asked, pointing at Johnny.

"I think you better leave," Johnny said, "before we call the law."

Charlotte rolled her eyes and flipped them her middle finger before turning and walking away. Ava's old van was parked behind Spurlock's Feed and Seed, and they watched Charlotte get into it and drive away.

"What was that about?" Johnny asked.

"Come in," Melissa said. "I'll tell you all about it."

Johnny examined the door where it had been pried it open and pronounced it fixable. While he repaired it, Melissa used her cell phone to order pizza and soft drinks to be delivered. She then searched the premises for anything Charlotte might have left behind. Finally, they sat down across from each other at the small table.

"Who was that little monster?" he asked her.

"It's such a long story," she said.

"I've got nothing better to do," he said. "I came all the way to town to check on you, to see how you're getting along. You are now obligated to entertain me, and that's what will entertain me best."

Melissa told him her whole story, how she kidnapped Tommy, how she came to Rose Hill, and how she had fallen in love with Patrick the first time she laid eyes on him. Meanwhile, the food arrived, and she kept talking, occasionally interrupted by a thoughtful question from Johnny.

When she told him about discovering Patrick was cheating on her with Ava, her eyes welled up with tears.

"I don't know why I'm telling you all this," she said. "You must think you done got trapped by a crazy lady."

"To me, the only thing crazy is how Patrick could prefer anyone over you," Johnny said. "I think you're better off without the guy."

"I know everyone thinks that," she said. "I can't help how I feel, though."

"Ah, feelings," Johnny said. "I am familiar with those. They can get you in all sorts of trouble."

"Why do people cheat?" she asked him.

"Because they lack character," Johnny said. "Honor, loyalty, true faith, and allegiance; those are huge responsibilities that are not easy to uphold. Weak people can't be bothered to try."

"I know I'll never be able to trust him," she said. "I just can't imagine my life without him in it."

"So, you've made your decision, then."

"I think I have to give it one more try," she said. "Then I'll at least know I did my best."

"I think I know how this will end," he said. "But who knows? Maybe you are the one woman who can change a man. I can see why a person would want to change for you. Here I am in town for the second time in a week."

"I'm sorry," Melissa said.

"Don't be," Johnny said. "I admire your devotion. I just hope he's worthy of it."

"Tell me about you," Melissa said. "How come you gotta live so far out in the woods?"

"Whilst serving my country I had what you might call a series of eventful experiences," he said. "When I came back, I determined that what was best for me, and probably for all those around me, as well, was for me to attempt to have a series of uneventful experiences. See this?"

He held up his hands and Melissa could see the tremor.

"That came back with me," he said. "When life gets too stressful, I can't cope. I fall apart. I find my little house in the big woods soothing; I feel safe there."

"But here you are."

"Here I am."

Johnny told Melissa about some of the things that had happened while he was in Afghanistan: battles he fought, friends he lost, and the unrelenting terror he felt every day and night, with little relief.

"Ultimately it turned me into a weapon with no safety on the trigger," he said. "I don't want to hurt anyone else, not for any reason."

It was cozy and warm in the little house because Johnny had lit the stove. Johnny smelled like wood smoke and something else, something she couldn't pinpoint but that was very pleasing to Melissa's nose. While they were talking, he had shifted his long legs, and now one rested against Melissa's. His big hands lay on the table in front of him when he wasn't gesturing or scratching his beard. His smile was so warm, so sweet.

As he talked, she felt herself allowing the growing attraction to bloom. She looked at Johnny's mouth and imagined kissing it, his rough beard again her soft skin, those powerful hands on her body, those lips on her ...

"I've got to go," she said.

She unintentionally knocked his leg sideways as she stood up. All of a sudden it felt so hot in the small space. She either needed to tear all her clothes off or flee into the cold night.

"Do you?" he asked.

The look in his eyes told her he was also painfully aware of the magnetic force field between them.

"I do," she said. "I'm sorry."

He stood up, and he seemed to fill the whole house.

"Don't be sorry," he said. "It's a difficult thing you're aiming to do, and I admire you for trying. I hope you will keep in touch, and let me know how it goes."

He held out his hand to her, and she knew before she touched it what would happen, but the snap of electricity still made her jump. He smiled at her, from a mischievous quirk of the lips to a sparkle in his light lake-colored eyes.

"I've lost count," he said.

Johnny left and Melissa, energized by her decision, compelled by the overwhelming need to see Patrick, to reunite with him, to not waste one more minute, locked up the little house and hurried up Peony Street to Rose Hill Avenue, to the entrance to the Rose and Thorn.

Outside, she could hear the traditional fiddle music and light from the interior shown out onto the sidewalk. She took a deep breath, opened the door, and entered the bar. There were six regulars at the bar, and half the booths and tables were full of tourists and college kids. Hannah was delivering a pitcher to a table. Sam waved to her from behind the bar.

Where was Patrick?

"Hey, chickie mama," Hannah said when Melissa reached her. "What're you doin' here?"

"Where's Patrick?" Melissa asked, ignoring the locals who were now vying for her attention.

Hannah gave Melissa a look that was equal parts embarrassment, pity, and compassion.

"Where is he, Hannah?" Melissa asked again.

"I don't know," Hannah said and ceased eye contact. "He had to go out for a little bit. Said he'd be back by ten."

Melissa looked at the clock over the bar; it was ten-thirty.

Melissa went behind the counter and wrapped an apron around her waist.

"What are you doing?" Hannah asked.

"I'm helping you out," Melissa said. "Shame on him for leaving you two with this many people."

"I'll go," Sam said and left as quickly as possible.

"This crowd?" Hannah said. "This is nothing. I'm a professional expectations adjustor. They want drinks? They have to wait till I bring 'em. That's not a problem, that's a teachable moment."

Melissa busied herself taking orders and delivering drinks while Hannah bartended. It had been over six years since she had waited tables but it felt like yesterday. If she and Patrick got back together, she would have to be here, by his side, working together, living together. There would be no opportunities for indiscretions if she were always nearby to keep an eye on him.

So what if Ava had bought the building next door? Melissa had never been keen on running a restaurant, and now she'd never have to. She could work with Sean all day and work in here with Patrick all evening. It would mean long hours and sore feet, but if she was determined to make this work that would be a sacrifice she was willing to make.

What about the little house Johnny had built for her? She could sell it; they would buy his folks' house, fix it up, and live there. She could still purchase the mobile home park and sell little houses; she would just not live there.

She thought about Johnny; that had been an intense attraction, a whirlwind of feelings for someone she didn't even know very well. She told herself it was nothing compared to what she felt for Patrick. It had been some sort of a test, maybe. And he lived way out in the woods, anyway. Melissa could not see herself living in such isolation; she'd go crazy. No, Johnny was definitely out.

As Melissa sorted out in her head what her life would be like with Patrick back in it, trying to reconcile what she wanted with what he wanted, she felt good; she felt like she had a direction in which she was excited to be going.

By 11:00 pm all the tables, booths and stools were filled, the noise was deafening, and Patrick had not returned.

"Where did he say he was going?" she asked Hannah.

"He didn't," Hannah said.

"Is Ava back?" Melissa asked.

Hannah shrugged.

"I really don't know," she said.

Melissa focused on serving the customers and tried not to worry.

At 1:30 am Hannah called time and kicked everyone out. She turned off the music, and the silence seemed to ring in the air.

"Call him," Melissa said.

"I've texted him every fifteen minutes since ten p.m.," Hannah said. "He's not responding."

Melissa took out her phone and called him. Surely if he saw her number, he would answer. It went to voicemail, and she ended the call rather than leave a message.

"Tell me the truth, Hannah," Melissa said. "Did he leave with some bimbo?"

Hannah sighed and put up her hands in surrender.

"He was flirting with a blonde when I got here, but you know him, he flirts with any double x chromosome with a pulse," Hannah said. "She left before he did. I don't know that one thing had to do with the other."

"Did he seem upset or worried?"

"No, not at all," Hannah said.

Melissa filled the mop bucket and added the oil soap. As she mopped, she thought about where Patrick might be.

If Ava was back, he might have gone to meet her. If he was with some random pickup, he could be anywhere. Either possibility was reasonable. Patrick was a flirty, sexually-tuned-in man. If he thought it was over with Melissa, he would turn to someone else – not for love – but for sex.

Melissa was irritated but not defeated. Once he knew he could come back to her, all that would stop. She would just have to make herself more available. After working all day and all evening she would probably be tired, but she would just have to make an effort. She didn't know how she could do all that and still have the energy to clean or grocery shop or spend time with friends and family, but if she wanted Patrick back, that was what she would do.

Work all day, work all evening, keep an eye on him as much as possible, and satisfy him in bed even if she didn't feel like it. A worn out, sexually satisfied man was a faithful man, right? She'd also have to keep tabs on him while she was working at Sean's during the day; maybe she could take him lunch every day and make surprise afternoon visits when she had time. She could put a GPS on his truck and track him with her phone like Will tracked Ava.

She'd have to keep track of Ava, too, somehow, know when she was around and might drop in on Patrick at work. She could ask the other waitresses to tip her off; they were women, they'd understand. But were they hitting on him? She'd have to make sure whoever worked the afternoon shift was old and ugly.

If she could structure her days around Patrick, and make sure he was never tempted, would it then be safe to marry him and have a child? Where she would find time to have a baby during all this, she couldn't imagine. She wouldn't be able to work all those hours, for one thing. Plus, she wouldn't have the energy. A baby would take up so much of her time, time she wouldn't be able to spend paying attention to Patrick. He would resent that, and go look for attention elsewhere.

So a baby was out of the question.

"Hey," Hannah said. "You're washing the finish right off the floor."

Missy realized she'd been so focused on her thoughts she'd quit paying attention to what she was doing, and had mopped the same spot repeatedly.

"Sorry," she said.

"He's probably at his mom's," Hannah said.

"It doesn't matter," Melissa said. "He didn't know I was coming."

"Why are you here?"

Hannah sat on a bar stool and patted the one next to her.

Melissa sat.

"I'm gonna take him back," Melissa said.

"Don't do it," Hannah said. "He won't change."

"I know that," Melissa said. "I'm the one who has to change."

"Why in the hell should you?"

"He's high maintenance," Melissa said. "He's weak-willed and needs a lot of attention."

"You're describing an adult," Hannah said. "How sad is that?"

"If I want to be with him, and I do," Melissa said, "I'll have to keep an eye on him; be more available. I need to be what he wants so he won't want anyone else."

"What about what you want?"

"This is about compromising to get what I want."

"And he doesn't have to compromise at all?"

"He'll have to quit foolin' around," Melissa said.

"Or just be sneakier," Hannah said.

"I'm not going to give him enough leash to do that," Melissa said. "I'm going to be one of those suspicious, controlling wives who always knows where her husband is and what he's doing."

"Sounds fun," Hannah said. "Maybe we could tag and track him, like a bear."

"It's the price of admission," Melissa said. "I want Patrick and the whole family back, and that's what I have to do to get it."

"I hope he's worth it," Hannah said.

Her phone rang, and she went behind the counter to pick it up.

"That was Delia," she told Melissa when she hung up. "Sammy's throwing up copious amounts of Halloween candy and his daddy does not do vomit. He will do poop, but only mommy does vomit."

"You go on," Melissa said. "I have a key, and I could do this in my sleep."

After Hannah left, Melissa took the bucket back to empty it in the washroom. As she rinsed out the mop, she wondered if she would be happy being that controlling, suspicious wife she just described to Hannah. It sounded sort of exhausting.

The side door opened, and Melissa peeked out to see who it was. A disheveled college girl, a tall and long-legged blonde, stumbled through the door giggling.

"You got me drunk," she said.

Talking to Patrick, it turned out, who followed her inside.

Melissa ducked back into the washroom and held her breath, her heart thumping.

"Hey, Kirsten," Patrick said.

"It's Kristen," the young woman said.

"Oh, yeah, right," Patrick said. "You see those stairs? You go up there and wait for me. I'll get rid of Hannah and be there in five."

"Don't make me wait too long," the young woman said.

"I'll make it worth the wait," Patrick said. "I promise."

Patrick disappeared into the front room while the young woman drunkenly made her way up the ladder to the loft.

Melissa left the bathroom and paused, trying to ascertain where Patrick was.

"Hey," the woman said from upstairs, looking down at Melissa. "Whose panties are these? Who are you?"

"Just a minute," Patrick said from the front of the bar.

Melissa slipped out the side door and met Ava walking up the wheelchair ramp.

"Well, the gang's all here," Melissa said. "The good news is Kristen just found your panties."

"What are you doing here?" Ava asked her. "Who is Kristen?"

"Nobody who will matter in the morning," Melissa said. "Just like me."

"Why are you here?" Ava said. "I thought you two broke up."

"We did," Melissa said. "He's all yours now."

"What's going on out here?" Patrick said as he looked outside. "Oh, crap."

"I guess we should each take a number," Melissa said. "Looks like you're rackin' and stackin' 'em this evening."

"Patrick," Ava said. "What is she doing here?"

"I didn't know she was," Patrick said.

Melissa saw the look that passed between Patrick and Ava, a look that said she was the one on the outside of this, looking in on the real deal.

"Y'all have fun," Melissa said. "I'm outta here."

They went inside. Melissa stomped down the ramp and stood on the sidewalk.

Where was she going?

She didn't want to have to tell Delia, or anybody else, what had happened, and she didn't trust herself to talk to anyone without crying. It was one thing to think about Patrick cheating, in the abstract; it was another to witness him cheerfully doing so.

Melissa walked down to the river and then along the bank between the water and the rail trail. When she got to the dock behind Will's bicycle factory, she saw a little rowboat tethered to one of the pilings. It was a restored vintage wooden model with a gleaming finish. She climbed up on the dock to look at it, almost stumbling over a pile of cinder blocks someone had stacked there. She pulled the little boat around so she could see the back end.

"Happy Wife" was written on it in an elegant script.

"She's back in business," Melissa said to herself.

She considered untying the boat so it would drift down and go over the dam like the first one. She actually had her hand on the rope before she changed her mind. It would be a shame to destroy something so lovingly restored, so valuable.

'I'm just a sore loser,' she thought.

Melissa went back to the little house and considered sleeping there, although there was nothing to sleep on. She was looking for her phone to call Delia so she wouldn't worry when she realized she had left her cell phone at the bar.

"Dammit."

She put her jacket back on and went back up the hill to the bar. All the lights were still on. She used her key to open the side door and yelled, "Hello!" but no one answered. She listened but didn't hear anything upstairs. She climbed the ladder and peeked over the edge of the loft, but there was no one up there. She climbed back down and looked around, wondering what had happened. She retrieved her cell phone from the bathroom.

She went to the front room and saw that the till full of money was sitting on the bar top next to two highball glasses, both partially filled with amber liquid. She picked them up to pour them out, mostly out of habit, and noticed there was residue in the bottom of one of them, a powdery substance settled beneath what smelled like whiskey.

When she turned around, she saw Patrick's cell phone, wallet, and keys on the back bar. His jacket was on the hook by the door to the back room where he always left it.

Her mind raced.

She picked up his cell phone and scrolled through his messages. The last one inbound was from Ava, earlier this evening, telling him she was back in town and wanted to see him. His response was "no this is over."

Melissa checked her phone and saw that there was a message from Patrick about a half hour earlier. It said, "SOS."

Hannah walked in just then.

"What are you still doing here?" she asked. "Skip called to tell me the lights were still on."

Melissa quickly told Hannah what she thought had happened.

"Patrick was the only witness to Ava killing that guy," Hannah said.

"And he tried to break up with her tonight," Melissa said. "She drugged him, and now she's going to kill him."

"Was her SUV parked outside when you left the bar?" Hannah asked.

"No," Melissa said. "Her new boat was at the dock."

They rushed to the dock behind the bicycle factory.

"There," Melissa cried, pointing to something on the dock.

"It's Patrick's pocket knife," Hannah said. "His dad got him that when he made Eagle Scout."

"He's leaving us clues," Melissa said.

Hannah called Ava's house phone, but no one answered.

"Let's drive out to Ava's," Hannah said when she hung up. "Maybe Will's gone, and she took him to the castle. The worst thing that can happen is we embarrass ourselves, and we'll be glad we're wrong."

"It will take too long to drive," Melissa said. "We need a boat."

"Ed has a canoe," Hannah said. "It's on the carport. I think we can get it without waking them up."

As Hannah and Melissa were stealing Ed's canoe, his dogs started barking, and he came outside.

"What are you doing?" he asked them.

Hannah quickly explained what was going on and what they were doing.

"I'm calling Scott," he said and went back inside.

"C'mon," Hannah said.

The two women trotted down Iris Avenue and then Pine Mountain Road holding a canoe upside down over their heads. They put it in the river at the bottom of the road. Hannah unclipped the oars and handed one to Melissa.

"See that red light," she said, pointing to the far shore. "That's Ava's dock."

The only sound Melissa could hear as they paddled across the river was the swoosh of the oars in the water, the roar of the water as it cascaded over the dam, the whistle of the icy wind through the trees, and the frantic beating of her heart in her chest.

Although they had aimed for the red light, the strong current brought them quite a way downstream from the dock before they reached shore. They pulled the canoe up onto the muddy bank and, using their phone flashlights, made their way toward the red light.

About ten yards out, Hannah put her finger to her lips and turned off her flashlight. Melissa did the same. As they crept closer, they could see two people on Ava's dock, and they seemed to be struggling with each other. Neither was large enough to be Patrick, however.

As they got closer, they could hear what was being said.

"I'm doing this for us," Ava said. "You have to trust me."

"I won't let you do it," Charlotte said.

There was a boat tied up to the dock, and as soon as she realized what was in it, Melissa clutched Hannah's arm and pointed.

"It's Patrick," she whispered.

From the light of the moon, they could see Patrick was lying on his back in the small vintage rowboat, with cinder blocks tied to him with rope. Charlotte was holding another rope attached to the small boat, and Ava, holding an oar in one hand, was trying to take it from her.

"I have no choice," Ava said. "You have to see that."

Ava grabbed hold of Charlotte's arm. Charlotte pulled away from her mother and turned to pull the boat closer to the dock.

"I won't let you do it," Charlotte said.

Charlotte started to tie up the boat, and in that instant, Ava lifted the oar with both hands and struck her daughter hard on the shoulder. As Charlotte fell she dropped the rope, and the small boat was quickly pulled away by the swift current and headed toward the dam.

Charlotte was writhing on the dock.

"You hurt me!" she cried.

"I told you not to interfere," Ava said. "Now see what you've done."

Melissa turned and ran, tripping and almost falling, down the muddy shoreline, trying to keep up with the small boat. Hannah followed.

"Go to the dam," Hannah called out. "We can catch it there and keep it from going over."

There was a large, broad mass of tree branches and sticks stuck at the edge of the dam, and Patrick's boat was stopped behind it. Melissa attempted to walk out on the dam's cement wall and almost lost her footing on the icy surface, so she was forced to back up. Patrick's boat was now turning so that it was parallel to the dam, pushing the pile of branches and sticks over, a few at a time.

Hannah caught up.

"I'm going in," Melissa said, as she handed Hannah her phone and kicked off her shoes.

"Wait for me," Hannah said.

Hannah threw both of their phones up the hillside and kicked off her own shoes as Melissa dove in. She came up with a gasp and then swam toward the boat.

"Jeebus it's cold!" Hannah said as she waded in. "Just get the rope, and we can pull him in."

Melissa reached the side of the boat and pulled herself up so she could see Patrick. She took his wrist in her freezing cold hand and was relieved to feel a pulse. The mass of sticks was now halfway gone; it wouldn't be long before the boat was next to go over.

Hannah reached the boat and worked her way around to the prow.

"Got it," she said, between chattering teeth, as she held up the rope.

Together, they turned the boat around and towed it to shore. Once they had it mostly out of the water, Hannah said, "I'll find my phone and call Scott."

Hannah scrambled up the bank and disappeared in the tangle of rhododendron bushes that masked the shore.

Melissa shook Patrick, but he was limp and unresponsive. Quickly, she started working on the knots to the rope that was wrapped around him and strung through the cinder blocks. Her body was shuddering from the wet and cold, and her fingers felt numb, which made it hard to use them with any dexterity. The only light she had was moonlight filtered through the fast-moving clouds.

"You," she heard.

When she turned, she saw Ava standing behind her on the shore, holding the oar up over her head. Melissa managed to dodge the first blow, which struck a cinder block that cracked the oar. Ava raised it again, but before she could swing it down, Hannah came from behind with a large branch and whacked Ava across the back.

Ava lost her balance and fell with a splash into the water. She struggled in the current, which swiftly pulled her out to the middle of the river and toward the dam. She called out for help, but a cloud passed over the moon, so Melissa could no longer see her in the darkness.

"I couldn't find the phones," Hannah said.

She climbed into the boat, straddled Patrick, and started working on a knot.

"Aren't you going to help her?" Melissa asked.

"Hell no," Hannah said. "If I'm the frog in this scenario then she's the scorpion."

"What?"

An outboard motor could be heard approaching, and light from a searchlight landed upon them. Men's voices called out.

"Over here!" Hannah shouted and waved.

Melissa returned to her work: untying the knot of a rope attached to the cinder block intended to drag the love of her life to the bottom of the river and keep him there.

CHAPTER ELEVEN - TUESDAY

When Melissa left Patrick's hospital room, she found his mother Bonnie, an alarmed look on her face, walking down the hall toward her, carrying a bakery box and a super-sized coffee. Patrick's wailing could be heard far down the corridor, where staff members at the nursing station were leaning out to look.

"Is that Patrick?" she asked Melissa. "Are you leaving?"

Melissa nodded.

"How can you leave him alone when he's carrying on like that?" Bonnie asked.

"He's not crying for me," Melissa said. "Now that you're here I can go."

"I need to talk to you first," Bonnie said.

She looked at the door to her son's room and seemed to weigh her options. The pull to immediately try to comfort her son was strong, Melissa knew.

"He'll be all right," Bonnie finally said. "Let's go down here."

Bonnie gestured to Melissa to follow her to a couple of chairs at the end of the hall by a window. Bonnie put her box and coffee on the table between the two, and they both sat.

"I would have come last night, but I had Ava's boys," Bonnie said. "Scott assured me Patrick was out of danger or I would have been here."

"They gave him Narcan in the ambulance," Melissa said. "He came out of it quick; he threw up and had a headache, but after we got him in a room he slept for several hours."

"I heard it was busy here last night. Scott said you all might have to stay in the ER for a while."

"Our nurse told us they brought over twenty overdoses in here yesterday," Melissa said. "They had to Narcan one guy three times just to bring him around. I guess not everybody made it."

"Thank goodness you found him," Bonnie said. "I hate to think what might have happened if you hadn't."

"I'm glad you're here now," Melissa said. "I'm plum wore out."

"Have you talked to anybody?"

"No, I lost my cell phone last night," Melissa said. "Why, what's happened?"

"Ava didn't drown," Bonnie said. "She didn't even get wet."

"What do you mean?" Melissa said. "Hannah knocked her in the river because she tried to kill me."

"That was Charlotte," Bonnie said, "and they haven't found her body."

"I know who I saw, and it wasn't Charlotte," Melissa said. "It was Ava. Ask Hannah, she'll tell you the same."

"It was dark, honey, and they do look alike now that Charlotte's all grown up," Bonnie said. "Ava says Charlotte was the one who tried to kill my son, and who tried to kill you."

"Wait a minute," Melissa said. "That's not right."

Melissa searched her memory. Ava on the dock with Charlotte, arguing, struggling. It was dark, with only the moon for light. How did she know who was who? Ava's voice was deeper, more mature, and she had thought the one with the oar in her hand was Ava. Why was that?

Melissa closed her eyes and pictured the scene on the dock. Something had glinted in the moonlight: Ava's big diamond ring, on the hand that held the oar. The one that had knocked Charlotte over; the one that had tried to kill Melissa.

Melissa felt dizzy; she reached for the arms of the chair to steady herself.

"Bless your heart," Bonnie said. "You need to sleep. You're not planning on driving yourself, are you?"

Melissa shook her head, rubbed her eyes, and tried to focus.

"No," she said. "Delia's picking me up; she should be here any minute."

"You get some food in you, and you'll feel better," Bonnie said. "I'll call the shop and have the girls send over some sticky buns."

"What happened to Ava?"

"Flew the coop," Bonnie said. "Will took her and Olivia to the DC airport this morning; they're probably somewhere over the Atlantic Ocean by now, on their way to England. He's buying a house there; they're not coming back."

"What about the boys?"

"I was just about to tell you," Bonnie said. "She came to my house early this morning, to give me instructions about the boys; where they were to be sent after Will made the arrangements. Instead, I told her how it was going to be. She didn't much like it, but I didn't give her any choice. Will was waiting out front, and she didn't want him fussed."

"What did you say?"

"I told her we all knew Olivia was Patrick's daughter; we also knew about the private investigator she had the affair with and killed. I told her unless she gave me custody of my grandsons I was going to raise a stink like she'd never smelled before in her life. Before I was done with her, I'd have Olivia, too, and she'd be in prison."

"Weren't you scared?"

"Sean was there, so no, not really."

"Sean was there?"

"He had the custody agreement ready," Bonnie said. "I've been busy this week; you didn't even know about that, did you? I can be sneaky when I have to be. Now, granted, Sam and Sean put their heads together and came up with the idea, but it was me that got to deliver the news."

"Y'all are sneaky," Melissa said.

"Sean was wonderful," Bonnie said. "He could tell she was going to call our bluff, so he told her that the FBI had all the evidence plus a statement from Patrick and they were going to arrest her as soon as they could get a warrant."

"Is that true?"

"Maybe," Bonnie said, but then winked at Melissa and smiled.

"What did Ava say?"

"She turned white as a ghost," Bonnie said. "Her sins had finally come home to roost. She signed those papers and lit out of there like her backside was on fire. She didn't even wake up the boys to tell them goodbye."

"And no one drowned?"

"They haven't found a body, so no, we think not."

"That means Charlotte is still around somewhere."

Bonnie shrugged.

"I love all my grandchildren, but I feel like I've lost Charlotte," Bonnie said. "Unless Patrick decides to press charges, I don't think she'll be in any trouble."

"He won't," Melissa said.

"Has he talked about what happened?"

"He says he doesn't remember," Melissa said.

Bonnie looked down the hall at the door to his room, and Melissa noticed Patrick had stopped wailing.

"Maybe that's for the best," Bonnie said.

Melissa sighed and then said, "I gotta go."

She stood up and steadied herself.

"Don't abandon him now," Bonnie said. "He needs you."

"No," Melissa said. "Whatever it was that held those two together is stronger than me. I'm not gonna spend the rest of my life playing first runner-up to that woman, never mind all the other ones he'll fool around with."

"Give him some time," Bonnie said as she stood up. "You may change your mind."

"I love you," Melissa said as she hugged Bonnie. "I'm only sorry you won't be my mother-in-law."

"I love you, too, darlin'," Bonnie said. "If it weren't for you my son would be dead. You'll always be special to me."

Melissa walked down the hallway, away from Patrick's room, past the nurses' station, to the elevator. When the doors opened, Hannah was standing inside.

"I'll ride down with you," Hannah said.

Melissa entered the elevator and leaned against the back wall. She didn't think she had ever felt so tired in all her life.

"How's the patient?" Hannah asked.

"Bawling and squalling," Melissa said.

"He's a big baby," Hannah said. "You're officially a superhero now, you know, just like me. I've been considering names for you. How do you like 'Tiny Titan?' You know, like for Tennessee."

"Perfect," Melissa said, as she closed her eyes. "I love it."

"Hold me closer, Tiny Titan," Hannah sang. "Saving cheaters on the river ..."

Melissa laughed and opened her eyes.

"We're friends now, huh?" Melissa said.

"Yep," Hannah said. "You're an honorary cousin. We took a vote, and it was unanimous."

"I'm honored."

They got off the elevator and walked toward the main lobby.

"Any news?" Melissa asked.

"They haven't found Charlotte's body," Hannah said.

"I can picture it so clearly," Melissa said. "The dark hair, the pale skin, the hand with the ring on it. That big sparkly ring. It was Ava."

"Ava claims Charlotte knocked her over and then attacked you," Hannah said. "She says it was Charlotte who kidnapped Patrick and tried to kill him."

"But it was Ava with Patrick at the Thorn when I left. I saw Charlotte at the little house earlier. Johnny saw her, too. She had Ava's van and planned to go to their house."

They reached the ground floor and left the elevator. In the main lobby, they sat down in two chairs well away from anyone else.

"Ava says she was never at the bar," Hannah said. "The blonde girl conveniently doesn't remember anything, so there's her paid off, I'd guess. Ava says she heard a commotion on the dock from up at her house and went down to see what was happening. She says she was trying to save Patrick when Charlotte hit her with the oar and knocked her over."

"I swear to you, Hannah, it wasn't Charlotte," Melissa. "Charlotte was waiting for her mother to leave town so she could stay at their house. She's probably the one who heard Ava at the dock, went down and caught her. Charlotte would not have tried to kill Patrick. The things they said on the dock don't make sense the other way around."

"It was dark," Hannah said. "I thought it was Ava hitting Charlotte and then attacking you, but I only saw her from behind, and they look so much alike. I'm sorry, I can't honestly swear to it."

"It doesn't matter what I say," Melissa said. "I'm the ex-con, and she's the queen of Rose Hill. No one will ever believe me."

"What does Patrick say?"

"He doesn't remember anything. That might be true, but probably Heathcliff just doesn't want Cathy to get in trouble."

"You really took that book personally, didn't you?"

"I'll tell you what I think," Melissa said. "I think Charlotte's tethered to cinder blocks at the bottom of the river or buried in the woods somewhere."

"You think Ava killed Charlotte, attacked you, fell in the river, swam to the shore, and then sneaked back and buried the body?" Hannah asked. "I know Ava's rotten, but that's like Mephisto-level evil. Besides, there wasn't time."

"Then that means Charlotte's still around here somewhere," Melissa said.

Melissa saw Delia crossing the street from the parking garage to the hospital.

"There she is," Melissa said, and they both stood.

"How are Timmy and Ernie?" Melissa asked.

"They're with Sean," Hannah said. "I don't know exactly how it happened because my husband is a veritable vault of secrecy, but it looks like they're officially Bonnie's now."

"They're better off," Melissa said.

"Ding dong, the witch is dead," Hannah said. "She had everything, but it went to her head."

Melissa walked out of the hospital with Delia to find that snow had started to fall; big, fluffy bunches of flakes that stuck together and melted as soon as they hit the pavement. Out in the parking garage, they saw Terese getting out of a car. When she got to where they were standing, Terese hugged Delia.

"You two gonna own up to me now?" Melissa asked them.

"Fine with me," Delia said.

"Sure," Terese said. "Can we sit in your car?"

After they got in, Delia and Terese up front, Melissa in the back, Delia started the car and turned up the heat.

Terese took out her ID and showed it to Melissa.

"Federal Bureau of Investigations," Melissa read. "Does that make you a good guy?"

"I think so," Terese said. "The majority of us are good guys; there are a few exceptions, of course, just like anywhere else."

"Have you been investigating Ava?"

Terese nodded.

"Not officially at first. I was here several years ago with my boss, investigating a drug-dealing operation," she said. "We stayed at Ava's B&B."

Melissa waited while Terese seemed to hold an internal debate over telling her more.

"You can trust Melissa," Delia said.

Terese shook her head, and Melissa realized the woman was trying not to cry.

Delia reached over and patted Terese's arm.

"Even though I watched most of this happen, there's still a lot I don't know," Delia said. "But I've given it a lot of thought over the years. I think what Ava does, and she's very good at it, is to present a lovely blank screen, and whatever a man projects onto that screen, she becomes. Whatever he imagines she is, based on his fantasies and her beauty, she pretends to be for as long as she needs to get what she wants."

"She's a shapeshifter," Melissa said.

"She is," Delia said. "So these men think they've met the love of their lives, when actually, what they've met is a dangerous con artist."

"My boss is a brilliant but arrogant man," Terese said. "He prides himself on being an excellent judge of character, and by the time he met Ava, he had built up a reputation as an honorable, straight shooter. For Ava, however, he was willing to throw it all away, to risk everything he had worked so hard for. He could have lost everything."

"Except you protected him," Delia said.

"He was a good man who made a mistake," Terese said. "If it came out it would have ended his career."

"What did he do?" Melissa asked.

Terese shook her head.

"I can tell you," Delia said. "You remember that Ava's first husband, Patrick's brother, Brian, abandoned Ava when their kids were very young. He got mixed up in selling drugs, had borrowed money from Theo Eldridge, and then disappeared. Right after Theo Eldridge was murdered, Brian showed back up in town, on the run because his second wife had died under mysterious circumstances."

"He was a bigamist," Melissa said, and Delia nodded before she continued.

"The FBI had agents living at Ava's B&B while they investigated the local drug ring, and Terese's boss fell in love with Ava. One morning, very early, he left the B&B in an SUV, and later that day, Brian was found dead in a ravine near the State Park. Do I have it right so far?"

Terese nodded.

"Terese's boss was pursuing him when Brian's car went off the road," Delia said. "Instead of stopping to help him, he left him there to die."

Terese turned her head to look out the window.

"Ava turned on him after that," Delia said. "She no longer needed him, so she dumped him."

"And took up with Scott," Melissa said.

Delia nodded.

"She dumped Patrick a few times," Melissa said. "He just never stayed dumped."

"I think Ava was the first woman Patrick fell in love with as a teenager," Delia said. "I believe he idealized her when they were young and he truly believed he rescued her after his brother left. She convinced him she was his one true love, and that except for all the complications that continually arose, they would be together."

"Men are so dumb," Melissa said.

Terese turned back toward them and laughed, but also wiped her eyes.

"Underneath her exterior, deep down, Ava is actually very insecure," Terese said. "She thinks she has to manipulate men to get what she wants, which is safety, and to feel safe requires money and social status."

"I don't feel a bit sorry for her," Melissa said. "She's dangerous."

"She's a malignant narcissist with sociopathic tendencies," Terese said. "The only emotions that matter are her own. Anyone else's are just weaknesses to be exploited, and anyone or anything that gets in her way must be destroyed."

Melissa realized then just how lucky she was to still be alive.

"We started out working on the drug dealing investigation," Terese said, "but after that ended my boss got me assigned to the Rose Hill mayor's political corruption case. During that time, while I lived here during the week and went home on the weekends, I kept an eye on Ava for him. She took up with the chief of police, Scott, and then after she got Theo Eldridge's money she dumped him and went back to sneaking around with Patrick. I knew she was never going to marry Patrick, but a fool in love will see what he wants to see; I should know. After the mayor's case was done, I went back to DC, but I still had contacts here."

"That would be me," Delia said.

"And eventually Karl," Terese said. "When Will rented the whole B&B from Ava, I knew what was going to happen. I was content to let Ava do her voodoo on anyone dumb enough to fall for it until she killed the private eye. And she killed him, there's no doubt about it. I've seen it from two angles now, and I've got Patrick's statement, so there's no question in my mind."

"Were you working with Karl the whole time?" Melissa asked.

"Karl's a retired agent, and an old friend of my boss," Terese said. "After Will's father died, his uncle, who is a very well-connected political donor, got in touch with my boss's boss, looking for someone to watch over Will. Will's a great guy, actually, and a good businessman, but evidently, he's always been an idiot where women are concerned. Will's mother reported her concerns to her brother-in-law, and he took care of it. My boss recommended Karl and Will's mother hired him. Karl, in turn, hired the private detective through an intermediary; the private investigator didn't know who had hired him.

"Karl had their house wired for video although Ava never knew it. She thought he was a

314

drunk, but he only wanted her to believe that. He saw her come and go from that side of the river, and the private investigator saw her come and go from this side. We knew right when the affair with the private eye started. She really is an incredible manipulator. She would have made an excellent operative."

"Or a notorious double agent," Delia said, "like Mata Hari."

"No doubt," Terese said. "The night Ava killed the private investigator, Karl saw her leave the house and then saw her husband try to leave. Will was out of it but insisted on driving. Karl talked him into letting him drive. When they got to the intersection outside the bar, Will grabbed the wheel, and they caused the coal truck to wreck."

"Isn't leaving the scene of a crime against the law?" Melissa asked.

"Karl works for Will's mother," Terese said. "He didn't see the private investigator get hit, and he's being paid to make sure nothing happens to the woman's son, period. Will was his first priority.

"Karl took Will back to the house and was going around to the other side of the SUV to get him out when Ava showed up. He hid and then sneaked back to his apartment, where he watched on hidden cameras while Ava disposed of her clothing and hid the victim's belongings. The next day he retrieved her clothing from the trash, and before she left the house that night after her party, he took the victim's belongings from the donation bag she asked him to put in her car."

"But not before Hannah stole the memory card," Delia said.

"We have that now," Terese said. "Between the video evidence from the bar and the funeral home, and Patrick's statement, it wouldn't have been hard to get a warrant."

"Why did you let her leave, then?" Melissa asked.

"I received a call from Patrick last night, before the accident, saying he wanted to rescind his statement," Terese said. "And there were other complications I didn't foresee."

"Your boss is still in love with her," Melissa said. "He's protecting her."

"Here's the thing," Terese said. "Will's uncle is closely connected to the current White House administration, he was a major donor to the president's campaign, and he's also a defense contractor. I heard from my boss this morning; the new head of the DOJ wants us to back off, or everyone's fired."

"She's getting away with it."

"Yes."

Delia turned on the windshield wipers to remove the melting snow and turned on the defroster to clear the condensation that had accumulated on the inside of the glass.

"I guess when you're beautiful and evil you can get away with anything," Melissa said.

"When you combine that with money and proximity to power," Terese said. "Will has both."

Melissa sighed.

"I'll always wonder if she'll come back," she said. "I don't think I'll ever rest easy."

"I don't think she'd dare," Delia said.

"I'm sorry," Terese said. "I wanted it, too."

"Do you think your boss will let her go now?" Delia asked.

Terese shook her head.

"He won't, but I'm done," she said. "I'm going to request a transfer as soon as I get back."

"Are you here to check on Patrick?" Melissa asked.

"Tying up loose ends," Terese asked.

"He won't ever get over her," Melissa said.

"I'm sorry," Delia said. "I think you're right."

"What are you going to do now?" Terese asked.

"I'm going to take my own advice," Melissa said. "It's time for me to make my life the way I want it, and let those old dreams die."

Terese held out her hand, and Melissa shook it.

"Don't worry," Melissa said. "I won't tell anybody what you said."

"I know you won't," Terese said. "I admire you, by the way, for what you did for your son and what you've accomplished."

"Thanks," Melissa said. "I guess you know us better than we can imagine."

"You're better off without Patrick," Terese said. "Although it took me a long time to come to that same conclusion about my boss for myself. I understand what it's like."

"I guess it's always good to have a professional opinion," Melissa said.

Terese got out of the car, leaned back in, and handed Melissa a business card.

"If you ever need anything, please call me."

Melissa smiled and put the card in the breast pocket of her coat. She watched Terese cross the road to the hospital and go inside. She got out of the car and then back in to sit in the front passenger seat.

"It's not as easy as you think to let somebody go," Melissa said. "It's like living with two people inside of you, and one of them's an idiot who doesn't want to listen."

"Let's get you home," Delia said and put the car in reverse.

Melissa's phone rang; she didn't recognize the number.

"Johnny Johnson here," a deep voice said when she answered. "I am calling you on a device that I suspect may utilize alien technology recovered from area 51. My neighbor and good friend Dee Goldman has graciously assisted me in the procurement of said device, and our mutual acquaintance Sam Campbell has facilitated the addition of a technological contraption to my windmill that amplifies the connection needed to operate it."

"You don't have to talk so loud," Melissa said with a laugh. "I can hear you fine."

"You'll have to pardon me," Johnny said. "I'm still a bit dizzy from my trip here from the last century."

"I can't believe you got a phone," Melissa said. "What made you do it?"

"I enjoyed our recent discussion," he said. "So much so that I wish to replicate and improve upon the practice over time. With your permission, of course."

"You have my permission."

"I am much obliged," he said. "Now let's move on to a contemporary topic with which I am much concerned. I understand you tangled with the devil herself and lived to tell about it. Are you all right?"

"Not yet," Melissa said. "But I will be."

Pumpkin Ridge by Pamela Grandstaff

30298088R00184

Made in the USA
San Bernardino, CA
23 March 2019